Crossing Allenby Bridge

Michael Looft

Ψ Proteus Publishing

For everyone *out there* whose path has crossed mine.

CONTENTS

Part I | San Francisco

1	Mark	1
2	Elena	4
3	In Dreams	10
4	And Nightmares	14
5	Mark Leaps	21
6	Tower on Fire	28
7	High Art	35

Part II | Outer Mongolia

1	I See Mark Again	41
2	Mongolian Style Indian Mexican Food	50
3	Chinggis Khaan and Turtle Rock	58
4	Mongolian Microfinance	65

Part III | The Philippines

1	Home	71
2	Manila	74
3	Pavement Dwellers	80
4	Shangri-La	88
5	The City of Gentle People	95

Part IV | Java

1   One Night in Hong Kong   107

2   Father Jack   114

3   Akademi Maritim   124

4   The Orchid   130

5   Crumbling Tower   137

6   Under the Rubble   144

7   Zach   149

8   Ratu the Dukun   155

9   The Watercourse Way   160

10 Leaving Java   172

Part V | The Middle East

1   Baltimore to Amman   181

2   Petra   185

3   Crossing Allenby Bridge   192

4   Jerusalem   201

5   Reunion   207

Acknowledgments   211

About the Author   212

PART I | SAN FRANCISCO

You are a wheel at which I stand,
whose dark spokes sometimes catch me up,
revolve me nearer to the center.
Then all the work I put my hand to
widens from turn to turn.

Rainer Maria Rilke

CHAPTER 1 | MARK

The first time I saw Mark I never would have guessed he'd inspire me to upend my life and travel to the far reaches of the Earth. On that foggy afternoon in late June ten years ago, a typical summer in San Francisco, he was just another guy sitting around the table at the bank. I'm not even sure why he was in that meeting, as he was a temporary programmer brought on to build us a database or a website or something like that—I really don't remember. I *do* remember that we were on a conference call trying to close a deal, so his job was to just keep his mouth shut and listen. He did that part well. So well, in fact, that as he sat perched at the end of the table, I recall studying Mark's carefree expression with casual interest. He was no one I thought of as extraordinary. Yet, the more I watched, the more irritated I grew at him for being so sound in his own skin. He had no business looking so comfortable. Nevertheless, I decided I wanted to find out more about this calm individual who'd drifted into my world.

A few days later I found Mark seated alone at a table in the outdoor café next to our building on Pine Street, his nose in an old library book. Dark curly hair hung down over his pensive face as he sat unmoved while I studied him for a moment, deciding whether to interrupt. I knew he worked on the second floor, where all the operations people sat and where few of us from the fifth floor had a reason to stop. So, I guessed this would be one of the rare opportunities I'd have him alone if I wanted to figure out what made him tick. Without a strong urge to talk to him, especially given my position at the bank, a subtle spark still drew me to his light. His suit jacket sat draped over the arm of the chair next to him. I took off my own jacket and lay it on the other arm, grabbing the seat opposite him. Even though I made a show of sitting down I had to harrumph to gain his attention.

"Oh, hello Mr. Stone. How are you?" he said, lowering the book and fixing me with purposeful eyes.

1

"Please, call me Harry. You're Mark, right? The programmer?"

"Yes," he whispered, closing the book and laying it down in front of us. It would have been easier had he revealed the spine with its title, but alas he forced me to intrude.

"What are you reading there?" I must have said it with a touch more interest than he expected, because he gave me a sheepish grin and spun it around for me to read–though I had to crane my neck sideways.

"*The Razor's Edge...*" I muttered, and paused to make a joke. "Business secrets of Gillette?"

"Not quite." He threw his head back with a hearty laugh.

"What's it about?" I'd heard the title several years back, but maybe it was a movie.

"I'm not too far into it, actually. I think it's about a guy that rejects the world and goes off to find himself. I found it at Green Apple Books the other day. I guess it just jumped out at me."

"I suppose that's the way it is with some books. Well, you'll have to let me know whether it's worth a read–whether he does in fact find himself. I'm guessing that's the case as no one wants to read a book where the main character goes off and gets lost and never comes back. Right? Though I can't say I read much these days." I leaned back and crossed my legs, letting out a breath and wondering what to say next. "I'm impressed; figured you computer guys only read stuff on binary code or something."

"Nah, not for me. I actually didn't study computer science."

"Really, how did you get into it then?"

"I've been going to night school over at SF State. I kind of fell into programming when I was doing some accounting work. The job was so boring I decided to automate what I was doing. One day the guy I was working for was looking over my shoulder and told me I should do programming–that I could make a lot more money doing *that* than what he was paying me to do. So, I just started doing it."

"You like it much?"

"I guess so. It's fun in a way–like doing crossword puzzles. I'm not sure how much meaning is in it, though. When you get down to it, it's all just *binary*." He over accentuated the last word for effect, chuckling to himself.

His comment touched a slight nerve, but after turning it over in my mind, I decided not to dig any further. "Well, we all have our calling in life, I guess. Maybe you just haven't found yours yet. At least you can make some good money doing what you're doing until you finish school."

"I actually just graduated a few weeks ago."

"Oh! Well then, congratulations!"

Our conversation was cut short when Don, the president, noticed me while walking by and stopped to chat about something important, forcing me to excuse myself. That was my life in a nutshell–brief exchanges related to my work that always seemed more important than anything else. Normally, it didn't bother me because I lived a narrow life with as few complexities or surprises as possible. I woke up at the same time every day and one could set a clock by my regular movements. My job was no longer "work", but rather routine chats with subordinates resulting in someone else doing the work. So, there was something about Mark, about the way we spoke and how his words struck my ear that made me want to continue without interruption. We'd only talked for a few minutes, but as I said goodbye and picked up my jacket and walked away I felt a slight pang, as though we could have sat there for hours. I suppose it had been years since I found someone else's words interesting.

CHAPTER 2 | ELENA

I saw Mark every now and then and always stopped him for a brief chat, but never longer than I wanted to. The rest of the summer was a whirlwind of activity at the bank. As head of lending, I oversaw the underwriting of the largest deal the bank had ever made. Determining the fair market value of retail businesses, particularly chain stores, had become one of my specialties over the course of my career. Unlike some businesses, the anticipated cash flows of retail stores required a bit of foresight into the future of that business based on consumer preferences. The Pet Rock was a brilliant idea in the mid-1970s, turning its creator into an instant millionaire. Alas, it fizzled out after a mere six months.

As a boutique commercial bank, we couldn't afford to make mistakes by casting our lot on a silly box of rocks. I had a knack for spotting long-term successes and failures, both in people and businesses, and because of that I'd made a lot of money for us even during the lean times. This last deal to allow a major big box electronics store to expand to a few key locations in the Bay Area gave us notoriety in the financial community. After twenty years of backhanded insults by the big boys who never lost a chance to refer to us as *quaint* or by some other diminutive term, just like that we became known. The deal insured a steady stream of income for several years—as long as the financial world stayed intact, which we saw as a given in those halcyon days back in 2007.

With the deal done and my divorce a few years behind me, along with my one-bedroom apartment on Telegraph Hill that gave my legs a good strong workout and access to some of the finest restaurants in the city, I guess you could say that I was living the good life. At least, that's how I thought of it back then. The one downside I noticed was that I sometimes had to step over a homeless man or two lying in the middle of the sidewalk—a ubiquitous site in San Francisco, where the city seemed to do nothing to help these people. That fall and into the winter, fate decided to pitch three curveballs my way.

The first one swerved in during a seminar organized by Kitty, the head of human resources. Kitty was a frail, thin, fake-blonde, politically correct woman in her early thirties with whom I never saw eye-to-eye. Maybe it's because she somehow just didn't fit into the culture we had created at the bank. Don had hired her a few years prior, when he felt we needed to "professionalize" after decades of doing things on our own. I didn't see the need for a dedicated human resources person as the executive vice presidents were managing fine without someone poking their nose into our business and disrupting well-functioning little fiefdoms. However, Don was worried about the trend of lawsuits tied to dissatisfied personnel and job applicants. So, he framed the hiring as an insurance policy to protect our bottom line. It wasn't her status as a woman that bothered us, because we were technically not an all boys' club. In fact, we had Judith overseeing operations to prove we were not. A few of the staff had nicknamed her "Nurse Ratched" though, a label so spot-on that it stuck for good and I even once overheard her calling herself that one night after a few drinks.

Kitty was cut from a different cloth than the rest of us, and I guess that's why Don hired her, to keep us all in check. After the second onsite ethics training seminar framed as a team-building exercise, some of us complained that these little digressions were becoming a nuisance. I was sick of looking at Kitty's face standing in front of the whiteboard wearing a passive-aggressive smile, introducing some theater major dropout trying his best to make us laugh our way through two hours of basic concepts most human beings already knew. Since some of my guys were in the room, I did my best to withhold snide remarks, saving them for Don later. He always had a way of shrugging these things off as things we had to *just suck up and do*, which summed up his attitude on Kitty. So, we were all just going through the motions like prisoners on the chow line, waiting to receive whatever mystery meat was plopped on our trays.

Everything boiled over after Elena drifted into the office one day in early September to teach us "mindful integration". The other trainings targeted senior officers and anyone else involved in legal transactions. This meeting was optional and anyone at the bank could attend. I planned to skip it, not bothering to sign up even after Kitty had popped her grinning face into my office ten minutes before to remind me about it. It was a gorgeous afternoon, and I headed down the stairs to squeeze in a walk, debating whether to take the rest of the day off.

I wonder what my life would look like today had I not caught Elena's flaming red hair and radiant smile bounce by me in the lobby and me turning to observe her elegant figure. I hadn't seen Kitty standing at the elevator, and she gave me a sour smile as if to say, "This is the kind of thing

I'm talking about!" It wasn't guilt that brought me back in to attend Elena's seminar. No, it was pure lust. Like an old dog sniffing his way through a season, I made my way to the elevator, trying not to focus on the curves underneath Elena's dress. No, I kept my eyes on the gold-plated walls for the most part, feeling her spirit fill the space. Kitty turned to me as we rode up on the world's slowest elevator.

"Harry, this is Elena. She's our special guest today." As she spun towards me, I noticed that despite the same radiance I'd noticed a few moments earlier and piercing green eyes set against smooth, amber skin, the rest of her features were rather plainer than I'd expected. *Earthy* and *powerful* popped into my head, which both comforted and unnerved me. It was as if she were looking right through me and thus impervious to any charm I could conjure up to win her over. She was still beautiful, and I felt drawn to her, but not in the usual way—not sexually. Karmically, whatever that means. "Elena, this is Harry, our Chief Credit Officer. He's in charge of all our credit activity. Basically, he makes sure all the loans we make are on the up and up. Right, Harry?"

"That's right. Mr. Straight and Narrow." I reached out my hand and met Elena's firm handshake. It felt like squeezing a beating heart. "It's very nice to meet you. I nearly forgot about the seminar today," I said, winking at Kitty behind her, who shook her head in causal annoyance.

"I'm very happy that you are coming, Harry. I hope you get something out of today's session," she said with a responsive smile in her eyes.

"Me too, but I do have a question. What exactly is integrated mindfulness?"

"*Mindful* integration." She corrected me with a slight pause in breath. "Just think of it as a way to come home to ourselves again. To be present for our Spirit and whatever it wants for us."

I didn't have a quick comeback for her. In fact, I didn't have any other response than to mutter a perplexing hmm. Moments later, we reached the fourth floor and the elevator opened with a ding. Saved by the bell. I followed the two of them out and we strode to the conference room. A mere ten people showed up. No one else from the fifth floor, but I did see Mark seated in one of the chairs arranged in a small circle. I took the chair next to him and gave him a nod and a wink. He nodded back to me, but didn't say a word, his eyes following Elena. I had trouble keeping my eyes off her as well. Her face had a soft glow to it, and the whole room seemed to fill with her presence. I couldn't quite peg her age, though. I once heard that the guys at the carnival who guessed ages often looked at the back of a person's hand to narrow it down. Judging by hers, she was somewhere in her late forties, but the rest of her seemed a bit younger. Maybe it was just the spirit with which she carried herself—like the world was a curious and fun place to be. The precise opposite of my world. The other attendees fidgeted in their seats, trying to keep their composure while Kitty stepped into the circle and briefly introduced Elena with some psycho-spiritual lingo. Elena then glided into the circle, rotating as if in the eye of a great storm.

"You're probably wondering what I'm doing here." Some of us grinned, recognizing the exact question on our minds. "But the question I want to put to you is, what are you doing here?" My stomach sank as I realized mine was tied to the sway of her hips. I glanced around and felt a few of the others sitting in uncomfortable silence. Of course, there were the two lefty women who only worked at the bank to pay bills–the type who went to yoga retreats and walked with intention. They both sat up erect in their cheap blouses, barely passing the business attire test. They were beaming at her in anticipation as if they knew what was coming next. Refusing to play favorites, she smiled at each of us and continued to twirl in slow circumspection. "You may not know the reason you came here. Maybe you had a break in your schedule and were curious. Or perhaps you've meditated once or twice and thought this might be fun. Maybe you'll learn a new technique. Who knows? Maybe you tried to get out of it, but the *Universe* threw a monkey wrench into those plans." She gave me a subtle wink, and then turned her back to me, and I let my eyes run down the muscles of her calves. "Whatever the reason, I'm glad you're here. I hope you get something out of this hour we have together."

"Let's jump right in, why don't we? I'd like you all to close your eyes and make sure your feet are flat on the floor. Try to relax into your chair and sit as upright as is comfortable for you." I shut my eyes, feeling anything but comfortable. Her voice was soothing enough, like a well-trained hypnotist. Although my discomfort persisted as she spoke, I began to think less and less about the shape of her legs or how I wanted to bury my nose in the long curls covering the back of her neck. "Focus your attention on your breath. Breathing in... and out.... As you inhale, imagine gold energy coming in and filling your body. As you exhale, imagine dark energy flowing out. Energy from your last conversation, your spouse, from anything that is not yours. Breathe in your gold, and breathe out everything else that's keeping you from being present–being here... right now.... Now picture a golden rose...."

We did this for about five minutes. At first, my stomach felt like it was fighting indigestion, and I also experienced waves of nausea wash over me. I'd expected to be good at it the same way I was at most things–even fantasizing that Elena would be congratulating me in front of the group for picking it up with ease. Instead, I wondered if I was going to pass out. Maybe it was the turkey sandwich I'd wolfed down at lunch. I hadn't drunk the night before, so it couldn't be a latent hangover. In fact, before I sat down I felt healthy and energetic. I decided to cheat and crack my eyes to catch anyone keeling over. I expected to see Elena in the middle of the circle, and surprised that instead she stood in front of me, her index finger hovering two inches from my forehead. I almost shouted out, but her eyes twinkled at me with a trace of empathy and I felt her gentle touch on my forehead, just above my eyebrows. It was as though her touch forced my eyes shut again, and I felt a tingling feeling throughout my body and the nausea fell away with my next breath.

As she spoke, I recalled a bumper sticker I'd seen once that read, "Don't believe your thoughts." That made me chuckle, and I again felt Elena's finger on the same spot on my forehead. I noticed the bumper sticker drift away from my mind and I began imagining the gold ball again. Several minutes later she invited us to open our eyes, and when I did, a comforting sensation swept through my body and the room looked a little more in focus, sharper. These wore off after a minute, but left a gentle residue tingling through my fingers and toes.

She began to ask for feedback, and I heard fantastical stories from my co-workers about images and breakthroughs that made me wonder if I'd been doing something wrong or if they were just making things up to impress her. One young woman, one of the tellers who dressed liked a hippie, held her gaze down at the floor as if she were in a trance saying that working for the bank was not her life path. I heard she resigned a few days later. Not the outcome Kitty expected, and I couldn't help but throw a "good going" barb at Kitty about it after our next weekly management meeting. I waited for Mark to say something, and when Elena looked his way he said in a slow, low tone, "I feel lighter, like a little weight has been lifted from me. The world's clearer, sharper." This sent a shiver down my spine. Stealing my thoughts also annoyed me. I glanced away and ignored Elena's eyes when they fell in my direction.

The hour went faster than I expected, with a few people lingering around after she dismissed us. I noticed Kitty giving her a curt thank you and bolting out of the room—no doubt still bruised from the teller's remark and writing-off the whole venture to be a waste of time. I sat amused in my chair, saying goodbye to Mark as he gave Elena an affirmative wave on his way out. He seemed energized by it, and his usual stoical nature replaced with a smile I hadn't seen on him before. You might even say he was glowing.

I stood up, staring at her email address on the whiteboard and glancing over as she talked to the two lefty women who I expected would approach her with those spiritual smiles. They spoke in what sounded like New-Agey jargon—blathering on about auras and shifting energies. It all sounded like mumbo jumbo to me and another example of people tricking themselves into believing they were enlightened because they played the part. Of course, part of me was a tiny bit fascinated by that side of the world, though not enough to venture too deep down the rabbit hole. I hesitated, wondering if I should write down her email address, say hello, or just skip out with a wave like Mark had done. I waited too long, for within moments the other two had left and Elena and I stood alone in the conference room. She gave me a soft smile and a knowing look.

"What did you think, Harry?"

"Honestly, I felt sick at first, but your poking my forehead seemed to help. What was that trick of yours?"

"No trick—just helping you open your third eye a bit."

"Third eye?"

"We all have a third eye that helps us to see what the other two can't."

"Interesting." I had been standing beside her as though I were about to leave, but now shifted my body to face her. With heels on she came up to my chin, and when she looked up at me I felt a jolt emanate from behind my eyes and spread throughout my body. "That was pretty cool... so, is this what you do? Teach meditation?"

"Among other things. I have a yoga studio out near the beach. That's my main source of income. I also do natural healing."

"I've always wanted to try yoga."

"Oh yeah?"

"Yes, believe it or not I'm fascinated by all that stuff—spirituality and religion. Always have been. You know, with a few drinks in me my subconscious mind steers most conversations over to the subject. Not sure why, but it just happens."

"Maybe the Universe is trying to tell you something."

"Maybe..." I trailed off, feeling like I'd better say something bold before the conversation lapsed into goodbyes. "Listen, Elena. I could sign up for your yoga classes and keep that up for a while before mustering up the courage to ask you to dinner. That might take weeks and we'd wind up in the same place we're at right now."

"And where's that?" She flashed non-committal teeth.

"I'm not quite sure. So, what do you say to dinner on Friday?"

"I'm busy this Friday. I *do* like your idea of signing up for a yoga class. Let's start there." She gave my shoulder a reassuring tap like I'd just grounded out, and with that said goodbye. I watched her pick up her bag and walk out with the same elegant gait when she first arrived. I wanted her, but I wasn't sure how. She wasn't my usual type—though I'd grown weary of dating high-maintenance types who ranked hair highlights too far up Maslow's Hierarchy of Needs. Elena was about as far from them as she was from me—or at least where I thought I was.

CHAPTER 3 | IN DREAMS

That night I had a dream set in the Caribbean. I had gone scuba diving there the previous winter, a hobby I picked up in my thirties. The dream resembled the wall dive we had done, a hole over a thousand feet deep. I recall the Divemaster warning us about a condition called *nitrogen narcosis*, often referred to as getting *narced*. Recreational diving sets a maximum depth of 130 feet and beyond that the risk of narcosis rises dramatically. Even the Divemaster warned us to watch our gauges because the symptoms of narcosis resemble drunken giddiness and before you know it you're welcoming your own death with a grin on your face. A bit like taking laughing gas and then plunging off a cliff, giggling all the way down. One of the crew called it the "rapture of the deep." The immediate and simple cure for this temporary condition is to ascend back up and stay there awhile. The dream started out very similar to the actual dive.

I reached the edge of the wall and hovered over its crest, fascinated by imaginative thoughts of what lay down there in the deep. The rocky crag of coral and rock stretched out over the horizon and sunk into blackness. I rolled into a rappelling position, descending in silence and watching tiny creatures zigzagging in and out of the crevices along the limestone rocks, some of which appeared stacked by humans. At one point, I noticed Elena's flaming hair swirling in bubbles and her gesturing at the stones. I shook my head and waved her off, descending further. 50 feet and the colors were losing their brilliance. I let my fingers slip over crusted barnacles. 80 feet into the deep black, looking up at hazy shadows. My ears squeezed and popped, and I felt a gentle tug beckoning me to continue my slow drift, like a dark hand clutching the end of my fin and pulling me down. I wanted to go deeper, driven by the desire to brag about reaching the 130 feet limit. I also marveled at the spooky sensation of dropping into an abyss and running my fingers over the fringes of death. The thought of hovering over that razor's edge reminded me of Mark and the title of his book.

200 feet. That didn't seem right. Seconds earlier it was half that. How could that be? I blinked and rubbed the gauge, shaking it free from any temporary defects. I felt a pang of terror, remembering the words of the Divemaster at how easy it is to slip down too fast. Oh, well. I was fine. I would not die, or maybe I would. A blissful feeling enveloped me, and I let the gauge drop, along with all judgment or even recollection of the life that I had beyond a few images that warped their way into my mind. Images of my dad watching television and me holding the block of balsa wood, asking for help to carve it into a racecar. "You get started on it and I'll be in to help you later," I heard him say. My ex-wife, staring me down until I felt like that child again, crying in the corner of my room with no one to help me. The profile of Mark's meditating face. Red blanket of fire smothering me, veiling me into a fathomless slumber. Then I saw Elena's bright face come into focus and she pulled me up out of the abyss and back into the light. When we came to the surface and I took a deep breath, I noticed that her face looked more like Mark's—eyes closed just as I'd seen him during the mindfulness session. Then it morphed into Kitty's face with that silly fake smile of hers.

I woke up, still feeling the dream working through me and unsure of the edge between fantasy and reality. I still had an hour before sunrise, and once I started coming to I felt antsy and restless to get up and do something. So, I slipped on my shoes for an early morning run along the Embarcadero. Intending to clear my head, all I could think of was Elena. Like a foreign disease infecting my mind: her eyes, her hair, her face plagued my every thought. Even if I tried to think of something else, she still occupied a little room in the neural pathways of my brain that seemed connected to everything else. The feeling itself was not so foreign to me, though it had been some twenty-five years since I recalled a similar intensity. Although this feeling ran deeper, softer and not hard-edged like in my youth. Yes, it was soft, like her. Yet, I didn't want it to take hold of me as I knew its deleterious effects from prior experience, like that one time I'd overdone it with flowers and false charm so long ago. By the end of the run I decided that I would pursue her just by showing up and learning yoga. Something told me the way to her heart was through friendship anyway.

Sunday morning, I found myself stuck trying to twist myself into the eagle pose at the back of the room of her studio out on forty-eighth Avenue. It was far out on the avenues, about as far away from my neighborhood as one could get, and just a block from the beach. Like most people in the city, I didn't own a car. So, the taxi ride seemed to take forever. It was worth it to hear her voice again among the two dozen students in her class. She struck a powerful pose, dressed in all black with her back to a large window looming over the Pacific Ocean. Her red hair was tied up in a ponytail, and I could see the bony features of her face that gave her a more masculine look—a sharp contrast to the feminine touch back at the office. It was like a different woman stood before me, and at first, I felt a slight repulsion to her. As soon as she started talking us through the yoga poses, and I heard the familiar mid-western accent intoned in her speech, I felt home again. At least, that's what being around her felt like in the beginning—arriving home to a warm fire on a cold night. I spent the next hour forcing myself not to blurt out any smart-ass remarks, something I slip into when nervous in a group.

I knew I would see her after the class, because in her email response she told me not to forget my running shoes. At least we had that in common, and I figured she took a chance that I was a runner and it might have been some test. Although, I was not prepared for chasing her down the beach and losing her in the distance, which is what happened. As a lifelong long-distance runner, I've never been a fast one, and it was obvious that she was part gazelle. I'm not even sure it was a date, because all we did was run for an hour and then she left for a lunch appointment, leaving me sputtering on the street outside her studio deliberating over asking her for a formal date or throwing in the towel. In fact, the first few months of our relationship consisted of her calling or texting, often at the last minute, to invite me out for a run or to walk down the beach and sometimes followed by a cup of her homebrew green tea. I remember how startled I was to get a text from her because before then I couldn't recall ever having received or sent one. It just appeared on my flip phone with a jingle I didn't recognize. The message wasn't even written in proper English, reading: "r u free? – Elena." At least she'd spelled out her name, otherwise I would have guessed it was spam or someone else's mistake.

I continued to pursue her that fall, the relationship moving at glacial speed. In fact, early on I mentioned something about it during one of our late afternoon walks and she whispered, "Slowness is a good thing. A lot happens in the slowness." That last phrase stuck for me and became the theme of our relationship. She even moved slowly. Except when she ran. This rubbed off on me a bit and I began noticing my own pacing in life slow down, whether I was walking or even talking to my staff. It was like she downshifted me a few gears. That was all the upside.

A downside was she insisted on romance taking the back seat. For Elena, friendship was the foundational connection from which healthy relationships grew, and she wouldn't dream of loosening the reigns of her heart and letting herself get swept up in passion. I found this strange, since many of our conversations revealed how free and open she was to ideas and experiences. Some of those ideas were far outside the bounds of reality and I sometimes had to check my tongue or try not to laugh when she explained life's conundrums through an astrological lens. I'll never forget when I complained of the bank's servers crashing and she remarked that it was likely a result of Mercury having gone retrograde. Yet these idiosyncrasies drew me closer to her and I recall confessing that it was like I took a space ship and crash landed on another planet—an interesting planet, but decidedly different than the one from which I had just left. So, meeting Elena was the first curveball thrown my way. I didn't realize how much so until she invited me to her friend's house one night for what turned out to be a séance.

CHAPTER 4 | AND NIGHTMARES

Elena later dismissed my calling it a séance as hyperbole. Just a gathering of friends, she said. Nevertheless, I was there and there was some creepy shit that went down. It was the Saturday before Halloween and the warm weather earlier in the month had started to turn cold, though still mild compared to other parts of the country. Elena invited me to a costume party and since it was the first time meeting her inner circle of friends, I went all out to make an impression. I agonized over costumes. I considered wearing one of my three-piece suits and going as a banker. Showing up as my real self would have been cliché and perhaps *too* scary.

I settled on Alex from Kubrick's movie, *A Clockwork Orange,* a costume I already had from a previous Halloween. Based on the reactions from a few of the other guests later at the party, I might have been better off going as myself. For one thing, most people saw my all white outfit, black boots, and black bowler hat and guessed wrong–missing the single eyelash and eyeballs on the sleeve. This was especially true of the younger ones who'd never seen the movie and one woman who even asked if I was Huck Finn. Elena was amused when I showed up at her house to pick her up. Early on, she had confessed that the wicked streak hiding my goodness was one of the things she appreciated about me. We shared the same dry and sometimes warped humor, and when no one was around we had a good time laughing at bawdy jokes. She told me these were hallmarks of old souls. Elena dressed as a belly dancer, and something told me she'd already had the costume for other occasions. When I asked her about it, she mentioned that she danced on occasion, but rebuffed my attempts to get her to perform before we left the house. Maybe later, she said with a wink.

The party was up in Marin County, on the other side of the Golden Gate Bridge. So, we took Elena's little Honda up there. The bridge gets fogged over most of the year, but we were in luck that evening, crossing with blue skies and a bright setting sun to the West over the Pacific Ocean. I didn't get out of the city much, always feeling like I was going on a long journey anytime I did leave it. I caught Elena's profile while looking over the bridge at the sky glowing red. She wasn't much younger than me, but years of healthy living spread across her cheeks and I couldn't help noticing how beautiful she looked in that light. Though her features were plain, and I suspect too much so in her youth to turn many heads, I presumed she was aging like a fine wine, made confident with time and temperature. Seeing her there, face both bold and placid looking out over the road in front of us, it was the first time it hit me how lucky I was to have met her. I even blurted something out to her, and her mouth wrinkled into a smile and she cast her green eyes on me. It was then that I knew I was falling for her. Sappy, but true. I also knew she saw something in me that I didn't see myself. Otherwise, I had no clue why she put up with my own plainness and mediocrity.

We wound our way around Mt. Tamalpais to a hillside house overlooking huge swathes of the Bay Area. Elena sensed I took time to warm up to parties, so she introduced me to the hostess, a buxom grey-haired woman dressed as the Fairy Godmother—complete with a starry wand—and then let me slink off to the deck with my glass of wine to watch the boats in the Bay switching over to their night lights. We were early, only half a dozen people having arrived so far. The house appeared bigger on the outside, and looking back in through the glass doors I realized it was no more than a large studio. The décor resembled Elena's, but with more art from the Far East than India. I noticed a small frame of parch paper with a quote in calligraphy hanging outside next to the door: "Respect Buddha and the gods, but don't count on their help." – Miyamoto Musashi, *The Book of Five Rings*. I had no idea who this Musashi guy was, but he tickled me with that line.

After some time out there, I made my way back into the house. The dark interior was lit with candles and lamps covered in soft clothed to dim the lights. I expected more people to show up, but no one did. Elena began introducing me to everyone. Each of their flamboyant costumes matched their personalities. One was dressed as Tinker Bell. She was as thin as a rail and laughed a lot, showing big teeth and gums when she did. She was with a large guy in a Bamm-Bamm outfit, complete with a massive wooden club. With his thick beard and crazed expression, I think he'd give real cavemen a run for their money—perhaps even frighten them. Elena seemed to know them quite well, and we were stuck talking on a field of pillows that served as a couch. I reclined into a comfortable position and observed the conversation. They were chatting about a guy who took an old shipping container and turned it into his house. Seemed like the kind of place Bamm-Bamm might live, but I said nothing except for asking how they'd get cell phone reception inside that box. They didn't have an answer for that.

Reclining behind Elena, our bodies lying opposite one another, I could feel the warmth from the back of her calf through my socks as I sipped my wine and grew more comfortable with my surroundings. She noticed what I'd always assumed was social anxiety–at least that's what my ex-wife labeled it–as something different. According to the books, some people possessing fragile nervous systems hold a condition labeled Highly Sensitive by psychologists, and she thought that its description suited me better. Of course, I disagreed, citing my ability to survive rigorous schooling at the U.S. Naval Academy and thirty years battling it out in the financial arena as proof negative. *Overcompensation* was her one-word response to that. I dismissed all of this, but it got me thinking about all the times I'd left parties early or sought refuge from crowds, loud sounds, and anything that annoyed me–lots of things! Even if she were mistaken, I began to appreciate her giving me the freedom and space to warm up to new information or suggest quieter places to go without hassle.

About an hour into the party, I noticed an old woman slide in through the front door wearing a burgundy gown that looked as old as her. Maybe she'd forgotten to wear a costume or maybe that was her costume–hard to tell. Her dark eyes were like those of a falcon, set back far into her skull, and it felt as though they were locking on to mine. I glanced away. I had long tuned out Elena's conversation into a muffle, but I wasn't in the mood to leave or to meet anyone new. I was happy with the bottle of wine that I kept tilting into my glass, with the slow aim of getting drunk. Elena glanced over at me a few times to make sure I was still there, and I would wink or do something else to acknowledge her presence. I heard lots of laughing inside the kitchen where the Fairy Godmother and a few others were standing behind a screen that separated it from the main room.

Before I knew it the woman in the burgundy dress was upon us. She knew Elena, of course, and came over to embrace her. I stood up as well, setting my glass down in a free spot on the bookshelf next to us. Earlier, I perused it looking for books that might catch my interest. They were all titled *The Power of Now*, *The Way of the Peaceful Warrior* and other ones that seemed like psycho-babble self-help books. Elena introduced the woman as Agatha, and I felt those eyes sink into mine like gigantic hooks. Her hand felt very cold to the touch, and it was so bony that it conjured up images of ghost stories about witches and other women that haunt little boy's dreams. Yet, she had a tenderness to her, and gave me an inquisitive nod while searching my face with curiosity. I was courteous to her, but did my best to sit back down and hide out in my little corner behind Elena. My instincts were correct about her–she was a witch. Had I not gotten drunk I could have easily avoided what happened later.

It was about three hours in, when most of us were either giddy or tired as the party hit that inevitable juncture where enough people went home to make the few who stayed more devoted to squeezing the last bit of fun out of it. I yearned to be on the list of those leaving, feeling my attraction to Elena swell and a desire to get her alone. Of course, she suffers from FOMO: Fear of Missing Out, and I was stuck there with the Fairy Godmother, Agatha, and somebody dressed as a Crash Dummy who had a mask painted on so thick I couldn't see the real person. He didn't say much, anyway, and the three of them were busy kneeling at a small table where Agatha had been turning over cards for the past hour. I'd been just out of earshot from the whispers of the people coming up to the table, but I could tell she'd been giving them important information while discussing the cards. Sometimes I'd see a face light up in joy, while at other times they were bathed in sadness or some other emotion that seemed extreme. Elena and I drifted over to them, and I asked what was going on. Elena whispered that she was a psychic working with a tarot deck. Agatha looked up at us, and I assumed Elena was going to sit down across from her. She nudged me over and after declining a few times, I felt myself slide down across from Agatha, a little amused at what might happen.

Agatha made sure my eyes stayed with hers, remaining very still and attentive. She then took a long, slow deep breath and asked to see the palms of my hands. I set my drink down and indulged her, casting a glance up at Elena and rolling my eyes in slight embarrassment. I made a crack about not believing in this sort of thing, and Agatha dismissed it with grace, telling me that believing was not a prerequisite: "only a willingness to be read." Her voice sounded distant when she said this, and I felt a tingling in my hands when she touched them. Hers were still cold and I wondered why that was–maybe she was half dead already. She appeared to be in a trance or something. The creepiness sent shivers up my spine.

"Now, I'm going to turn over three cards. The first is where you've been. The second is where you are now. The third, of course, is where you are headed." She shuffled the deck and flipped over a card faster than an Atlantic City dealer. It was of a man in robes and a flat crown sitting down, holding a circle, with another on top of his head and two below his feet. Each of them inscribed with a star. Behind him lay a small city. "The Four of Pentacles," she muttered. "As you see, the man here is hoarding, making sure no one touches his coins–clutching them for dear life, fearing loss. He cannot move because his feet are too busy holding the coins down. He is tied to his possessions and cannot do anything else. As you can see from the eyes, they are tired. He is tired. Yet, he is also smiling, betraying self-satisfaction over his accomplishments." I shot Elena a scornful look. She said nothing, just placing a warm hand on my shoulder as I turned back to Agatha, who took in a deep breath and began speaking again. "This is where you've been Harry. How you coped with the past, doing what was necessary for your survival."

She turned over a second card with the words *The Tower* on it. It was a dark and ghastly image of a tower on fire with lightning bolts striking it, a golden crown tumbling off the top and people leaping to their deaths. *Just great*, I thought, already feeling swept up in the moment. For all my steadfastness in weighing risks at the bank and making prudent choices, I must admit that I could be gullible when it came to the occult. Even though part of me passed it off as rubbish, I still had another part that believed there to be some truth in it. When no one was looking I read my daily horoscope each morning, hoping for a five-star day. Anything less than four stars and I didn't bother reading it. Deep down, all that stuff gave me the heebie-jeebies.

"This can't be good!" I blurted out in a half-joke, downing the rest of my wine.

"I don't place any judgment on the cards, Harry. Indeed, Mars has come to shake up your world. It is time. This card is one of transformation, which will come after the destruction of ambitions built on false premises. Remember, the Universe only brings about change when we are ready for that change—even if we don't think we're ready for it. Old towers need to be destroyed so new structures can be erected that fit our new selves, our transformed selves. The best thing to do is surrender to it. Just surrender."

"My life is going fine, so I'd say you're one for one at best on the cards, Agatha."

"The cards don't lie." She gave me a pitying look and then turned over a third card. "Five of Cups... very interesting...."

"I've had at least four cups of wine, so maybe the card's saying I need one more."

"It wouldn't hurt," she teased and we both laughed. "But as you can see, three cups are overturned on the card. There are two yet to be filled. So, if you're not driving, you could fill them both." She paused and then her voice lost its playfulness, taking on a dark tone. "You know, Harry, you will need that humor to help you weather the storm. You see this figure in the black cloak? He is dealing with great loss and looking down in despair. If you look closely, he is focused on the three fallen cups and doesn't see the two behind him waiting to be filled. So, no matter what happens, don't forget to look around you. Off in the distance is the bridge that will take him back over the fast-moving river and home again. So, don't forget the cups, and don't forget the bridge."

"OK, will do," I said in a conciliatory tone. I made to stand up, but her hand motioned for me to stay where I was.

"But there is one more thing here. If you noticed, when I initially turned the card over, it was upside down."

"It matters which side they come up?" I'm sure she detected the incredulity in my voice.

"Absolutely. Everything matters in this world. Not just in the cards. *In everything.* Everyone you meet is important. Every sign you pass is a marker on the path."

"So what does it mean then? Being upside down?"

"Well, taken with the Tower card, it signifies that you have a chance of moving past loss and regret and to a better place of forgiveness and acceptance. Moving on, so to speak."

"Who am I supposed to forgive?"

"Yourself, among other people, and the choice will be up to you."

"Isn't it always?"

"Yes. The divine is the great potter spinning the wheel of life, continually reshaping the world based on our choices, opening up new ways. So, do your best to make her job easier."

"*Her job?* So, the divine is a woman now?"

"Of course. Always has been. Women give birth."

"And what is the role of men?"

"Maybe it is to listen." She pursed her lips in satisfaction, scooping up the cards and knocking them back into the deck.

"It's my turn," Elena said with zeal, faux kicking me until I rolled over onto a pillow to watch her reading. Of course, hers was filled with magic and pleasure–unlike mine. I wrote off the entire show as a sham and Agatha yet another feminist charlatan who took pleasure in mocking men in front of their dates to take them down a notch. I poured myself another glass of wine and then another until all the wine was gone, and I would have left the party with the same taste in my mouth if I hadn't experienced something just before we left that to this day still makes the tiny hairs on the back of my neck stand up.

It must have been after midnight and I had just come out of the bathroom, exhausted and hoping Elena wouldn't take too long so we could go back home on the other side of the bridge. Only Agatha and the Fairy Godmother remained, and they were in the kitchen talking about levitation when I broke in with a snide comment. With an arched eyebrow, Agatha asked me if I wanted to see it for real. Of course, after the wretched tarot reading I was more than happy to unmask her as a fake. Before I knew it, she'd hauled over a tall wooden four-legged barstool and asked me to place my hands atop the flat seat. I did as instructed, and then she overlaid her own hands on top of mine so we each stood hunched over the stool. She invited me to concentrate on a vision of the stool rising in the air, and I played along. She closed her eyes, but I kept mine open.

At first, nothing happened. Then, just as I was about to call bullshit, I felt the stool rumble. It rumbled a second time, reminding me of fish

19

nibbling on a line, coming every few seconds and working up into a rapid crescendo. I looked around to see if Agatha was doing something with her feet or some other form of trickery. Perhaps she was gripping the flat seat in a way that allowed her to move it, but my hands were on it and hers on top of mine. We were pressing down on it while a force from below pushed against us. Then it happened; I felt something change in the room or my mind or something, like another presence filled the space around us. The pit of my stomach dropped as the stool rose up on its side and then three legs, still rumbling and shaking as if the force of my mind's will struggled against it rising in the air. I was so astonished that I could concentrate on nothing else and my mind went clear as it envisioned the stool and tried to make sense of what was happening even while looking at it. The world slowed down, and I sensed that the last leg, though barely touching the floor, remained tethered to the earth. I could not let it happen, I thought, while another part of me danced with joy like a child experiencing his first magic act. Just as the final leg left the floor, I pulled my hands away from Agatha's and let the stool tumble over on to its side. Noticing the terrified look on my face, Agatha gave me an empathic pat on my forearm like a mother would her small child.

I said very little after that, just a few goodbyes before stumbling to Elena's car. I didn't say much on the ride home either. Elena, no doubt sensing that the Newtonian world I thought I'd been living in had just been shattered to pieces, kept quiet for the most part. At one point as we were crossing back over the bridge she told of how the psychologist Carl Jung thought all this stuff bunk too until a few incidents changed his mind. I waited for her to elaborate, maybe described the incidents, but she remained quiet, driving me straight home and dropping me off with a sideways hug in the car.

Of course, I woke up the next morning wondering how much I'd experienced at the party was due to wine. A throbbing headache convinced me of this, allowing me to get through the day without having to adjust to some new world. I've thought about that stool a hundred different ways over the years. Sometimes I concoct an entire schema where everyone else was in on some grand joke involving hidden wires or something. I even researched illusionist acts to see how it might have been done. Maybe they set the cruel joke up beforehand as some dark magic to knock my belief system for a loop. On rare occasions, I believe it all happened as it did, feeling a wave of gratitude for having been shown another plane of existence that only a select few get to see. That's usually when I've had a few drinks and my mind wanders back to that night. I guess I'll never know, but one thing is for sure and that's that I wish I had been sober that night.

CHAPTER 5 | MARK LEAPS

I already mentioned Mark, and I could count him as the second curveball thrown my way. At least in terms of how our relationship went from the occasional chat to a deepening friendship that inspired me to follow him. He was thirty years my junior, and like Elena, moved in a world of deliberate slowness that both attracted me and sometimes left me one step away from a contained rage. Of course, at work I donned a thoughtful persona to project leadership. I read all the Jack Welch books, and I knew the game. I played nice most of the time and cut a few throats when I had to, but it also went against my grain and sometimes I would come home exhausted from the effort. Mark's way seemed effortless. His status as a contract employee gave him the luxury of staying above the fray. He didn't have a stake in anything, and the heads-down technical work he performed was so far beyond the reach of our expertise that in a way he was in an ideal position to adopt a Zen monk style of relating to people. I often wondered if his steady and calm demeanor warped into something sinister when no one else was around.

I saw deeper into Mark one night after we were celebrating a big investment we'd received from an Asian bank, which would allow us to expand our mortgage lending portfolio. Don decided to throw a lavish party at the Tonga Room inside the Fairmont Hotel. He had just given a charismatic speech about the effect this influx of investment capital would have on our bottom line. We were about to become a major player in the Bay Area real estate market. The guffaws of excitement and congratulations spread through the room, infecting everyone. Well, just about everyone. I caught Mark standing in the corner trying his best to blend in with a palm tree, but he seemed down in the mouth.

"Well, it's a whole new world, Mark." He shrugged off my platitude, staring down in his drink with the look of a man so utterly bored with his surroundings. I thought it might be because he wasn't a full-time employee and thus not reaping any of the potential rewards like the rest of us. "You don't seem to be enjoying yourself. Are you?"

"Maybe that Max Weber guy was right. We *are* stuck in an iron cage of materialism."

I stifled an uneasy laugh, and would have brushed this off, but I'd already had a few drinks and his comment triggered deep anger in me. I'd heard that line before, and I was sick of people living in one of the richest cities in the world blaming their troubles on avarice. I grabbed his elbow firmly, and he struggled to hold on to his drink. This startled Mark, and he gave me a surprised look, but he sensed the intensity in my eyes.

"Mark, I want you to come with me." I didn't give him a chance to respond, pulling him outside onto California Street. Once we caught our breath in the chilly evening air, I motioned to the posh hotel across the street. "You know what that is?"

"It's a hotel, right?" Mark listened to me with strained patience.

"The Mark Hopkins. Have you heard of it?"

"The Top of the Mark? Who hasn't heard of it?"

"Yes, with the famous glass-walled bar on top, serving overpriced drinks. You pay for the view. It's been around for eons; has changed hands a few times. Big deals worth lots of money. It's now part of the InterContinental chain of hotels. In fact, it's the oldest of them. This hotel we're in here, the Fairmont. It's a landmark too. These were built by successful people who invested their money wisely. *This* is what we do. We help those people invest their money wisely and thus make the future happen so that our sons and daughters can enjoy the fruits of hard-working labor."

"But what is *our* labor? Doing math? I'm sorry, Harry, but I just spent three months on a database and some spreadsheets that are making rich guys richer and I cannot point to anything beyond that. Future... future of what? So, people can sit down and order an overpriced drink and feel all happy about life?"

"What are you, some kind of socialist, Mark?" I tried to lighten the mood with a patronizing smile, and I caught Mark's face wavering to pull himself out of a maudlin downward spiral.

"Of course not, I'm American. I just wish I was doing something a little more for the *common man*."

I placed my hand on his shoulder and gazed into his eyes, feeling myself slip into an avuncular posture. "I understand, Mark. Believe me. There's a lot that I *don't know* in this world. One thing I *do* know is money. Money can buy freedom. It can open the door to opportunities we never knew existed. That doesn't mean that those who earn it, even those who earn a lot of it, are bound in an iron cage. Some people are ruled by the almighty dollar and a slave to it. That's their problem, but that's a psychological problem, not a social one. People always get that wrong. No, as bankers we've chosen to earn our living, our promise of a better future for civilization—which I do truly believe is what we are doing—by making sure we are just a little smarter than the other guy. We get to build the future the way we want it, not the way the other guy wants it, and we are rewarded for it. As simple as that. Not positive or negative. Just is. Most people are worried about money. What they should be more worried about is making sure they have their head screwed on straight. Then the money will come. Those of us holding the purse strings are *not* the problem."

Mark heaved a long sigh and looked up and down California Street as if he meant to catch a taxi. I watched his shadowy face in the moonlight, and he shot me a look of indignant resignation before turning away. I knew I was right. Yet, I felt a foreboding loss in those sad eyes, and they cleaved open my heart, exposing overwhelming pain and loss I had spent years learning how to bury under layers of success and moderate living. He thanked me in a quiet voice and turned to leave. I stood there watching him for a few moments before heading back down into the Tonga room, feeling him still walking up the hill into the night air.

I didn't see Mark very much the rest of that fall, but I still thought about him a lot and the conversation we had in front of the Tonga Room. When the Christmas party rolled around I attended it but planned to slip out after the customary rah-rah speeches. I couldn't spot Mark during any of the commotion, scanning the room for him the entire time I stood at the podium during my own short homily on the record-breaking yield on our burgeoning real estate portfolio, which was threatening to dwarf our business lending. We held the party onsite in subdued temper since after the party in September the management of the Tonga Room politely asked us never to return due to a drunken mishap. The centerpiece of the South Pacific themed Tonga room is a shallow pool complete with a floating band. They had to scuttle it in the middle of an Abba song after a table was hurled into it. I suppose the boys can get a little rough after a few too many drinks.

Spotting an escape route, I patted my way towards the side stairwell, and as I reached for the handle I felt a strong grip on my arm. Before I turned I knew it was Mark's hand. In a sea of dark suits, he wore a white tuxedo as if he were auditioning for the role of Rick in a Casablanca remake. I thought of making a joke of it, but demurred when I saw his peaceful smile, the same one he wore both the day I saw him at the outdoor café and after the mindfulness session.

"Merry Christmas, Harry." I looked back at him with my best December smile.

"Happy Holidays, Mark!" I moved to leave, but his grip tightened.

"Could I talk to you for a second?" He glanced around, "Someplace private? Looks like you were heading out anyway."

"Sure, Mark, follow me." We both bolted through the door and I motioned us up a floor, where we sneaked into my office. I locked the door behind us. "Have a seat."

"Thank you, Harry. I really appreciate your taking the time—"

"No worries. My pleasure. I haven't seen you around much recently." I handed him one of the bottles of beer I pulled out of the small fridge I kept in the corner. I was drinking a little more these days, so sharing a beer with Mark seemed normal; although, drinking in the office outside of scheduled parties was frowned upon. I sat in the chair beside him, resting back with a slight twist towards him, beer dangling from my fingers. "So… what's up, Mark?"

"I just wanted to let you know that I'm not returning in January." He said after exhaling a deep breath.

"Your contract up already?"

"No, but I talked to Judith and I'm at a place where things can easily be handed over to someone else."

My heart sunk, and I regretted spending the past few months dodging phantoms around the office. I had been too harsh on him back on California Street. All I could muster was a questioning hum. He carried a bit of sadness, but appeared excited to be telling me this. I swigged my beer and felt my lips curl up in frustration masquerading as deep thought. He let the words penetrate in the silence and after several seconds I wondered who should speak next. So, I broke in with a question, trying to hide the distress from my voice.

"Well, I'm sorry to see you go. Where are you off to, young lad?"

"To figure out what I'm supposed to do in this world."

"Do you have another job lined up?"

"Nope." He gave me a laughing shake of the head only the young without a care in the world could pull off.

"That seems rather bold." I could hear that avuncular tone slipping out in my voice. "What are you going to do without a job?"

"You remember in the summer I was reading that book by Somerset Maugham?"

"Maugham?"

"Sorry, *The Razor's Edge*… I was reading it that day in the café."

"Oh yeah, right."

"Well, it had a *profound* effect on me."

"Yeah, so?"

"It's just that I really identified with the main character. He rejects the so-called *good life* and travels the world, goes to India to find himself."

"Intriguing. Does he find what he's looking for?"

"I suppose so. The title of the book comes from a verse in the Upanishads, 'The sharp edge of a razor is difficult to pass over; thus the wise say the path to Salvation is hard.' Or something like that."

"You know, Mark. I hate to bring this up, but you *are* living in San Francisco. Best city in the world as far as I'm concerned, but it's a transient one renowned for its part-time Buddhists and general flightiness. I really hope you haven't succumbed to these spiritual vices. I'm no expert. We both know the path to enlightenment is not about practicing yoga and drinking expensive bottled water. It's also not about going off to India to starve oneself and live a life of abject poverty. There's a middle ground one needs to strike."

"Yes, but if it's as narrow as a razor's edge, I have to find out where that edge is."

"But why?" I felt over-reactive heat rise to my head.

"I don't know. Something inside of me, a little voice, just keeps telling me this is not it and I need to leave. Perhaps the seeds were planted by this book and maybe even that mindfulness seminar we had here. I don't know. What I do know is that like Larry in the book I need to find my *own* truth... and if I don't do it now I'm afraid I'll wind up like..."

"...like who, Mark? Like me?"

"I wasn't going to say that!" He shot me an incredulous look. "Besides, you seem to have it all figured out, Harry. At this point, life is probably a piece of cake for you."

"Hardly, but thank you for the vote of confidence."

"Well, I'm just trying to figure out which way is up for me, and right now that means going out there, somewhere."

"Is this about a girl, or a boy, depending on which way you swing? Because if it is, let me just tell you that this city is the worst for single people. Everyone's looking for perfection—and frankly, most of them are aiming a bit out of their league."

"I just broke up with someone, but it's not about her. It's about me and what I want for my life. So, I need to just go somewhere."

"And where might that be? I mean, what's your first stop? I hope it's not India because from what I hear that place is a total mess. Teeming with typhoid, I'm sure."

"I've always wanted to go to Mongolia. Maybe that's where I'll go first."

"Mongolia! My God, man! It's the middle of winter. You'll freeze like a stone. Why don't you pick someplace warm, like Fiji? I'll tell you what, if I were seeking enlightenment, that's where I'd start."

"I'm not joking, and I didn't say I was seeking enlightenment or truth with a capital 'T' or anything like that. I'm just trying to figure stuff out, maybe figure out *my* truth, like I said."

"Fair enough, but I still think you could do all that right here. I'm not just saying that because I like having you around, I just don't think it's out there. Listen Mark, let *me enlighten you*. I've been around a bit, traveled to some countries–been places. This may not be the politically correct thing to say, but it's close to the truth: most of the world sucks. It just does. Sure, there are nice places outside of this city, outside of the state, but really, the vast majority of it sucks. Everyone thinks Paris is nice, but they don't pick up after their dogs and all you do is step in other people's dog shit. Sure, they've got great food, but the people are snotty, and Europe is just filled with socialists who are hanging on by an economic thread. Asia, Africa, Latin America–they are called the *Third-World* for a reason. From what I hear, nothing works right and it's just one big shit show with people fighting for their lives. Might as well park it here and enjoy the best parts of all those cultures from the safety and confines of one of the many restaurants this glorious city has to offer. See, we don't need to go out there. Just bring the people here."

"You crack me up, Harry. You know, if you decide to quit this place you could carve out a great career marketing this city to the rest of the world."

"They should be so lucky!" He snickered at my joke and I had to laugh too.

"Listen, Harry." Mark's voice became subdued and I was no longer talking to some City College boy, but a man who had already spent a thousand years on a mountaintop. "I appreciate you caring for my well-being. We're all spiritual beings. So, I'll be fine no matter what. Even if I run out of money, I'll be in the bosom of the Divine. It's all good."

"You seem so sure of yourself." I felt my tone shifting to skepticism bordering on lambast. The room suddenly became dark and quiet, reminding me of the spooky energy of the séance.

"I am not afraid of destitution or even death. Believe it or not I have faced both already. What I fear beyond those is walking the wrong path for too long. I don't want to waste this life on things I don't care about, and right now I don't care about this city or this bank or the way my life is going. Does that even make any sense to you?"

"Of course it does, on some level. Mark, I may not know you all that well, but I see in you someone with such great potential and I'd hate to see it wasted by sitting around in some cave or going stark-raving mad trying to figure out where your next meal is coming from, or one day waking up to the fact that you could have done so much more starting from a solid footing."

"There is no solid footing, Harry. We're all skating around on melting ice and none of us truly knows how thick it is and whether it will crack for no reason."

"Well, you may have a point, Mark," I said in resignation, not quite believing my own words. "Anyway, I'm glad you pulled me aside to tell me your plans. I'm leaving for a scuba diving trip over the break, so this may be the last time I see you for a while."

"Probably."

"Drop me an email once in a while and let me know how things are going." He nodded with pursed lips and I wanted to make sure he knew I was serious. "And this goes without saying, but I'll say it anyway. I'm not sure where you're at finances-wise, but if you ever need any assistance, let me know. I don't want to find out you froze to death in a gutter because you didn't have enough money for a hot meal or you were slaughtered like a sheep because you couldn't come up with the bride price for a Mongolian lass you knocked up."

"Thanks, Harry. That means a lot to me. Again, no need to worry about me. You know, I have a feeling everything is going to be alright. As a wise man once told me, if you get your head screwed on straight, the money will come." It took me a second to catch his smirk and realize he was throwing one of my lines back at me.

"I might have said that, but it may be bullshit, too. Even if it's true, it's far easier to make a smooth transition. This cutting and running off to a godforsaken place in the middle of nowhere *and* in the middle of winter is just plain madness."

"Yes, it is madness; but like Virgil said, *Fortune favors the bold.*"

"I hope you're both right, Mark. I really do."

"Me too."

And with that he downed his beer, shook my hand, and like a man without any cares in the world, disappeared out of my office.

CHAPTER 6 | TOWER ON FIRE

The Monday after the holiday party Kitty and Don gave me their own Christmas present. Kitty had already scheduled a meeting first thing to catch me before I flew out of town mid-week, and I knew something was up since the curt subject line read "touching base." She and I never touched base on anything, especially after I made it clear that her attempts at team building were a waste of everyone's time. I suppose I could have been more diplomatic with her, but I couldn't stand the preachy tone and always going on about how our main role was building people up so they felt good about themselves. I wasn't from the unearned soccer trophy generation, so her pleas fell on deaf ears. Besides, my guys were kicking ass with the strong financial incentives I put in place. Pats on the back were nice, but padding the bank account was a better way to keep morale up. Or so I thought. Kitty gave a slight knock on my door just after I sat down in my chair. I'd already seen her red shoe poking out from the Persian rug runner.

"Good morning, Kitty." I forced a smile as she came in.

"Good morning, Harry. I trust you had a nice weekend."

"I did, thank you. How about you?"

"It was great, thank you. Listen, Harry. I included Don on this meeting as well. He wants us to swing by his office."

"OK. Must be important, then," I muttered, fishing for a clue to her designs.

She didn't respond except to turn on her heels and head down the hall to Don's office. I noticed a folder under her arm, so I grew curious about what was happening. I knew we had a problem with one of my newer loan officers who'd been caught making too many mistakes on the applications, and I guessed it might have something to do with that–though I'd already warned him that he needed to stop making mistakes if he wanted to keep his job. So, it didn't seem like an HR issue at this point. I also remember seeing the Credit Manager a little too cozy with one of the female tellers at the holiday party. I was aware of his lechery with new hires, but he knew where to draw the line most of the time. Besides, his job performance was stellar, so I wasn't about to fire him over a drunken grope. By the time I arrived in Don's office, Kitty was already sitting, and both wore sober faces.

"Somebody die?" I asked, stifling a laugh.

"Can you get the door, Harry?" Don said, and I took a deep breath, turning to shut it. Normally chummy with me, I recognized something was amiss by his tone. I took a deep breath and prepared for battle. Once I sat down in the chair next to Kitty, Don's massive mahogany desk separating him from us, he leaned back and looked at Kitty. "Kitty, why don't you get us started."

"Sure, thank you Don." She opened the folder in front of her as if to read something to me, but then glanced at both Don and me and uttered in a patronizing tone. "Harry, I'm looking at a complaint here."

"What sort of complaint?"

"It's a complaint about some foul language and other inappropriate comments made in staff meetings."

"Okay. What does that mean?" I gave Don a puzzled look, then turned back to Kitty, whose long-faced dramatic display was so typical of her making a big deal out of nothing. "What staff meetings are you talking about?"

"Yours, Harry."

"OK, is this is a guessing game? Who is complaining about what exactly?"

"Well, I can read through some of the examples of the language used, but I am obliged to protect the identity of the persons filing the complaints."

"Persons? Complaints?"

"Yes, there are a few complaints filed by more than one person."

"Great..." I grumbled with more than a hint of sarcasm, my neck feeling hot. Kitty kept glancing down at the folder as though she were trying to hide inside of it.

"The complaint points more to a culture that is non-inclusive, gender demeaning and possibly racist."

"Gender demeaning? Racist? What the *hell* are you talking about?" I felt my voice crack in anger and fear.

"Perhaps you can give him one or two examples," Don butted in.

"Sure." Kitty nodded her head and flipped through a few pages.

"Harry, did you recently use the expression, 'let's open the kimono a bit'?"

"Gimme a break! There's nothing wrong with that phrase." I rolled my eyes and appealed to Don. "Don, you know I've been saying that years.

29

Heck, we've all said it, probably. Perfectly acceptable."

"What does it mean to you?" Kitty asked with a self-important tilt of the head. This caused me to stumble through in my reply. Instead of answering her, I wanted to wring her obtuse neck.

"Well, in the context of a discussion about revealing information, it simply means we're going to need to open up a bit more about it. I don't recall when I said it last." I let out a hefty sigh. "Look, Kitty. I realize you're trying to do your job, but let's not get caught up in politically correct language. We've got a job to do here, and last time I checked we're doing a *really good* job."

It was as if she didn't hear me at all. "There are more phrases; some are attributed to you, and some to your leadership team. Shall I read them?"

"Sure, indulge me."

"OK… getting one's panties in a bunch, being thrown over a barrel, who do I need to screw to get a cup of coffee around here…"

"Well, I don't drink coffee," I mumbled, but she continued as though I said nothing.

"Then there are the complaints about the Credit Manager engaging in sexual misconduct with a few of the tellers. I'm afraid this all points to an unhealthy boys' club culture that is opening us up to some serious lawsuits." She glanced at Don with a frown, refusing to even look at me until she sensed that Don was on her side.

"Don, what is this shit? You know I run a tight ship and my guys are kicking ass. So much so that we're an attractive buy right now."

"You're right, Harry. We *are* an attractive buy. In fact, I'm looking at a deal with an Asian bank right now that just may do that. So, we can't afford to have any lawsuits on our hands. No one's going to want to buy us if we've got internal problems, lawsuits. You know that!"

I've only heard Don raise his voice a handful of times since I've known him, and I could sense the stress in his last sentence. He stopped, took a breath, and then glanced at both of us, inviting Kitty to leave the room. Once she shut the door, I thought of trying to defend myself, but I knew him well enough that sometimes it's better to just sit there and listen. He stood up and put his back to me, pouring two glasses of scotch. It was nine o'clock in the morning and I was in no mood for a scotch, and neither was he. I guessed he didn't know what else to do and needed a few seconds to gather himself. He handed a glass to me, and I stood up to take it and then sat back down again, holding the glass as though it could slip from my hand at any moment. He downed his own and then gave me a steely look.

"Harry, you and I go back a long way. We were at the Academy together."

"Yeah, and I used to cover your duty shift for you when you were out banging townies back in Annapolis. Remember?"

He stifled a half-laugh, but then his face fell ashen and his eyes filled with tears. "You were one of the first I brought on here when I started this bank. We got this place off the ground."

"Those were the days, weren't they?" I said, slipping into a conciliatory tone. "You know how grateful I am for that. I've worked very hard all these years."

"Yes, you have. You've made us all a lot of money, including yourself. I'm grateful for all that, but Harry, times have changed. It's a different world than when we started. You know that. I'm not sure if I'm going to sell to these Asian guys or what. I'm not sure what's going to happen. What I *am* sure of is that your time is up here. It's been up for a while and deep down you may know that too. At least I hope you do. Harry, I need someone who can manage people in a way that steers us into the twenty-first century, and frankly, it's not you." Don's words struggled for a landing, but bounced off me in the shock of the moment. He looked at me, his eyes glazed with tears, but not crying.

"What am I going to do?" I heard myself asking in a low childlike voice, looking down, my world spiraling down a drain. Don said nothing. All he could manage was a look of deep pity as I crumpled in front of him, my heart breaking in two. I did my best to keep my composure, and I remember hearing a booming voice inside commanding me to keep a stiff upper lip. The Academy had taught me to bounce back from anything, and that I did. I collected myself, stood up and shook Don's hand. It was strange, but after I stepped out of the building and as I walked up Sansome Street, stunned and reeling in distress, I remember stopping and taking a deep breath. I looked all around me at the buildings, some new and some over a hundred years old. I looked up into the blue sky wondering if there was a God up there. I wasn't sure of that any more than I am now ten years later. I do recall feeling a rush of energy through my body lifting me up and leaving me light on my feet—empty and refreshed. Then it hit me. A single word came into my mind: *surrender.* I laughed at that, thinking of Agatha's old face less than two months earlier, and the image of Elena's profile with the red cables of the Golden Gate Bridge and the setting sun behind her. That moment on Sansome Street was the clearest I'd been since as far back as my days at the Academy, sailing on the Chesapeake on cool afternoons in late autumn.

Before I had left Don's office he requested I take a few days off to decide whether I was up to coming back for a month to ensure a smooth transition. The choice was mine. It was gracious of him since the usual practice in the industry was to give people the boot without ceremony as though they never existed—have security escort them off the premises. We had too much history and goodwill for that. So, I considered this and a moment later put it out of my mind as I trudged up to my apartment and changed into hiking clothes. I wasted no time renting a car and heading up to my favorite hiking trail just north of Bolinas. The trail started as a cliff side coastal trail and like an uncoiled snake wound its way down into the forest to a small lake.

Still upset over the firing and trying to make sense of it all, I considered leaping off the cliff, feeling a hidden force rise within, urging me to do it—even pulling me to the edge. I shrugged it off and stopped myself for two reasons. The first was that even though it was December, the sun was shining so bright it made up for the cold breeze and it just felt great to be out there on a day like that. The second reason, and no doubt the one that won me over, was that I wasn't certain if the ten-story drop from the cliff's edge to the rocks and sprays below would be enough to do me in. With my dumb luck, I might wind up in a wheelchair after some miserable Good Samaritan climbed down to save me. I saw no one else out there that day, but it was a possibility, and a risk I didn't want to take.

I went back to the bank on Wednesday, hours before my flight to Grand Cayman. I kept my upper lip stiff while working with Don and Kitty to lay the groundwork for a smooth succession. Finding a replacement was not a problem with so many qualified candidates in the city. Three weeks later and we had someone in the chair. Two weeks after that I was gone. It took skill and fortitude to steer the departure conversations over positive waters, and I had enough gray hairs to make the case for early retirement. Those closest to me, particularly staff who'd worked under me for several years, went through their own stages of grief—or at least that's what they showed me. I told them that a year later they will have forgotten all about me. That seemed to make things worse. So, for the most part I just did the best I could to go out on a high note. I had to chuckle at the card my staff presented to me at the going away party. It was a hand-drawn woman wearing a kimono, with two flaps that when opened revealed signatures of best wishes, etc. from everyone on my team. I knew the officer who'd created it—the one person in the office with enough creative talent for that. If only she'd known how close to home it hit. I loved that card!

Some of my old friends advised me to file a lawsuit, or at the very least tell Don to go to hell—I didn't owe him or the bank anything. Vindictiveness did not flow through my blood, and besides, they were wrong. I *did* owe him and the bank something. They'd both given me decades of a professional life and promising financial security for the rest of it. Years later, I would feel deep gratitude for Kitty and Don setting me on a new path, even if they were unaware of it. At the time, I felt no anger towards either of them, only sadness knowing the hand I played in my own fate. I'd been on the other side of this several times. So, I accepted being driven off the mound like an old lion. It was bound to happen sooner or later. I just wished I'd been given some heads up earlier that it was coming.

I found strong support from Elena. She became my rock. Of course, she took no time in pointing out that this was all part of the Tower crumbling away and giving me the chance at a new life, and as she put it, learning that I'm defined by the Universe and my connection to it and not some job or station in life. After I returned from my scuba vacation and finished out January at the bank, I spent most of my afternoons throughout February and March cuddled up on her couch that overlooked the ocean. My apartment was too close to the bank, and after my last day there I didn't even want to be on that side of the city during the day.

Turning my mid-life crisis into a cliché, I bought an old black Triumph motorcycle. I used it to zip over to her place in the mornings and catch the 8:00 a.m. yoga class. Then I would stick around until she kicked me out sometime after dinner. I didn't do much else during that time aside from the occasional long run on the beach on days when it didn't rain. I was growing more used to Elena's place with her warm tea mugs and Bohemian couch of fantastic colors, gazing out over the ocean. The contrast between our apartments became a source of amusement for both of us. Whereas my furniture and décor bore a resemblance to a sparkling new espresso machine, hers felt like a hippie shrine filled with Buddha statues, vases of peacock feathers and other strange flowers, and colorful knickknacks. A comfortable mess where I alternated between feeling deep relaxation and wanting to haul a garbage can in there and toss everything into it and start over again. On the rare occasion that she made it over to my place, she giggled at how bare and clean to the point of obsession it was. "You really don't need to fold your socks and underwear, you know."

While our relationship developed like a tiny plant struggling to unfurl leaves, six months in and I still hadn't had sex with her. No blossoming flower. Her rebuffs were gentle at first, and then we had *the big talk*. Seems she saw something deeper in me and had it in her head that big love did not thrive on sex. In fact, I still remember her shouting it to me across the couch while I felt torn in two. Harry the man, the *virile man*, demanded she capitulate to my basic human carnal needs. As she put it, she needed to sidestep that brute and make direct appeals to my so-called *Higher Self* to break free from trite relationship patterns reinforced by Hollywood. As she put it, we needed to take a chance on a relationship built on friendship. I had no clue what a healthy one resembled, and a side of me wanted no part of that. So, I remained skeptical and kept one foot outside the door while the other stood holding visions of her, burgeoning memories of our moments together: my hand on her cheek and nose buried in the other, the crackle of tofu in an iron skillet and wishing it were a steak, slapping cards down during a cribbage game on a rainy day, listening to her voice singing on the veranda, bearing my soul by accident.

Once, when I tried to stare her into sexual submission her eyes squinted, and she flung an obscure quote from Goethe my way: "That is the witchcraft you poor deluded fool. Each man sees in her the sweetheart of his soul." Perhaps a man in love does in fact project spiced-up reality onto a woman. What's the harm in that? "However *'natural'* it might be," she retorted, "we must not turn our loved ones into gods and goddesses. It only slights the real ones and gives them cause to betray us."

"Where do you come up with this stuff?" I hurled at her. As much as I railed against her lofty appeals to my Higher Self, part of me appreciated the intellectual rigor it required to keep up with her, not to mention invoking classical imagery that fed my imagination. She didn't fall for my usual charm and tricks and other ways of winning a woman over that had worked so well in the past, including on my ex-wife, who never quite lived up to the promise of Aphrodite, who I tried my best to fashion her into with poor results. No, she was a different sort and demanded a *real* connection. As strong as I am, I felt myself seduced by her promise of eventual lovemaking separate from, but on a par with the gods.

CHAPTER 7 | HIGH ART

In late March I received an email from Mark just after I'd woken up.

Dear Harry,

Greetings from Ulaanbaatar (UB for the locals)! I hope you get this message because I tried your bank email, but it bounced back for some reason. I found this one online.

As you can see from the attached picture, I didn't take your advice and some days wish I went to Fiji after all. I never knew cold until I moved here. Things haven't really gone as planned, but do they ever? I left SF just after the holidays and landed here, not knowing a soul. I wandered around UB a few days and found the expat crowd at the Mongolian barbecue of all places. It's not a real Mongolian thing—some American guys came over here and opened one up to cater to expats—a weird concept if you ask me, but the food is great!

Anyway, through someone I met there I found a place to live and a job selling felt covers to the nomads to put over their ger tents (outsiders call them "yurts", but if you want to sound like a local, you need to call them "gers"). These covers reduce heat loss, so they don't need to burn as much fuel in the wintertime to stay warm. I'm also selling clean cook-stoves and other things to fight pollution. Did I tell you how cold it is here?? Most days it doesn't get above zero Fahrenheit and isn't light out for all that many

35

hours. It's also super smoggy because people burn their trash to stay warm. My coat is covered in a layer of soot just going to the corner store and like everyone else I have to wear something over my mouth if I want to go outside! Old London has nothing on this place!

Anyway, I'm reading a lot (and drinking lots of vodka to keep warm). I'm writing to see if you can send me a few books to read since I've devoured everything I could get my hands on here and the bookstores don't carry many English translations. I would really appreciate it. Feel free to come for a visit if you'd like. It's not Fiji, but it has its charms!

All the best and I hope you are enjoying life as usual.

Mark

I closed the email and printed out his attached picture. He was standing in front of one of those gers with a big pile of furs draped around him. He was smiling and the whole scene looked comical. I felt tears trying to flood my eyes, unsure why they were coming. I guess he didn't know I'd been fired from the bank. Resourceful guy, though. I grabbed my leather jacket and headed over to Elena's place. After yoga, I was sitting on her couch gazing out over the ocean while I could hear her making tea over in the kitchen.

"You know that guy Mark I told you about?"

"Yeah, I remember you telling me about him." She responded, sitting next to me with a tray of Kava tea. It was my favorite tea as it reminded me of Fiji.

"I received an email from him this morning." I yawned, taking my usual cup—a cheerful monk etched into the side of it—before she set the tray down next to her.

"Interesting."

"I think I told you he set off for Mongolia just after the holidays."

"That's right. To go find himself. After reading that Maugham book."

"Good memory, sister!"

"Well, I like that one too, so it stuck out in my mind. Anyone who appreciates that book has a little substance. As I recall, you took a liking to him."

"Sure, nice kid." I slid the printout of the photo he sent me from my pocket and handed it to her. She unfolded it and studied the picture for several seconds.

"Gentle soul. He has the face of a seeker," she said with resolute authority.

"He asked me to send him some books. Said I should come for a visit too, but it's still winter over there, and it will probably last a few more months."

"Yeah, I had a friend who served over there in the Peace Corps. She said it's a bit like New York with just two seasons: winter and construction."

That made me laugh and I pulled her on to my lap, burying my head in her neck. We sat there motionless for several minutes.

"You could send him some books, but why don't you bring them out to him?" I heard her say, feeling the vibrations in her chest. I lifted my head and scanned her eyes to gauge her seriousness.

"Mongolia? You kidding me? It's a frozen wasteland of... well, mongrels."

"I think you mean Mongols." She shook her head as if I were a small child. "Ever since you left the bank you've been moping around here in the rain. Maybe it'd do you good to see a little bit of the world beyond Europe and tropical islands."

"And freeze to death? No thank you. Besides, I'm still trying to convince you to come to Fiji with me."

"Maybe in a few months. We're still getting to know each other, and I'm not ready to take that next step with you yet. That's too much."

"Too much? What's it been, six months... sort of? All I'm talking about is parking ourselves on a beach and doing some occasional snorkeling."

"Well, as I told you before, a lot happens in the slowness, and as much as I love getting to know you, going anywhere like that right now is just too fast for me." She stood up and moved to the end of the couch, easing herself down as if she were entering a hot bath.

"I thought you New-Agey chicks were all about free love and such."

"Yeah, well, you missed me by twenty years. Sorry. These days I'm seeking a higher connection, and that takes time and patience. Are you still up for that?"

"I suppose I have to be up for it since you're holding my heart hostage."

"I wish you didn't see it that way. I wish you saw it from a spiritual perspective."

"It's not my fault I was born lusty and I appreciate the finer things in life, sex being one of them."

"*Evolved* men are sexy."

"I'll take your word for it. Besides, I'm only hanging in there because your cooking is so damned good–and this tea isn't too bad either."

She snorted into her oversized cup and scrunched her eyes–a sure sign of deciding whether to be amused or offended. She set the cup down on the tray, casting one of those searching looks as though trying to locate the spot on my head that would allow her to peel off a layer. Her adeptness at nudging me in the right places made it work between us, though most days I considered dumping her–until I would catch sight of those legs or the way her shoulders twisted during one of her sideways glances. One glance into her eyes and I felt the same way I do when stretched out on a hammock on a warm day, a cool breeze on my face and sparrows singing in the trees above. No, I couldn't leave her then even if I tried. "Based on what you told me of Mark, I think you should bring him some Hermann Hesse books. My intuition is telling me that's what he needs right now."

"First of all, I'm not going to Mongolia. I thought I just said that. Second of all, I don't think he needs any hippy-trippy books. A man struggling to find himself should be reading *Unlimited Power* by Anthony Robbins or *The Wealthy Barber* or someone else who's made it big in this world. You're always going on about how great fiction is, but fiction is just that–fiction. Dreams. I live in a world of facts and like Churchill said, *facts are better than dreams*. Everyone else is basing their life on some false hope that makes absolutely no sense."

"One day you just might learn that fiction is high art, Harry, root of the truth. The great works of literature describe layers of what it means to be human–and some of us find meaning in those stories as they point to universals. I wonder about some of those books you read, which you don't really need at this point. They may help a few people by marking out the path of one successful man, but their value is more in the way they can motivate the few people already standing on the precipice of success and needing a gentle nudge. The rest of us are too far back and wrestling with some pretty powerful demons for that to work just yet."

I dismissed her with a wave of the hand.

PART II | OUTER MONGOLIA

CHAPTER 1 | I SEE MARK AGAIN

A week later I was on a flight to Mongolia with a bag full of books, two of them written by Hesse. I felt a sense of relief and freedom looking out over the Pacific Ocean. Elena's gentle prodding made me feel I was somehow in divine hands now, and as much as I teased her for the unconventional views she went on about, a tiny part of me believed them too.

Some of my tropical vacation destinations could be considered third-world countries, but I never noticed the poverty since I often traveled direct from airport to resort. Leaving the Ulaanbaatar (UB) airport and passing over the roadway into town made for a jarring experience. I expected to see those ger tents Mark wrote about dotting a sweeping landscape like some picturesque brochure. Instead, I noticed thousands of them wedged together in slums covered in dirty speckles of snow. With a charcoal gray sky and the occasional grim face on the side of the roadway, I felt like I landed on the edge of the world with the next stop somewhere between the *Twilight Zone* and the harsh mining conditions where the little girl worked in the beginning of *Doctor Zhivago*. Perhaps it was the dullness of the end of winter or the idle cranes and half-completed buildings downtown, but my initial assessment of UB was that it lacked the aesthetical character needed to be considered a world-class city. It was late, and I was tired and needed a hot shower and warm meal. The hotel promised a shiatsu massage, catering to Japanese businessmen who appreciated that sort of thing. So, after an early dinner I treated myself to a not-so-gentle walk on my back before laying a leaden head on my pillow to sleep for thirteen hours.

My muscles staged an open revolt the next morning. While Benadryl helped with the overnight sleep, my head felt like it needed to be held up by someone else. I decided to postpone the search for Mark. In an act of indulgence draped in necessity, I went for another shiatsu massage, drawing an older man with hands like a linebacker. I spent the rest of the morning in a steaming pool inside a spooky cave, then took in a late lunch at the hotel restaurant, finishing out the day propped up in bed watching American movies on the television set that hadn't even made the cut on American cable. I fell asleep around seven, grateful that I took another Benadryl before dozing off so that I could sleep through the night. It was an old trick that prevented the dreaded 3:00 a.m. bug-eyed wake up that plagued most overseas travelers trying to switch over to the new time.

The next morning, I woke up groggy, but fresh from rest. I was ready to go find Mark. After breakfast, I hauled the backpack full of books over my shoulder and trotted down to the lobby to rustle up a taxi. I approached the friendliest-looking person I could find at the front desk, a boy about the same age as Mark.

"Good morning, sir. How is your stay?" he said with a chipper smile. Seeing the imposing Genghis Khan imagery everywhere, I half-expected to be greeted by brutes clutching longbows and sabers. Instead, he and everyone else I encountered so far displayed a courteous gentleness bending towards hospitality. I kept waiting for the warrior edge to emerge on their faces, but that history must have been wiped clean by centuries of Buddhist influence. Of course, as a general principle the hospitality industry doesn't hire beastly people. So, I reserved final judgment until after I rubbed elbows with a few more people on the street.

"So far so good," I responded to him. "Everything has been pleasant and comfortable. By the way, I think we spoke the other night when I checked in. Sorry if I was a little grumpy with you all."

"It really is no problem, sir. It was a long flight from America, I'm sure."

"Miserable. By the way, your English is very good. Not like some of the others. Where did you learn it?"

"Ohio, sir. I went to Ohio University in Athens, Ohio."

"Really? Athens? Didn't know there was an Athens in Ohio."

"Yes sir. I studied for my bachelors after spending my last year in high school there as a foreign exchange student."

"Did you like Ohio?"

"Oh, yes, sir. Ohio is really a wonderful place. I love it there. I still have many friends who email me. Someday I might go back for a visit."

"Did you travel much outside of Ohio?"

"I went to Washington, DC once, but that is all. Very nice, the White House and Washington Monument. Someday I hope to bring my family there."

"I'm curious; would you rather live here or there?"

"I don't know. My family is here. I love Ohio, and there are many opportunities in America, but I like it here. Here is home. I miss some things, though."

"Like what?"

"Football games and keg parties." He said this with a youthful laugh. "So *crazy!*"

I looked at his nametag. "Listen, Zul. I was wondering if you could help me with a taxi. I need to find an address."

"Of course, sir. I am happy to help. Do you have the address?"

"Yes, it is here." I showed him a printout of the address Mark had given me to send the books to, and he studied it for a few seconds with a searching face. I waited for the aha moment to wash over him, but it never happened, and he seemed to plunge further and further into confusion. After asking me to wait in a polite tone, he showed it to one of his colleagues, who then showed it to another, the three of them all staring at it like an unsolvable riddle. A few minutes later, Zul came back over to me, holding the paper between us.

"Excuse me. Is this a business or residence, sir?"

"I thought it was his home address. It's from a friend of mine, but I don't know if he's living there or not. Why?" As I spoke, I realized how stupid it was of me to fire off a single email a few days before telling Mark I'm on my way but giving him no other notice that I was coming. He might have thought I wasn't serious, and I hadn't heard back from him yet. The idea of surprising him revealed how reckless and unwise I'd become in such a short time.

"Well, looks like it might be in the ger district. On the edge of town, I think. I really don't know. The roads are not marked well. They keep changing as people are moving. Do you have a phone number for your friend?"

"No, sorry."

He stood deep in thought, and I wondered if this request either went above his pay grade or outstretched his mental capacity. Nevertheless, I was touched by how much time and effort he and the others were putting into something they could have shrugged off as not their job.

"Listen, Zul. Why don't you find me a taxi where the guy speaks a bit of English? I don't mind driving around a bit to find it. I've got time."

"I will go with you, sir." He stunned me with a matter-of-fact resoluteness. "Just let me fetch my coat, please."

Something told me not to argue with him, but to just let him come with me. I was already piling up curious experiences over the past few days, so I just rolled with it. The two of us jumped in a dirty old taxi and drove across town, Zul playing tour guide as he pointed out Sukhbaatar Square and its massive bronze statue of Genghis Khan seated on a throne. I always thought it was spelled and pronounced *Genghis*, at least that's what I was told growing up. Somewhere along the way either the locals changed it to Chinggis or the rest of us were wrong all along.

I suppose I expected more of the downtown area, with a few high-end shops and not a single five-star hotel. I marveled that a city hundreds of years old still looked like it was just getting started. Zul must have read my mind, because he discussed its roots as a nomadic Buddhist monastic center evolving vis-à-vis a culture where moving around a lot is the norm. For a people who spent millennia living in tents they could pick up and take with them to follow the food, the notion of a city that stays put is still new even after hundreds of years. I began to see more and more of these round tents as we moved beyond the city square and toward the outskirts of town. As Zul put it, UB is a small city surrounded by thousands of gers. Some of those communities, particularly along the outer edges, are more fluid as families make a temporary stay, while the ones closer to the city center form more permanent peri-urban neighborhoods. Many of those neighborhoods resembled some of the shanty towns I'd seen in southern Maryland during my youth whenever we'd drive down from Baltimore to my grandfather's place.

I heard Zul in the front seat, talking with the driver while they both kept glancing at the envelope as a touchstone for finding their way. I could sense we might be getting close as the taxi stopped and backed up, trying a different route, then turned around again while they studied sides of buildings interspersed among gers. At one point, the driver stopped to ask a crusted old man standing on the corner in layers of drab clothing and a huge furry hat. The old man grumbled something and cast a curious glance at me; my window rolled down to let me escape the driver's choking cigarette smoke. The neighborhood looked a bit rough, though I found the Mongolians themselves, despite being gentle when in conversation, very tough looking. Of course, as a product of the Cold War era, etched faces underneath giant babushka hats always looked rough to me. Nevertheless, I was determined to buy one of those hats when I had the chance. They looked warm at a time when every part of me was cold. In the end, we stopped in front of a small red brick building that looked out of place among the gers. I couldn't make out the Cyrillic lettering on the sign over it, but Zul turned to me and nodded, his demeanor shifting from slight anxiousness to quiet triumph.

"I think this place where your friend is." I could tell from the way his English was breaking that indeed this venture had stretched him far out of his comfort zone. "We will wait here, or I can come with you if you'd like."

"Thank you, Zul. I can take it from here. Why don't you head on back to the hotel? I've taken up enough of your time." I slipped him 25,000 Tugriks (about $20 U.S. back then) and after some hesitation, he took it.

"We will wait to make sure you find your friend."

I glanced around, noticing a few people on the muddy street noticing me. My blond hair, blue eyes, and sleek businessman's coat set me apart and while I didn't quite fear these faces, they gave me a bit of a stir. I rapped four times on the door and waited. A single window seemed to be covered in brown paint, so I had no way of knowing if anyone was inside. I glanced back at Zul's placid face—an expression I would come to associate with Mongolia—then knocked again. Maybe I should have listened to Elena and at least gave him the date I was coming so we could arrange a meeting. I heard an inner door slam and then the movement of someone approaching. A bolt popped and then the door cracked open, an unfamiliar face on the other side. It scrutinized me and then opened wider, so I could see it was an oversized man on the verge of middle-age, with rosy cheeks and western features.

"May I help you?" The thick accent sounded European.

"My name is Harry. I'm looking for a friend of mine, Mark." At that, his face softened into a smile.

"Oh, Mark. Yes. You're a friend of Mark's? Please *do* come in out of the cold." I thanked him and sent Zul and the driver off with a confident wave, shutting the door behind me and pulling the heavy backpack from my shoulders. I let it land on the carpeted stone floor with a thud.

"I am Stefan. Can I fix you a cup of tea?"

"That would be great, thank you."

Stefan motioned for me to sit down and made a quiet shuffle into the back room. I moved over to an old fabric couch and at the last moment decided to sit in one of the two large wooden chairs with red velvet cushions. I felt an annoying fluorescent light bearing down on me from above—bright and humming. While I found some comfort in the chair after enduring an hour of old springy seats in the taxi, between the harsh light and the slapdash décor I remained uncomfortable. The air also carried a musty smell that reminded me of my graduate school apartment where the only cleanup that occurred happened when someone's girlfriend couldn't take it anymore. An overused ashtray stared back at me on the wooden coffee table, along with an old copy of the German magazine *Der Spiegel*. Stefan returned a few minutes later with two large steaming mugs, placing one of them on the table beside me and plopping down on the couch with his, pulling his feet underneath him as the Buddhists do.

"You from America, no?" he said with a pleasant smile.

"Yes, Mark and I used to work together. I came to bring him some books and to see what he's been up to." I motioned to the backpack beside the couch.

"Oh, he didn't say. Anyway, would be good to have some new books around here."

"You are from Germany?"

"Yes, but I'm half Swiss on my mother's side."

"I was in Germany once upon a time. Whereabouts are you from?"

"Oh, a little town near the Austrian border."

"I passed through there in the summertime on my way to Salzburg. Seems like a great place to visit in the winter."

"I could ski before I could walk, actually." That made me chuckle.

"Any skiing out here?"

"Mongolia? No." He waved his arm in defeat. "People here just drink vodka to get through the winter. I thought the Swiss Alps were cold. Your man Mark came here at the very worst time, in fact. *Der hat eine meise!*"

"Where is Mark, by the way?"

"He is working. He has a job selling environmental products."

"Oh, is that where he is now?"

"Yes. He returns late afternoon. You can wait here for him, but that might be a long time and there's no telling when he'll return."

"Any idea where he might be, exactly?"

"Hard to say, really." He looked around and then made a self-conscious twitch. "I work for GI Zed, if you are wondering why I am home today. I usually work from the house on Mondays. Sometimes Mark returns home for lunch, though I am not sure about today."

"What is the GI Zed?"

"It's the development agency for the German government."

"Interesting. What are you doing for them?"

"I am working in the energy efficiency program area. Clean cook stoves, solar panels, products like that. Mark is working with one of our affiliate partners on distribution."

"That's fascinating. With all the pollution, I would say you have your work cut out for you."

"For sure. In the summertime the skies are clear. Today, it is overcast, but most of that is pollution. Did you know that this country spends the equivalent of four percent of its GDP on health costs directly associated with the pollution in winter? Climate change is driving the nomads to UB, but they have no livelihood here, so they cannot find work and are very poor. Sixty percent of the population lives in the ger district. Some build houses, but most still live in their gers. They wind up burning whatever they can get their hands on just to survive. I've seen people burning old truck tires. Pay attention when you're outside as you can sometimes see different colored smoke coming out of the chimneys: yellow, green, red. Almost no one has running water. Imagine having to get up in the middle of the night, negative thirty-five degrees Celsius, just to take a crap in some hole outside? It's a big mess."

"Wow, I had no idea." I'd heard much of this environmental rhetoric before from the tree-huggers back home. So, much of what he said I softened in my mind. Although, the precision and authority with which he spoke, along with the burning tires comment, swayed me to consider his perspective. No doubt I was taking in some of those toxic fumes while we sat in the living room, which was still cold, but being warmed by something. "By the way, how do you heat this place?"

"Ah, good question! We have installed solar panels on the roof that generate some electricity. So, we can use energy-efficient radiators. Most of the people in this community use coal-burning stoves. We are trying to switch them over to more energy-efficient devices, with limited success. They are still *quite* expensive."

I drank my tea, its spice filling my head with energy. Stefan seemed to have a wealth of knowledge about clean energy, Mongolia and pretty much any topic I mentioned. He had been living in UB for the past four years, and from his demeanor appeared both committed to staying on indefinitely or traveling back Germany at a moment's notice. Perhaps what gave that impression were his fashionable eyeglasses pointing toward a futuristic world juxtaposed against thick cashmere socks and embroidered felt slippers. While his jowly face and short-cropped hair edged with specks of silver gave him a comical look, there was no mistaking the intensity of his steely gray eyes. He appeared a man who ate life, both in the literal and figurative sense. He wasted no time on pretention, directing his energy to a professional drive aimed at wielding technology for the common good. His erudition and ease of navigating a conversation with polite sincerity and a hint of humor very much reminded me of the Europeans I'd met over the years, who often seemed more educated and sure-footed than my countrymen—or me, for that matter.

From Stefan I learned that Mark was very lucky to have found him and his friends at the Mongolian barbecue restaurant because not that many locals speak English and his first few weeks in the country were rough going. The large monastery in UB rejected him first, assuming he was a tourist and he couldn't convince them he wanted to stay. Something in Stefan's voice gave me the impression that perhaps Mark hadn't tried very hard. I've heard these monasteries are famous for turning people away to test their mettle. So, without any options he approached a table of laughing expats and therein found a job and a place to live. I detected a bit of self-praise in how Stefan told that part of the story as though he and his friends had rescued Mark from a grim fate.

After an hour of listening to Stefan, the unease of overstaying my welcome began to set in. Waiting there for Mark was not an option I considered worthwhile. I could wander around looking for him or come back later. Instead, I chose to leave the contact information for my hotel and the backpack, telling Stefan to feel free to rummage through it since he also seemed to be deprived of reading material beyond the magazine that looked several months old. Stefan threw on a massive Russian coat and flagged down a taxi that was in even worse shape than the one that brought me there. He gave the driver the name of my hotel in Mongolian. After a firm handshake, I was off again. Stefan seemed to be taking care of Mark, and from the way he spoke of him, enjoyed having him around. That was reassuring and not altogether unsurprising. Mark's innocent vulnerability made him the kind of guy people wanted to help.

As we wound our way through the narrow muddy streets, I observed the fuel gauge on the taxi nearing empty. This had been the case with the other taxi, and I wondered if these guys lived hand-to-mouth and couldn't afford the cost of filling up the tank. Who knows, maybe they feared thieves who might siphon off a few liters overnight. While I considered this, and observed the passing scenes of people trudging through a thick mix of snow and mud, I caught site of Mark's unmistakable bright face passing by. He stood away from the road, talking with two Mongolians. I shouted for the driver to stop, and he bounced his body sideways, but it didn't seem to register with him. So, I clutched his shoulder and again shouted for him to stop. I felt the car lurch to a stop, and he stared back at me, face burning with surprise. I pointed out the window and mumbled something even I couldn't understand. He answered with a shrug. So, I shoved a fistful of Tugriks at him and bid him farewell, stepping out of the taxi and slamming the door. Oh well, another botched interaction.

Mark hadn't seen me, and even as I approached the trio standing beside a puffy white ger, he seemed deep in conversation and unapproachable. I hung back several yards behind him, like a stalking lion waiting for an opportune moment. The younger man standing next to him could have been an interpreter, as I watched Mark pause a few times while the other spoke to the older man in their tongue-twisting language. I circled around them to place myself within Mark's view, but he remained focused on the conversation. This went on for several minutes, and during that time I took notice of the surroundings, wishing I had a warmer hat on. Mark wore local garb, complete with a fur hat that covered his ears. His looked different— more Soviet style than most of the ones I'd seen. When his conversation ended and he shook hands with the older man and turned to walk away with the younger one, I belted out in a Russian accent.

"Eh, comrade!" He glanced over his shoulder, gradual recognition twisting into a smile.

"Harry? What the hell…" His voice trailed off and so did the color in his face. I wondered if he thought I brought horrific news. "Wow, you're here! I didn't expect you so soon… is everything OK?"

"Couldn't be better." I moved closer and saw the other one scrutinize me with protective eyes. "I was in the neighborhood and just thought I'd come and check on you in person."

Mark reached out an ungloved hand and shook my own, still in shock seeing me in person and trying his best to appear welcoming. It was difficult for both of us not to feel awkward, and again, I regretted not taking Elena's

48

advice to send him my arrival date. It would have been challenging anyway since I booked my flight last minute.

"Well, welcome to the edge of the world! I got your email, but didn't know when you were coming. So, this is a pleasant surprise." He shook his head as if I were a toddler with a hand stuck in the cookie jar. The color trickled back into his chapped face and we stood there gazing at each other. "I'm so glad you're here, Harry. It's really great to see you."

"Absolutely, and you'll be happy to know that I brought some books for you. They're at your place. I was just there. I met Stefan."

"Oh yeah?"

"Seeing you just now was purely coincidental. I was actually on my way back to the hotel."

"Well, lucky me. Why don't we go warm ourselves up somewhere?" He turned to the other man, "Harry, this is Tsenguun, my friend and interpreter."

"Nice to meet you, Tsenguun." I butchered his name, stuck out my hand and he gave me a firm shake and pleasant nod.

"Tsenguun, I think we're done this morning. Do you want to join us for an early lunch?"

Tsenguun demurred, not wanting to be a third wheel, I suppose. They agreed to meet up again after lunch, and once he said goodbye the two of us started for the direction of Mark's place. Walking beside him, I detected a slight shift in his gait. Could have been the cold air, but he seemed to walk with a bit more spring in his step, as if leaping into the future. His presence and the way he spoke about his work as we made our way through streets and people displayed an effortless quality, like when the sails are trimmed just right on a sailboat hitting its sweet spot. Indeed, I sensed Mark had found a sweet spot, if but a temporary one. As we neared his little house, he stopped and put a hand to his brow.

"Just remembered. I don't have a *thing* to eat in the house. Unless you want leftover mutton that didn't taste good the first time around. Why don't we jump in a taxi and go someplace decent?"

"Sure, I'm up for anything."

"I know a great Indian-Mexican restaurant," he said, hailing a passing car. I shot him an incredulous look as we climbed inside.

"Indian-Mexican food in Mongolia? Sounds like a recipe for indigestion.

"Believe it or not, it's quite good."

CHAPTER 2 | MONGOLIAN STYLE INDIAN MEXICAN FOOD

I didn't get sick from the Indian-Mexican culinary fusion. In fact, Mark was right. The food delighted my taste buds despite none of the dishes tasting either Indian or Mexican–more like a smorgasbord of curried bean dip wrapped in various tortilla-like flatbreads. After a few days I had already grown tired of the Japanese cuisine at the hotel and the occasional local dish I tried and set aside after a bite, or in one instance, a single glance. During lunch I began probing Mark on his life and new job. In addition to Stefan, he had another roommate. Her name was Sarah, a twenty-four-year-old ex-Peace Corps volunteer trying to set up a website for people to give to other people. Mark didn't know enough about it to clue me in on the specifics, but as he spoke about her I observed the subtle cues of romantic interest. He knew more about his job selling environmental products, and I relished in learning the details on something that up until then I'd only read about. Even when I watched him earlier with the old man in front of his ger, I could tell he was good at the soft-sell. Others trusted his face to tell the truth.

"They sell themselves, Harry. People here need them, and that's what matters most. A clean cook stove means less coal burned, which means their monthly expenses go down. Of course, the family and even society benefits from reduced pollution. They're still burning coal and maybe other things, but a lot less of it. Some of the other products are a bit tougher to sell because clients cannot see the immediate financial benefits. An extra felt cover reduces heat loss and solar panel kits give them access to electrical options, particularly for those who are not on the grid–people living on the fringes, but I'm finding that these don't sell as well. Most of the kits are first generation, so they break down a lot. Besides, they're very expensive."

"I saw you had an interpreter. Why don't they just have local people selling to local people? Would save the cost of having two of you pounding the pavement—or muddy snow in this case."

"Well, sadly, *innovative* products sell better when outsiders... especially westerners, are presenting them. Somehow our ideas are worth more, even though they're not even made by us, but have words written in English, which is good for marketing. We represent the future, I suppose."

"That makes sense. That guy back there was looking at you like you had all the answers. I bet you could have sold him a pile of nuts and bolts and he'd be happy."

"Not exactly. These people aren't stupid—especially after years under the Soviets and now the Chinese trying to spread their influence. They're suspicious of outsiders. There's a strong nationalist undercurrent flowing through the country right now. So, I'm a little surprised that they are so accepting of western influence—albeit technological. By the way, all we've done is talk about me. Which I notice you have a habit of doing—steering conversations away from you." He drew a deep breath and his eyes twinkled under the dim light of the restaurant. "When I got your email, I was surprised that you were coming for a visit. I mean, I asked and all, but why come all the way here?"

"I just retired from the bank, and I'm scouting out some investment opportunities as I'm kicking around the idea of maybe starting my own fund." This was an on-the-spot fib that flashed into truth as my mind grabbed hold and ran with it. "I'm off to China next, but I figured I'd stop in and see how you were getting along on the other side of the Great Wall. Besides, I hear there's some mining opportunities here, so I may poke around a bit. You mind that I'm here?"

"Not at all. Of course not! Like I said, I invited you. It's just a surprise to see you come all the way out here—and so fast! But it's awesome and I can't wait to see the books you brought. Can't thank you enough, Harry." The mood eased after his comments, and I could sense both of us relaxing into our cups of tea. "You seem curious about my work. Would you like to see more of it? This afternoon's not good—you look jet lagged anyway. Are you free tomorrow morning? Say 8:00 a.m.?"

"Sure, I would love to see you in action again as long as it won't interfere."

"Don't worry, if anyone asks I'll just tell them you're a potential investor. Who knows... might help!"

The following morning, I arrived at Mark's place a few minutes early. Despite a warm head from the new fur-lined hat I bought the previous afternoon, my extremities were freezing. I rapped on his front door. Once again, Stefan answered, and I wondered if he had taken on the role of

Hausmeister as he seemed to relish greeting visitors and serving them tea. When I sat down on my same chair, I noticed the open backpack and ten books stacked neatly on a wooden side table. The eleventh one was missing, one of the Hesse books: *Demian.* Interesting. Elena had insisted that I choose that book, along with another one I'd never heard of. I read *Demian* on the flight out there, though much of it was lost on me. Strange little book about strange little kids. I wanted to meet Sarah, or at least catch site of her, but Mark appeared alone and within minutes we were off, trotting through the snowy mud.

We found Tsenguun on the corner. Underneath his coat I noticed a cheap grey suit hanging over his skinny frame. He could have passed for a high-school kid, with a face full of pimples and hair crying out for a wash and comb. After chatting with him while the three of us walked abreast, I learned he was taking a semester off from Cornell and had gotten the interpreter job to earn enough money to finish his degree. A mere three years away from the motherland and he already sounded like a wise-cracking American kid, slipping in expressions like "my bad" and "that's so dope".

We walked together through the ger district, piles of litter everywhere and the neighborhood worsening—tattered clothes and grimy faces like I'd seen in *National Geographic* pictures of poverty-stricken countries. There was also an air of melancholic desperation hanging over everything. I had friends come back from various third-world countries saying that the people were poor but happy, as though they had something to teach us about the true meaning of life. I didn't see any of that where Mark brought me. No, the people appeared tired and worn out and the misery so thick I could feel it weighing me down. I'm not sure, but maybe places like India and Thailand are different given the milder climate, as the cold weather in Mongolia no doubt compounded the woes of the poor. I know my edgier side used to creep out more during the winter months when I lived on the East Coast. Though it did make me wonder if vacation travelers to any of these countries see more than the odd beggar or a passing slum corridor. Walking with Mark and Tsenguun through the thick of economic hardship endured by people used to living somewhere else ripped my mind into a thousand tiny thoughts that engulfed me.

We approached a ger and the two of them stepped up to the wooden door. Tsenguun shouted something through it and we stood there waiting until a thin-looking man appeared and motioned us to enter. I followed as the others did, removing my boots at the threshold and placing my hat down on a small table near the entrance. A pleasant hint of incense floated into my nose. The dingy white covering on the outside belied the beauty of its interior. I was surprised at the spaciousness and cozy atmosphere inside the ger. Carpets and furs lined the floors and the walls, and it seemed like every space was made to serve a purpose, though it was obvious that these people were poor. An old man sat on a bed covered in layers of blankets that doubled as a couch. A woman in her early twenties with a young baby wrapped in beautiful red fabric sat on a stool a few feet from the warming center stove. The baby looked up at me with curious eyes as the young man motioned for us to sit down on the couch-bed beside the old man. The entire scene felt awkward as the four of us huddled together and I overheard the woman shout something to an older woman moving about on the other side of the ger, presumably to rouse her into doing something for us.

Our host pulled over a faded and chipped green plastic lawn chair and sat down across from us with a proud mist in his eyes. Both he and the old man seemed happy to see us. I tried to hide my discomfort, wondering which local custom or protocol I might have inadvertently breached. Mark appeared well at ease, and I heard him say a few words in their language: *sain baina uu* to break the ice (later I had Zul at the hotel write out this simple greeting and practice it with me). The old man turned to me with a pleasant smile, patting my arm as if sharing an inside joke. I nodded and tried my best to become invisible. It was Mark's show, and I didn't want to ruin it with any bombast. Nevertheless, Mark tried to fill me in on the discussion as it seemed like he'd already met this man before. He spoke just loud enough for me to hear, but no louder.

"His name is Bold. He and his family used to live in the countryside. The old man is his father. Both of his parents live with them, which isn't *that* usual for Mongolia, but in this case his father was injured by a horse and they had to move in with his son's family. They were all herders up until about a year ago, when the harsh winter killed off most of his flock. He sold the rest of it and they moved here. He's been looking for steady work, and is mainly doing odd jobs. He wants to purchase a clean cook stove to save money on coal and to reduce the smoke in his house, but he hasn't the money. He's asking about financing to pay it off."

"Can you do that?" I asked.

"We normally go through a small bank, but they ask for collateral for non-business loans. Some people can use gold or silver jewelry, but he doesn't have much. So, it may not work out unless we can tie it in with a business loan. I've heard of some people *creating* businesses just to qualify for a loan and then they use part of the money for our products. Not ideal."

"Can he use the cook stove as collateral?" I asked.

"Yes, but it's not enough to cover it since the unit loses its value too quickly."

"How much do the things cost?"

"Our units run about forty dollars U.S."

"Christ, that's nothing!"

"But for this man that is a lot of money," Tsenguun broke in to remind me where we were.

"Then I guess he can't buy it," I muttered in resignation, looking around the ger as if I might spot a worthy piece of collateral—a throwback to my days as a loan officer.

I heard the baby cough and glanced over at it. It was still studying us from its mother's arms and I felt precious eyes fall on me.

"Who is this little guy?" I asked with a smile, never quite sure how I felt about babies. They are cute as long as I don't have to hold them.

"This is Altansarnai. *She* is seven months old," Tsenguun answered.

"Does her name mean something?"

"It means golden flower. Golden rose."

"She is coughing. Does she have a cold?"

"No. Actually, she has been coughing blood and the doctors think she might have a lesion on her lung," Tsenguun answered with a solemn glance at the girl.

"Lesion? Like lung cancer?" I was astounded.

"Yes. This is not that uncommon," Mark said, and my heart tumbled into a dark abyss. "The pollution level is so high here during the long winter months and babies are most at risk. In the countryside things are different, and many of the wealthier people send their families out there to ride out the winter, but here it is just too much for their little lungs."

"I'll buy the damned thing and give it to them!" I meant to say in a whisper but wound up almost shouting into Mark's ear, feeling the anger rise in me. Tsenguun heard me from the other side and I noticed his head lean forward and catch my eye. I'm sure he was trying to warn me that raising my voice in such a manner might put off my host, if not outright offend him. I leaned back in defeat, looking out over these people, not caring anymore what my face looked like. The older woman approached with a teapot and cups on a small tray. She set them down on a small plastic table that Bold had swung over in front of us.

"Please," he said in his language and gestured an open hand to the table. I only knew what he said because Mark whispered the translation in my ear.

We sat in silence for a few minutes, the five of us including the old man sipping tea and not saying a word. The more uncomfortable and intrusive I felt, the more Mark seemed to relax into it like he could have stayed all morning. How could he expect to earn a living selling forty-dollar stoves at this rate—sitting around drinking tea with people who couldn't even afford one? The child continued to shine her eyes on me, and I felt a compulsion to pick her up and hold her. Strange, given I was never much of a baby person, especially after losing the only one my ex-wife ever delivered.

After the tea, I expected us to bid farewell and head out to the next house, feeling an anxious twinge pulling at me. Instead, Bold brought out a packet of cigarettes, and Tsenguun and Mark accepted his offer to smoke. I couldn't stand the things after having quit the habit decades earlier. While the four men smoked away, I slid a hand into my pocket and felt for a few large Tugrik bills. I didn't want anyone to notice me tucking a few of the bills into the cushion behind me. The older woman brought out a large open leather sack and some bowls. Bold and Tsenguun said a few words, and then Tsenguun turned to me.

"He asks if you want to try the traditional Mongolian drink."

"What is it?" I asked.

"We call it *Airag*. It is a kind of milk." Bold gave an approving nod as Tsenguun spoke, holding a bowl out for me.

"Well, I don't want to be rude." I spent the previous twenty years telling everyone I was lactose intolerant, but after my little outburst I was eager to make up for any offense.

"Careful." Mark placed a warning hand on my wrist and spoke in a low whisper. "Just take a small sip. Don't chug it or you'll be sorry."

I followed Mark's advice and took a tiny mouthful of the unpleasant stuff and its sourness stayed in my mouth for the rest of the morning. Mark also took a sip, and I wondered if he ingested any of it. This seemed to please Bold, and after a few moments in a grand sweep of his arms he motioned for all of us to stand up and took both of my hands in his. He gave me a deep, penetrating stare and grasped me like we were brothers-in-arms bidding one last farewell before the great battle. This poor man with his rich self-respect beyond what I'd encountered in most wealthy men both intimidated me and inspired my own spirit to rise up.

Bold's wife sidled up next to him and I could feel the love woven through the family as Altansarnai looked up at me with those inquisitive eyes. In that moment, I wanted to *be* Bold. He had it all. Nevertheless, he would soon know the deep grief that comes from losing one's child, perhaps his only one. Peering into his hopeful face sent a hairline fracture through my heart, and I wanted to go and hide in my dark corner. I left his ger asking Mark if Virgil's quote about Fortune favoring the bold might come to pass for him. Mark shrugged off my remark without a word.

The rest of that day was a blur of stepping in and out of gers, most of it lost on me as I couldn't take my mind off the sweet girl with trusting eyes. She bore a slight resemblance to Mila—that poor little thing that didn't live past a week. Her eyes still carried a glow with remembrances of the soul's journey before this lifetime. When I drifted back into Mark's conversations, I stared at his profile next to me, his head growing distant. Did he feel the same as I did? He'd been doing this for a few months, with hundreds of conversations under his belt. Had those experiences desensitized him to the same pain I felt? If so, where had that pain gone? But he was still young with little life experience and personal hardship, and perhaps these things flew under the radar. I couldn't know for sure. These musings flew through the sky of my mind without leaving a stain of judgment.

I nibbled on jerky and trail mix hidden in my coat pocket throughout the day when no one was looking. It didn't seem appropriate to eat in front of poor people whose ceremonial offerings of tea and sweets taught me a mountain of lessons in hospitality and humility. Between missing lunch and holding nine cups of tea in my bladder, I was ready to return to the hotel by the end of the afternoon. Mark must have sensed that I was a wreck and he patted me on the back and said I did well, as if I were a trainee. Perhaps I *was* in training.

Before I left, Mark asked me away for the weekend. Since his crew didn't receive too many visitors in the winter, he suggested we use the occasion of my visit to head out of town to enjoy the countryside and some clean air. While it didn't seem like the end of winter from the snowy remnants and frigid temperatures, the weather was "turning nice" as Tsenguun put it. After only a few days in UB and spending the past two seeing the worst of it, I leapt at the invitation to get out of Dodge. I declined both an offer for dinner that evening and another round of ger visits the following day before taking a taxi back to my hotel.

Later, as I stood in the hot shower, hand propping me up and gazing down at the water flowing through the drain, it was the first time in my life I realized what a luxury that would be for someone like Bold, or the majority of UB, to experience. I could wash away a few of the day's emotions and step out feeling like a new man. They could not. I could put on clean clothing and enjoy a meal of my choosing from a variety of international cuisines, eating as little or as much as I wanted. They could not. I could visit the *kyabakura* hostess bar and have slender, scantily-clad young Mongolian women fawning over me, stroking my ego while I drank and sang karaoke songs, trying my best (without success) to lure one of them back to my room. They could not. I could finish out the evening lying down on clean, fresh scented linens in a climate controlled room set to a perfect temperature and humidity levels. They could not. I could sleep all night without hearing a pack of dogs fighting over a dead animal or the sound of a baby coughing up bloody phlegm. They could not. In the morning I would forget it all while reading the *Wall Street Journal* on my laptop. Some things I could not forget.

The next morning, I lay in bed for several hours, exhausted. The pitiful gym at the hotel consisted of a single treadmill, a few dumbbells, and some steel contraption that I couldn't quite figure out. So, between the cold weather, lingering jet lag and whatever workouts I could muster, my descent into sluggish depression arrived swiftly. Heading out into the countryside for a change of scenery might do me some good. Sometime midmorning the dated telephone on my bedside table rang and when I picked it up I heard Elena's chipper voice bursting out of it.

"You sound different," she said after pleasantries and my apologizing for not having called her since I arrived, which she brushed off with a huff. "Something's happened, hasn't it? I can feel your heart through the line."

"Oh, just a bit of jet lag."

"Jet lag? Are you sure it's just that?"

Early on in our relationship she had introduced something absent in all my other friendships. These were brief periods of silence, which I accepted after an initial struggle to fill the uncomfortable void with noise. She called them "centering moments"—an opportunity to let our real selves *climb out* as she put it. At first, I wondered if they were manipulative tactics couched in New-Agey mumbo-jumbo language, but I played along without mentioning anything to her. Yet, as I began to give over to the silence, I felt a calm liberation wash over me. Over time I grew not only to appreciate them to quiet down my incessant mind chatter, but to look forward to the serenity enveloping both of us. Of course, the silence seemed much longer on the phone than in person, and in my mind, became more a test of wills to keep it going rather than break its healing connection.

A silly thought ran through my head as I sat there on the phone with Elena. I wondered how much an entire minute of silence was costing her. Five dollars? I shrugged it off, realizing we were connecting through the stillness. When I began talking to her, my heart cracked open and the previous day's events tumbled out in a flurry of words. Elena listened with a gentle ear, and like a midwife she allowed me to give birth to a side of my heart I'd not seen before. I told her about everything: about Mark, about the ger district, about the Indian-Mexican food, about seeing the past reflected in a baby's innocent eyes. Later, I would identify that conversation as a turning point for me. In fact, it was also the moment when I realized that the world I had known before, the world that was so easy to navigate, no longer became so easy because I had stepped out of it and into another one more alive and real. Nevertheless, this new world provided nourishment to a deeper part of me that had been hungry for a long time. Maybe it would get easier someday.

CHAPTER 3 | CHINGGIS KHAAN AND TURTLE ROCK

Two days and three shiatsu massages later we headed out of town in a gleaming white Land Cruiser on a crisp sunny morning. They picked me up at the hotel after breakfast and as I shut the door on the passenger side, I glanced back to see Stefan and Tsenguun spread out on the bench seat behind me, while Mark and a young woman sat in the rear. It was my first glimpse of Sarah. She had a plain face and gums that showed when she smiled, but her warm glow filled the vehicle as she spoke, like a vortex where all life connected and pulsated through her. She had a down-to-earth quality and a look in her eye that spoke of kindness to the bone. She made people feel good about themselves just by talking to them. At least that's what she did for me. I wondered if she'd committed Carnegie's book to memory or won friends and influenced people just by being her natural self. Either way, she struck me as one of the most genuine people I've ever met.

We rode out east of UB. Our driver, a middle-aged Mongolian with aviator sunglasses and the look of a man who did what he was told without much talk. He remained in the backdrop during the entire trip. Once past the peri-urban ger settlements the landscape morphed into sweeping plains. I was surprised to find that aside from the white caps atop the surrounding mountains, little snow lay on the ground, only dust mixed with the hints of new grass. With each passing minute, the country grew more majestic and brimming with beauty. After my experiences in UB the previous week, I had all but written the entire nation off as a cesspool of hungry nomads huddled together to survive an unforgiving climate. In a country with a land area over twice the size of Texas with half of its 2.5 million people packed into a capital that holds the reins to most of its resources, it's easy to miss its magnificence if one never leaves the city.

I chatted away with Sarah, learning of her passion for using computer technology to help the poorest of the poor. I also discovered that she was a preacher's daughter, a fact that helped to explain the heartfelt way she related to others as though she already knew them quite well. Not in a phony way, but rather with the touch of divinity in her every move. I could feel Mark's love for her in his smiling gaze, and at the same time I wondered if she felt any different for him than anyone else. In another time and place she might have been misunderstood like Daisy Miller for her gregarious personality and general openness to life. In our time she was a rare gem that gleamed with the brilliance of the best humanity had to offer.

Stefan explained the agenda to us through a mixture of broad strokes and scintillating details, rivaling a seasoned tour guide for his effectiveness in piquing my interest. We would first stop at an enormous stainless-steel statue of Chinggis Khaan an hour outside the capital, which was just completed and stood 40 meters tall. We would then proceed into the vast Gorkhi-Terelj National Park, visiting a place called Turtle Rock, a Buddhist monastery and several other tourist sites before spending the night in a ger tent.

The drive to the statue was supposed to take an hour, but a few kilometers before reaching it our vehicle veered off the road, engulfed in a fierce sandstorm. Enmeshed in the sand equivalent of a blizzard whiteout, we sat motionless for twenty minutes. I marveled at its ferocity and the ability of nature to grind our plans to a screeching halt with scant warning. Like watching the flames of a roaring campfire, I fell into a daydream, envisioning us trapped inside a capsule propelled through an artery, each grain of brown sand representing a molecule of blood. We could continue to fight against the current, or give in and be sucked downstream into the beating heart. None of us spoke, mesmerized by the piercing sound of sand pellets skittering around our vehicle. Then, after at least a full minute, the light of day began peeking through and in an instant the sand all but disappeared from the sky. Stefan cheered first, and the rest of us soon followed with our own whoops of relief.

Eventually, we made it to the Chinggis Khaan statue. I wasn't prepared for the sheer size of it, a gargantuan 250 tons set against the backdrop of a sweeping landscape of snow-capped mountains and little else. Perhaps because it was just completed and still winter, we found the area surrounding it barren save the stone archway at the entrance. We stood under that archway, some distance away from the statue itself. Chinggis himself straddled a shining horse (said to be the largest equine statue in the world), both of which rested on a round building made of stone. He faced eastward, symbolically pointing towards his birthplace. When I asked why the Mongolians chose this site, Stefan answered that legend had it he found a golden whip on this spot. He pointed out that inside contained an elevator that would be able to lift people to the top of the horse's head, which we should come back for in the summer. Despite its breathtaking enormity, standing on the open plain made us vulnerable to the bitter cold wind and we dashed back into the vehicle.

After leaving the statue with a storm of dust trailing us, we drove out to Turtle Rock, a massive pile of stones resembling a turtle lifting its head. Despite the cold and a bit of ice that I slipped and fell on more than once, we scaled up to a place inside the shell that served up stunning views of the ger-dotted steppes. This was the Mongolia of brochures! No wonder people were miserable in the city, pining away for a spot in the countryside with its clean air and simple beauty. I later heard that every Mongolian was allotted a small plot of land outside UB, but few people had the money to build anything permanent on it, much less visit it very often.

After I shuffled my way down to the small vendor encampment below the rocks, I bought a simple painting of a black horse, which still hangs on my wall at home today. Horses figure prominently in Mongolian culture, as long-distance horse racing is one of the trio of celebrated "manly" sports, archery and wrestling being the other two. Tsenguun told me jockeys as young as five participate in those races. I noticed its iconography everywhere, so it was no wonder they decided to put Chinggis on the back of one for the grand statue marking national pride.

Never a fan of riding horses, I still appreciated its significance in what little philosophy I remember from school. The allegoric image of a charioteer struggling to maintain control of a white and a black horse pursuing separate courses from Plato's *Phaedrus* always kept me wondering whether my own passions and desires could be kept in check by a higher reasoning function. I suppose I keep the black horse on my wall as a reminder to pay attention to the demands of my irrational side, but with an eye of keeping it from wresting control of my life. Of course, it keeps me in a constant state of struggle where some days, like the time with Bold and his family, I feel each horse gaining primacy over the course of a single hour.

Tsenguun chose to hang back both at Turtle Rock and at our next stop— a long, steep hike up to the monastery. I'm sure he'd climbed both several times over. While curiosity drew me to follow the others up the stairs to the monastery, I reveled more in stretching my legs and feeling the welcome ache of working them out after a week of botched exercise sessions punctuated by tricking myself into believing that deep tissue massage and sitting in a hot pool served as adequate substitutes for self-driven cardiovascular training. The red-roofed monastery didn't move me as much as the spectacular view of the valley below and the peaceful feeling of perching on top of the world. Aside from a few gers and other small structures, the valley remained untouched and made me wonder how long it would be before big developers moved in to change the landscape for good. Perhaps that might never happen. The empty monastery seemed to be a sign that even the Buddhists got tired of sleeping out in the cold, desolate wind and took shelter back in the city.

Stefan explained that we were too early in the season to enjoy the archery and other touristy ventures out there. The best thing to do after the slow hike back down the mountain was to find our lodging and settle down to lunch and drinks. He put the emphasis on *drinks* to remind everyone that it would be an integral part of the weekend. I thought we would be staying in one of the ger settlements near Turtle Rock, but Stefan knew of a more remote place that I'm guessing few people in the country knew about. He also struck me as the kind of guy whose network extended far beyond what satisfied most people, like the scavenging character in prison movies that could get you anything you want. We drove for about an hour through a rough mountain pass and wound up at the edge of a small lake, three gers nestled a few hundred feet away.

"Incredible!" I shouted as we stepped out of the car and looked on the crystal blue water contrasted by shining white gers. The backdrop of pine and edelweiss made me think of the Alps. "You done well, Stefan! Reminds me of where you come from."

"Yeah, Stefan, you've been holding out on us. I've been here almost three years and I never knew this place existed," Sarah said as her body leaned toward the lake.

"A friend of mine has been developing it as an eco-tourist camp. So, we are one of his first guests. It's not completed yet, so be prepared for Spartan conditions."

"A real gem," I heard Mark say, and when I looked back at him I could see the flash of pride on Tsenguun's face. This was *his* country, *his* land.

A European-looking man came strutting out from behind one of the gers, wearing a sleek black jacket and jeans, smiling as he approached Stefan and gave him a convivial bear hug. He turned out to be another German named Dieter, and welcomed us to his camp, with two locals helping to carry our bags into the gers. The five of us shared a single ger, with carpets and décor plusher than the ones I'd seen throughout the previous week. We took our meals in the community ger, essentially a small kitchen in the middle of the tent, surrounded by thick wooden tables. My guess was that this part of the camp remained under construction, as it seemed to be missing a few tables and a general feeling of completeness. A small desk that resembled a podium stood toward the entrance, and Dieter leaned behind it at one point to sign some documents in a subtle display of leadership. The third ger presumably housed the crew, though I never saw them go near it. It's also where I believed our driver stayed while we were there. A small shack that could have been a cabin sat tucked away behind some trees some distance away from the camp, and I wondered if Dieter lived there, but I never thought to ask him.

"I hear you experienced a sandstorm on the way here," Dieter said to me in a thick German accent after Stefan introduced me as Mark's recent visitor from the States.

"Yes. I think that's my first sandstorm."

"Stick around. All sorts of crazy weather around here. By the way, have you had much local cuisine?"

"Not much. I wish I were a more adventurous eater, but frankly, much of what I've seen so far frightens me."

His knowing laugh gave me the sense that customer service was his strong suit. In fact, Mark had surrounded himself with friendly, fun-loving people that didn't take themselves too seriously. Not the world I was used to. I wondered if far-off lands tended to attract affable expats who could roll with the punches, and the ones who couldn't stomach it either moved on or stayed home to begin with. I knew a lot of people that wouldn't set foot outside the U.S., and in that vein Mark was my sole reason for venturing out of my usual geographical comfort zone. Despite the unfolding beauty before me, I still wasn't sure if I would have gotten on a plane to Mongolia if it weren't for Mark. Even when his quiet ways placed him in the background, he still stood in the foreground of my mind. Like an owl casting wise glances down from the darkened branch.

Dieter introduced me to local dishes that made me wonder if I was going to be sent home in a wooden box. Lunch consisted of *Boodog*, a skinned marmot sewn back up with a hot rock in its belly, cooking the meat from the inside out. I washed this down with *Airag*, which I'd sipped earlier in the week not realizing I was being served milk from a horse. Stefan's vodka chaser gave me some comfort in believing that I might thwart trouble through its *healing effects*, as he was careful to point out. Even pondering this showed just how far out of my mind I had gone. I was putting my faith in two Germans that showed a deep conviction that these foreign objects would not harm a delicate system weakened through a steady diet of organic vegetables and farm-raised animals. Marmots were free-range, right?

After a hike around the lake and a long rest, we were served a dinner of mutton cooked over an open fire, a staple of the Mongolian diet. I had given up hope of survival and just plowed through whatever food they put in front of me, believing the beer and vodka might help kill off whatever was already trying to destroy me from within. Of course, the others, particularly Tsenguun and Sarah, giggled at the change in my face whenever they described the contents of each dish. I couldn't help but join their laughs as I pushed off concerns of how many nighttime visits I'd have to make to the little bathhouse hut that Dieter pointed out earlier but that I had yet to inspect. Sarah was sitting across from me, and though she and Mark sat close to each other and I noticed an arm stretched out over his thigh, she seemed more interested in my side of the table, leaving Mark and Stefan to a technical discussion on the solar panels Dieter was trying to install on the property.

"I hear you're developing a website?" I asked her. She nodded her head and threw back a shot of vodka—at least her fourth of the evening. "What is it about?"

"It's a site that allows people to loan money to other people."

"Interesting. Tell me more." When she sensed genuine interest and not just sauced-up conversation, her face lit up with a radiance that almost hurt to look at.

"Well, I was a community economic development volunteer with the Peace Corps. Just finished. Lots of people need loans for businesses but even some of the MFIs won't lend to them."

"MFIs?"

"Sorry, microfinance institutions. They're small banks that serve the poor. The bigger ones don't want to work with them because it just doesn't pay to give someone a five-hundred-dollar loan, much less open a bank account for a few dollars." Her comment reminded me of when I opened my first bank account with five dollars on my seventh birthday. Back then it might have been manageable for banks, considering they counted on roping a little boy in for a lifetime of deposits.

"Yeah, I think Mark mentioned something about these banks. So, why won't these MFIs lend to them? Collateral reasons?"

"Sometimes, depending on the type of loan. It often comes down to basic supply and demand. MFIs have a different mission than regular banks. Serving the poor is expensive, so attracting investment is difficult. To fund their loan portfolio, many of them have to borrow that money in the market just like everyone else."

"Makes sense."

"Yeah, so they reach their limit on how many people they can serve. My site will help them get access to that capital not from the financial markets, but from everyday people over the Internet. If somebody needs a loan for five hundred dollars, I would put that up on the website and somebody else out there from the U.S. or wherever would fund it."

"How much interest would you charge on the loan?"

"I'm not sure yet. That's a big question. I would love to charge no interest at all, but that doesn't seem sustainable without some kind of fee. Anyway, it's still in the design phase and I don't have all the details worked out yet. It's also a little out of my reach when it comes to programming. I can do a little, but this would require transaction processing, and that's way out of my league."

"I'm sure Mark can help you with that, though." I winked at her and she shot Mark a quick loving glance." I'm not sure how much Mark told you, but I used to be in banking and I'm very intrigued by this idea, Sarah. I think you've got something here—giving people access to finance through the general public and bypassing the banks altogether. How do you intend to attract investors? I mean, the people who are going to fund these small loans?"

"I plan on posting a picture of the entrepreneur and a story about them—just a few paragraphs about their business and family life. I figure that even if somebody's half way around the world, they can still connect with someone else in need and lend them a hand. A picture and a story can be quite captivating, don't you think?"

"Disruptive! I think it might just work. Let me know if you ever need any help. I mean that."

"Well, thank you, Harry. That means a lot to me, and I might just ask for that someday." She leaned back with a soft smile and tilted her head at me. I could sense we were two souls seeing through all that surface clutter and saying, "good to meet you" to one another. Elena referred to those as *Namaste* moments. It wasn't much different than the time I sat down with Mark at the cafe nearly a year earlier. Sarah's mention of these MFI banks intrigued me, and I wanted to learn more about them. Of course, all of that was on hold because the *Boodog, Airag,* and whatever else I piled down my throat hit me like a mule kick after we returned to UB, forcing me to spend the next several days no more than ten feet from a toilet.

CHAPTER 4 | MONGOLIAN MICROFINANCE

Once I recovered from whatever hammered away on my vital organs, I decided to leave Mongolia before it killed me. I was determined to first establish a connection with these MFI banks. If MFIs were indeed working with the poor, people like Bold might be able to receive the loan they needed through some creative financing avenues. A handful of them operated in Mongolia, and Sarah knew them all. She made appointments for me to meet with the chief executives and since they all held a decent command of English, I could travel there by myself if I wanted to.

Of course, I hired Sarah to accompany me to the meetings, though she refused to let me pay her. My intuition about her proved correct as everyone we met lit up when they saw her coming through the doors. She also spoke their language quite well, or at least it seemed that way from the pleasantries she exchanged with each person she encountered. Like the rest of Mark's new friends, she represented a breed apart–whip-smart young people hungry to tackle poverty head on using sustainable business models rather than sink-hole aid programs. Of course, I was still skeptical of the efficiency of sitting around drinking tea and trying to sell forty-dollar cook-stoves to people lacking the wherewithal to buy it.

Despite their forward-thinking brand of poverty alleviation, the Mongolian MFIs seemed to have a similar hierarchical undertone to the world I had come from, where age and gender remained key ingredients to the ladder of success; although recent events in my life were revealing widening cracks in that old paradigm. At one meeting I found a University of Chicago trained MBA hunched next to his imposing father who played the role of board chair like a great Khan letting his fledgling son lead a small band into battle–a son who would no doubt rule over more kingdoms than the father. The head of another MFI, an octogenarian expat from the UK, bragged of driving out the local staff and replacing them with "good" people—ones who resembled younger versions of him. I could country bash with the best of them, but I found it a bit queer that a man who'd spent the past five years trying to help people would say, "This whole country is a bloody mess. What it really needs is a benevolent dictator like they have in Singapore. That would shape them up!" I passed on investing with either of those organizations.

I did find a small MFI pliable enough to take on a term loan just below market rates. This put me at ease because my fallback was to loan money outright to Mark's organization, but that would have been a much smaller sum since I was leery of the risk given their lack of lending experience. After spending three days in due diligence meetings with their able leader named Zorigoo, along with his staff and the clients they serve, I struck a tentative deal to let them use my money for a year for business loans, with a portion set aside to allow some of Mark's clients to finance his clean energy products without the need to conjure up a fake business. I set an effective date for the following month to finalize the terms to give me a chance to do a little more homework—specifically on the whole microfinance industry—before committing any philanthropic capital.

Spending time with Sarah, I learned a great deal more about economic development and the various actors working in Mongolia. The entire concept of helping people through small banks devoted to the poor appealed to me: *micro-finance* vs. *macro-finance*. This meant no big government aid programs or giveaways that often amounted to bureaucrats lining their pockets and wasting time and resources. Knowing that people got to use my money and had to pay it back in return without losing their shirts comforted me because there's nothing worse than enabling other people to sit on their asses and do nothing on someone else's dime, especially mine! I felt some connection to this avenue of finance beyond what I expected. After thirty years hyper focused on mitigating risk, I wasn't about to throw good money after bad just because some little baby made me cry. My reasoning faculty still held the reins, though I sensed I was stepping into a potential minefield that I knew little about.

I spent a few more days in UB, poking around and buying some cashmere presents for Elena. I was missing her warm touch and although the weather in UB started to warm up in the afternoons, I was ready to fly back home to some clean air. Stefan threw me a small party at their concrete house before I left. I regretted not having spent much time with Mark beyond that first week, much less than I anticipated. He was a contemplative soul to be sure, but I wondered if his own personal journey was much more difficult than I imagined. He seemed to be in love with Sarah, and while at the eco-tourist hotel I couldn't help noticing them taking a slow stroll that next morning around the lake, holding hands and moving at an easy pace. In her and Stefan he had found a pair who seemed to be guiding him in a healthy direction.

The cynical part of me imagined that they saw in me just a pseudo-philanthropic mark who could fund their ventures. They were all too idealistic and genuine for that sort of thing, though, and the many deep conversations I had with them over the three weeks I spent in Mongolia gave me glimpses into the purity of their souls. Even so, it wouldn't have mattered to me since most friendships carry some measure of utility no matter the connection; and the world that they were opening me up to already proved much more promising and meaningful than the one I had just left.

PART III | THE PHILIPPINES

CHAPTER 1 | HOME

For the first three days after my return my apartment transformed into a catacomb of delivered meals and sleep depravity. The Benadryl didn't work this time and I suffered trying to switch back over to San Francisco time while force feeding fresh organic vegetables into my system. Few people mention this part of long-range travel and jet lag–getting one's bowels back in order. Normally, I could set my watch by my morning movements. Getting that rhythm on track was a long time coming, and for the first week I felt like the lower half of my body had transformed into a sewer system. No doubt the salt and chemical-ridden airline food contributed much to that. Elena stopped over on the second day to bring some beauty back into my life. She had a way of saying a lot without saying a word, and I snuggled into her bosom for a mid-afternoon slumber. After years of an iceberg marriage punctuated by short romances based on utility disguised as lust, I reveled in her warmth and gentle touch. She also taught me a few short meditations, which helped me relax and keep my mind from racing at times when I couldn't sleep.

The next few weeks I committed to researching as much as I could on microfinance and to get a handle on this alternative method of financing. I read the book *Banker to the Poor*, written by Muhammad Yunus, a Vanderbilt trained economist from Bangladesh who saw that the trickledown economic theories he was teaching in the university were having little effect on the poverty in his country–a country dominated by the poor. So, he went out to a village and loaned twenty-seven dollars out to a group of forty-two people. That was enough money to either start their own businesses, or at the very least use the money to purchase raw materials they previously had to borrow for at exorbitant rates. Later, this would grow into millions of dollars as he created a microfinance bank and named it *Grameen* (meaning "village" in Bengali). Reading his story and how he spent four decades transforming the lives of millions of people felt like a profound wave crashing over me and I knew I wanted to be part of it. What most intrigued me were his statistics on the high repayment rate of borrowers–hovering around ninety-eight percent. I had heard hints of this in Mongolia, and as it was explained to me, for many people this might be their first and last chance to take a loan. As such, they didn't want to screw it up. Even the loan sharks wouldn't take a chance on most of them. The lending was often done in groups. So, people relied on social support, and even peer pressure to help pay back a loan. One thing I remember Zorigoo in Mongolia saying to me was that everyone was born an entrepreneur, and it was up to MFIs to tap into it. As I read Yunus' book, I came across the inspiration for Zorigoo's statement:

> *If all of us started to view every single human being, even the barefooted one begging in the street, as a potential entrepreneur, then we could build an economic system that would allow each man or woman to explore his or her economic potential.*

Those words resonated with me, as I'd spent decades supporting entrepreneurs of all shapes and sizes. Of course, none of this material was covered in any of my MBA courses over at Wharton. The basics were easy to grasp, essentially loaning and collecting small amounts of money to poor people, often via weekly group meetings. I had to adjust my opinions around creditworthiness. I'd grown up believing that poor people were lazy and prodigal, forgetting the dire straits my own family faced throughout my childhood. What I'd seen on the ground in Mongolia, buttressed by strong repayment rates captured in financial statements, dissolved that belief.

While I spent the next few weeks reading up on this new world, I also got my body back into shape and spent as much time as I could with Elena. She said she noticed a gleam in my eye that she'd caught mere glimpses of when we first met–a gleam that was now burning brighter the more I waded into this world of banking for the poor. I didn't notice it myself. All I knew is that I was finally excited about something beyond my own little world and what advantages I could wrangle out of it. Of course, I did see myself in the role of rescuing people from a miserable existence. Is that so bad?

I was home a month and had just signed the paperwork on the loan to Zorigoo's MFI. I was still a bit skeptical of how people were going to be able to pay back their loans, and it was half a million dollars, more than I planned to give. I still had a good chunk of equity at the bank, which I would receive in a lump sum once Don sold off the bank in the fall, so I wasn't too worried. The next day I received an email from Sarah. With the end of the long winter and the air quality in UB improving by the day, it seems folks in the ger district were not setting their sights on buying products they wouldn't use much for the next six months. Sarah had been in touch with an organization down in Manila willing to hire both her and Mark. They planned to head out there at the end of June.

I took pleasure in her invitation to come visit once they got settled. The first thoughts I had were around the scuba diving given all the islands down there. Then I considered Mark. Her postscript mentioned how much he appreciated the books I brought and had devoured them all. "Maybe you can bring more, and a few fun ones for me?" she wrote, adding a little smiley face at the end with a short list of requests. He snagged a winner in Sarah and I hoped he wouldn't blow it. He didn't seem like the kind of guy who would, though. That was more my territory, where I was kept wondering if Elena would be bored with my loafing around. I was eager to get back out of the country and to see both Sarah and Mark again.

CHAPTER 2 | MANILA

I flew to Manila in late July with another bag full of books and the appropriate clothes this time. After UB, I assumed I could handle any third-world city. That was a mistake. The taxi ride from the airport to my hotel took over three hours. I had spent a week in New Orleans once, dealing with oppressive humidity. Manila was worse, far worse. My driver shrugged when I asked about air conditioning, and I collapsed in the back seat overcome with sweat, exhaustion, and nauseating fumes. A warped-humor uncle once told me that the one phrase a traveler needs to know in the language of a foreign land is, "how do I get back to the airport?" I laughed, shaking my head at the memory and wishing I knew enough Tagalog to get him to turn around. Where was Charon taking me? Amidst the slow-moving honking and violent poverty, I felt I'd entered the fringes of hell. I booked the Shangri-La hotel in Makati because I wasn't taking any chances this time, and the online reviews promised that it lived up to its namesake. As we pulled into the circle with its ostentatious portico and smartly-dressed porters running about, I knew I would find comfort within its walls to help me adjust to a land that already drew unease in me.

Two days later, I emerged from a sleep cocoon to take on Manila. This time Mark knew when I was arriving, and Sarah had arranged a dinner with her boss for the evening. She asked me to come a few hours ahead of time to the *Center*, as she called it. So, I made sure the hotel fixed me up with an air-conditioned taxi so that I could at least arrive without sweat rings under my arms. On the ride over, the sluggish movements of people trudging through the afternoon heat made me realize why the global South had fallen far behind northern industrial societies. How can anyone consider work while buried underneath such energy-sapping wet heat? I spent a summer swinging a hammer on a construction site in my teens. The Maryland humidity all but killed me, and it didn't even come close to Manila.

Within a few blocks, the taxi moved from the cleanest part of town to trash-littered streets displaying visible signs of residential decay. Children tapped my window at stop lights, holding out their hands for some form of compassion, just a few pesos. While I felt my heart twinge a bit, I dared not roll down the window and let the heat disrupt the cool air in the cab. Besides, I wasn't about to create a mob scene by tossing money out the window. We turned down a narrow street filled with dirt and broken asphalt. The rainy season in full tilt, the taxi rumbled through a sudden downpour that seemed to get worse the further we rolled along. Groups of people peered out at me beneath plastic corrugated roofing abound with leaks. I noticed a family of five huddled on a small mound of dirt under a narrow overhang, skinny little faces buried in their mother's arms while the squatting father smoked a cigarette and gazed off into the distance. As we approached the end of the lane, we passed through a chain-link fence opening to a large gravel area surrounded by freshly painted buildings that seemed out of place for the rest of the scene. My driver tapped the horn, and I saw Mark's head pop up from behind a bush. He caught my eye and a broad smile spread over him. As soon as the taxi stopped, he rushed out with an umbrella to escort me to the safety of the building. The raindrops were so thick I saw a bird plunge to the ground and fumble helplessly in a thick gravel pool. Mark's umbrella also had a hole in it and one arm bent, leaving both of us drenched after the eight steps back to the building. The storm had exposed every weak spot in both man and nature.

"Welcome to the Philippines!" Mark shouted over the thundering sound of pounding raindrops on corrugated metal roofing. He looked thinner than I remembered, with a glowing tan.

"When are you going to listen to me and go to Fiji?" I jested, giving him a quick hug and knocking him in the ribs. He merely laughed and as he initiated a subtle interrogation of my trip so far, our conversation was hijacked by a loud screech.

"Harry!" Sarah came running from the back of the building and tackled me. For a diminutive thing she could hug like a grizzly bear. At once it seemed both overdone and just what I needed, and I enveloped her in my arms. She collapsed inside me and then sprung back to look at me, an arm sliding behind Mark's back. Had Mark actually found himself a genuine angel that loved others without condition? Time would tell.

We drank bottled waters during the tour of the Center, an extensive complex of separate units providing care for the poor. A Christian organization, the Center referred to these units as *ministries* and those who ran them as *servants*. As we skirted around the buildings to avoid the rain, which had started to abate, I noticed several large crosses on the sides of the buildings. A lapsed Catholic with a deep suspicion of religious influences, I nodded at each reference with concealed disdain. The Center ran a multitude of ministries out of the complex, including one distributing healthcare and supplies and another that picked starving people up off the street and gave them food and shelter in exchange for helping around the place. At one point, I noticed an enormous cylinder constructed out of gleaming metal, resting on a four-foot platform. Mark pointed at my bottle of water and talked about the ministry team devoted to providing purified water to the area residents. As he described it, the Center lay in the heart of one of the poorest sections of Manila. I glanced at my bottle, wondering where the water was being tapped and checking for any impurities floating around.

"Don't worry, Harry, it's clean," Mark cackled, and he gave me a light slap on the back.

We were followed by another man, a local they introduced as Edwin. He stood a foot shorter than me and wore glasses that magnified brilliant eyes charged with life. He had on a pressed light blue uniform, along with the dozens of other people I saw wandering about the large complex. Everyone seemed to move about with purpose, drawing a sharp contrast to the aimless wandering I'd seen outside the gates. A few of the others wore yellow shirts, and I asked Edwin about that.

"Sir, they are part of our pavement dweller ministry." He spoke in a very slow and deliberate manner. With his slight sing-song accent I wondered if English were his mother tongue. "As Mark explained earlier, in our ministry we help families transition from living in the streets to becoming productive members of society. Many of them are living and working at the retreat center that we are currently constructing outside of Manila. Some still work here to help out. Mostly maintenance and keeping the grounds tidy. If you have the time, you should come visit the retreat center."

"I would like that. By the way, how do you fund all these ministries?"

"Over there." He smiled and pointed to a small two-story building. "That is our microfinance ministry. Perhaps you would like to meet with our team, sir?"

We spent the next hour seated in the office of the microfinance ministry, which turned out to be a local branch serving the surrounding neighborhood. In fact, the Center itself did not house the headquarters of the parent organization, which I was told was in a small building located in a more industrial neighborhood of Manila not far from my hotel. The *Branch Servants*, as they were called, worked just like loan officers and branch staff I'd encountered in Mongolia, but they had an additional person on staff identified as the *Branch Pastor*. He was a burly man in his fifties with a kind face. He was tasked with making sure everyone followed the path of Christ, whatever that entailed. He also met with borrowers having trouble paying back their loans, sitting with them and praying that the money would come from God. Upon hearing this I nearly fell over in my chair, wondering if I was lost in a dream or had stumbled into a cult. From where I sat I could see the front gate through the window. It was still wide open. I looked at Mark, who raised his eyebrows and smiled as though I just had to roll with it. *Welcome to the Philippines.*

As Edwin explained in the spotless minivan that drove the four of us to dinner, the microfinance ministry provided the locomotive engine that enabled the boxcars of the other services they offered. Indeed, they charged high interest rates on their loans, sometimes carrying an annual percentage rate of sixty percent. This not only compared to other organizations offering microfinance loans in Manila, but their clients also received access to training programs and other *transformative* services to help them rise out of poverty, including Bible study. The rates were a bit lower in Mongolia, although I had already gotten over my initial shock of the high prices for doing these small loans. Regular banks wouldn't even serve these people and the prices were nowhere near what loan sharks were offering. This is because serving people at the base of the economic pyramid is expensive. It required a shift in mindset altogether, particularly once I looked at how high revenues on loan interest collected were wiped out by all the costs associated with those loans. I suppose paying a fleet of loan officers traveling around to disburse and collect small amounts of money adds up.

The minivan dropped us in the old section of Manila where cobblestoned streets and colonial architecture adorned the area. The sole reminders of the four centuries of Spanish rule were this tiny neighborhood and other ubiquitous hints found in last names, food, and facial features on most of the people I saw. Edwin led us into a quaint restaurant near a massive cathedral displaying architecture one might find in Europe. I reveled in the possibility of eating some local food that hadn't been deep fried first. We were seated around a large round wooden table, and within minutes a tiny well-dressed middle-aged woman strode in flanked by a small entourage. She had the same shining light in her eyes as Edwin, and at first, I wondered if they might be related. She beamed at me, thrusting out her hand and introducing herself as Ms. Luisa. She had a mixture of powerful energy and playfulness, wielding both by grabbing my arm and forcing me to sit next to her in a brilliant display of gender reversal. I just rolled with it, delighted at her charming bravado.

"Your first time to the Philippines, Mr. Harry?"

"Yep."

"And how do you like our little country with its seven thousand islands?"

"I've only been to one of them, and thanks to jet lag I've not seen much of it yet. I was quite impressed with the Center. Edwin is a wonderful guide."

"Yes, he is—and we like your friends Mark and Sarah. They are a big help to us." She settled in and hesitated a moment while the waiter took drink orders from everyone, and then hurled a question at me, "Tell me, who is your father?"

"My father?" I was flabbergasted. No one had asked about my father in years, and at my age it was likely due to the strong possibility of blundering into a conversation about his death. I later learned that in this part of the world people often asked others about their ancestors, with an unconscious desire to learn where they fit into social hierarchies. "My father was a fisherman. He is very old now."

"Do you see him often?"

"Oh, every now and again I do."

"I see." She held me in her penetrating gaze for a moment, wondering what to make of me. Then she broke it with a firm smile and maternal pat on my arm. "Well, no doubt the *other* father is always with you."

I wish I could say we all navigated the rest of dinner without incident, but it wouldn't be true. I ordered a beer. Everyone else drank water or soda. Someone asked me what church I went to. I said I didn't. Living in a land of secularism, I hadn't eaten with devout Christians in decades, or ever. I took a bite of my adobo just before Ms. Luisa called for grace, feeling a wave of foolishness wash over me. Despite trying so hard to be the quiet American, I instead kept revealing the ugly one. I caught Mark giving me a downward smile with a hint of remorse for not giving me a heads up on protocol first. Of course, how was he to prepare me for a day with hard-core Christians? It was as if I kept stepping in shit and washing it off again, but at each turn I felt a stab of terror followed by a gentle easing of my heart. The Center people were a forgiving sort, and I could sense that a few of them found my foibles endearing, especially Ms. Luisa. In fact, the more I messed up the more she warmed up to me.

"Let me tell you a story, Mr. Harry," she uttered after taking her last bite and tapping her mouth with the cloth napkin. "I studied for my master's degree in your country. In Iowa. It was cold, but I *so* loved it there. In fact, I wanted to stay, but an ill family member drew me back to the Philippines. It was my first time back in three years, and between you and me I was a little angry to have to come back. I was also shocked by the poverty. I had seen so much of it growing up, but being in your country and coming back brought out the contrasts. I didn't see any poverty in Iowa, yet I came home to beggars in the street. Entire families living in a box in an alleyway. I wanted to help them, all of them, but this was the problem: how? You know that beer you are drinking (having already crossed the Rubicon, I had ordered two more during dinner)? It is the same beer maker that laid off five thousand workers, many of whom had worked at the factory for countless years. They could not find jobs. It was painful. I saw this pain and I internalized it—and in that pain, I struck upon an idea."

"And what was that?" By this point, I had fallen under the spell of her mellifluous voice that thumped with passion.

"I would help them see who they were in God's eyes, not in the eyes of someone else. No, I would help them appreciate their worth as human beings created in *His* image, and realize that this—their intrinsic value—was not in any way contingent on their work in some factory. So, with an initial grant I created the Center to train people to start their own businesses and to live with dignity built upon self-reliance."

"Sounds like the American dream."

"Perhaps we did learn a thing or two from your country's hundred years out here. Like everything else, we put our own Filipino stamp on what we do. Most of us have not lost God and our connection to Jesus Christ. After all, *He* is the one who creates through each of us."

Back home I would have shuddered at such religious talk, but in her I sensed a strong belief in a divine hand guiding the work she was doing, and not some spiritual sales pitch. So, what if all these people tricked themselves into believing that something higher was guiding their path rather than human will and determination? Maybe they did have some help from above, who knows for sure. I thought of Elena and how much she would have enjoyed this strong woman and her story. Although Elena's blend of Hindu-Christianity, if one could even call it that, would not fly with this group. *God, I missed her.* Mark and Sarah seemed to be enjoying themselves, and they seemed just as spellbound by Ms. Luisa and her unabashed claim that the answer to poverty rests in Jesus. She picked up on my skepticism—maybe it was the way I scratched my cheek—and responded with an invitation to visit the retreat center they were building a few hours south of Manila to "see how the hand of God was shaping their ministry," as she put it. How could I turn that down?

CHAPTER 3 | PAVEMENT DWELLERS

Edwin, Sarah and Mark picked me up at my hotel two days later in a minivan marked with the Center's logo—the word *Center* with the "T" fashioned into a crucifix. We left at the crack of dawn to avoid the morning commute traffic. I was eager to get out of Manila as I'd spent the previous day wandering around what seemed like all of it, exploring as much as I could. Something both fascinated and repulsed me by the culture. The people expressed a warmth that stretched far beyond what I'd experienced outside America—which as a country could not hold a candle to others in terms of hospitality. Of course, as a swaggering American I represented wealth and my walking path became strewn with people creating jobs on the spot. Whether it was opening doors for me everywhere or trying to help me find my direction, I felt like both a mark and the ultimate guest.

One thing that got under my skin and I fought hard to let go of was the way everyone made direct attempts to engage my attention by referring to me as "sir" in an inquisitive tone that smacked of passive aggression. While beginning as an endearing annoyance that I shrugged off with a smile, it soon devolved into a constant verbal bombardment driving me to the edge of madness. Was I that hypersensitive, or worse—ungrateful? At the end of the day I collapsed onto my bed in a heap of mental and physical exhaustion.

Once outside Manila, the urban setting slipped away as we blazed along two-lane highways cutting through lush jungle. For two hours Edwin explained more about the conference center and other projects under the Center's poverty alleviation umbrella. As he put it, God was working miracles through each of them. When we reached the grounds of the conference center, Edwin pointed to several construction workers wearing yellow shirts, noting that they were former *pavement dwellers*. A row of small huts lined the steep valley behind an enormous partially constructed white amphitheater that resembled a small open stadium. The men in the yellow shirts lived in those huts with their families during the construction phase. I could count over a hundred people scattered over the property that covered at least thirty acres atop a hillside stripped bare of most of its vegetation. In fact, I'll never forget the wave of thick red dust that swept over us when we stepped out of the minivan.

While somewhat subdued in Manila, Edwin grew more animated as he showed us around the property, pointing out each detail. He had grown up nearby, and this mountainous area was a popular spot for wealthy Filipinos to build vacation homes. So, the satisfaction of rising out of poverty to become the right-hand man of the Center's founder and then returning home to build a dream was not lost on me. He was proud of every feature of the place, showing off such mundane details as European-styled toilets in one of the completed dormitories–making sure to point out that each room had its own private bathroom. When completed, the three conference centers would be able to house over five hundred people, who if they wanted to could spend their days in the conference halls and evenings packed into the massive amphitheater for singing and devotion. As we passed from the dormitory section to the rest of the completed building, I wondered who would drive the two hours down here and use these facilities. With the question hovering in my mind the answer came around the corner as we stumbled on a small gathering of people seated in a circle inside an atrium lit up by skylights, the sun beaming down on them. It was a group of businessmen from Korea, who I suppose took advantage of the bargain prices offered during the construction phase.

"Edwin, you said the families of the pavement dwellers lived in those huts down there," I asked him when we arrived at the crest of the hill, taking in a full view of the entire site. "Where are the children?"

"They are not here at the moment." His hands rose up and he sighed, turning to consider my eyes. "We didn't want them to get hurt from the construction, and they also need to stay in school. So, we are housing them at one of our orphanages just thirty minutes' drive away. They come to stay on the weekends. It is not perfect yet, but once the construction is finished we hope to find permanent jobs for the men now that they have more construction experience. They are learning many new skills here. So, then perhaps the entire family can be reunited and stay together, God willing."

"Hmm...." He caught my curiousness.

"Would you like to visit them? Go to the orphanage?"

"Is it out of the way?"

"Of course not. We should go there. I think you will like to see it."

"Wonderful. Thank you."

Adept at reading people, Edwin gave my forearm a gentle tap, stopping me from walking away. "Is there something else? Another question perhaps?"

"Only that I wonder how much of this... all of this, could be financed through that microfinance engine you talked about. Is this whole operation here and the orphanage and giving out water to people, all of this done through interest earned off thousands of two-hundred-dollar loans?"

"No. I wish we were completely sustainable. When this retreat center is up and running, we hope it will be our main source of revenue. For now, we must also rely on grants and a few loans from social investors."

"Social investors?"

"Yes, these are people who don't mind loaning money out at a lower interest rate to help organizations like ours. They earn a smaller financial return on their investment, but the social return is much higher, if you understand me. It has been a long road realizing Ms. Luisa's dream of running social businesses that employ people and generate profits that can be used to help even more people and to serve God."

"Well, it's astounding. Simply astounding."

Sarah and Mark bumped into someone they knew from Manila, another Center worker, and began chatting with her. Their conversation receded into the background. Edwin and I shifted to a shady spot under a mango tree. In fact, it was the only tree saved from the clear cutting they performed on the hill. A few plastic buckets lay scattered about underneath it, and we turned two over and made seats out of them. He and I each took in a deep breath and let out a long sigh.

"It's very hot in your country, Edwin."

"Ah yes, and humid. So humid." He faced me, arms resting on his thighs and fingers intertwined as though at any moment he might drop to his knees and pray. "Tell me, Mr. Harry. Are you a Christian?"

"I was raised Catholic, but I don't go to church anymore."

"Why is that?"

"Well, I guess I grew out of it. Didn't make sense anymore and all that business with the young boys just turned me off for good."

"I am the same, you know? I was raised Catholic, but for some of us it is not the way anymore. So, we have become Protestant. The poor need hope, not charity."

"But you *do* offer them charity, no?"

"I am oversimplifying, I know, but yes, only the most desperate need charity... but not for long. As you can see, they play a part too. Everyone works here. We all have a calling. If we have strong faith and work hard, the money and blessings will come from God. This is not about greed, you understand, but about rising up out of poverty. No longer are we bound to the station in life we are born into. We can spread our wings through our faith in Jesus Christ. I loved growing up Catholic, but I was never taught this by the priests."

"It all sounds good, but can I be frank with you, Edwin?"

"Of course."

"Why do you need Jesus in the picture? Can't you just help the poor and go on about your business? Jesus may have said 'help the poor', but do people really need to follow him and pray to him and all that? I'm sorry if this is rude, but I don't see the connection between some man in the Middle East two thousand years ago and a bunch of people here helping one another. If it's about people just being good and needing a set of rules to keep them from messing up with one another, do we really need all these churches and prayers and everything?"

"That is the precise reason why I am no longer a Catholic. I now have a personal relationship with Jesus Christ—not through some priest—and through that relationship I am forgiven my sins."

"That's another thing. What's all this focus on sins, as though they are bad? Isn't that a pessimistic view of humanity?"

"Do you know the Greek word for sin is *amartia*, which literally means *missing the mark*?"

"Hmm, I've never heard that before."

"Yes, I like the image of an archer shooting his arrow and not hitting the target. Most of my life I've committed these *sins* somewhere along a spectrum—missed the mark, so to speak. That mark is the true path for me in all things. That is the hole in which I strive to fit myself and for me that hole is Jesus Christ. That is my path, but even when I miss the mark, it's okay because it is teaching me humility. That is what God wants for me, to become humble… to serve others and not let my ego take over and run my life, ruin it. I already did enough of that before I was saved, so I am quite an expert on sinning." I detected a wistful smile cross his face.

"Interesting, what is it you did before the Center?"

"I was very lucky to get the opportunity to go to school and there I studied finance. I then worked for a large bank for several years, mostly operational stuff. The more I worked my way up, the more depressed I became."

"Why is that?"

"Well, when I was young, and my family did not have much money. All I wanted to do was to grow up and earn a good living and support the family. So, I focused on the most successful path I could and when I started to make a little money I was so happy and so was my family. I could buy what I wanted and do what I wanted. It was total freedom. Or so I thought. Then, I realized that I was making enough money and didn't need any more. So that hole was filled, but there was an even bigger hole in me I could not fill. I also realized that my bank was not serving people like the family I grew up in. There was no connection to the work I was doing and my own past—which is what I initially wanted anyway. So, for many years that was just okay. However, that is no way to break from the past. Over time I became aware that God gave me that childhood for a reason and it was to find a way up the ladder and then help others to climb out. I began to realize that I had abandoned the ladder and was not helping anyone else besides myself and my family. So, over time I became more and more miserable. I started to drink and to stay out late with my friends and soon became lost in my own wilderness. It is a dark place, you know? I became like an automaton, just going through the motions of life.

"But one day I saw a child begging in the street and something about her spoke to me. I still cannot tell you or anyone else what it was, because I've seen thousands of children begging. But in *her* eyes, I saw the eyes of Christ looking on me and begging me to help her and everyone else like her. I cannot explain more than that, but from that day forward I started to change my life over to one where I was serving that girl–serving God. Of course, it took a while because I was very resistant to the change. It was a slow battle to gain control over my soul, and eventually I started to see Christ in everyone's eyes. So, after many false starts, I got my life back–a life I never knew I even had. Now I am rich in what matters to God. Everyone who comes into my life is a gift and God is never beyond embrace. He is ready for my embrace whenever I am ready. I must always be preparing myself for it."

"Interesting way to put it," I said, not knowing what else to say.

"I have also learned something very special about money."

"What is that?"

"That money can become an instrument in the search for self-knowledge. You can learn a lot about yourself and others when it comes to money."

"How so?"

"I once lent five thousand pesos, about a hundred dollars U.S., to a friend of mine–a good friend. I never saw him again. I've also lent half that to thousands of people I barely know and most all of them have paid it back. Money can be a bellwether for testing one's character."

"I know what you mean. So, Edwin, with all this work that you are doing, I have one question. Are you happy now? Really happy?"

"Yes and no, to be honest. My life has much more meaning now, and I am very happy with the work that I am doing to serve Christ through helping the poor. I still have days, just like anyone else, where I am not so happy and even lonely at times. Those are just normal things like coffee spilling on me or the traffic in Manila, but that is to be expected. So, in some ways my life is reversed. I am no longer always happy on the surface, but that is just like a sliver of an iceberg, and everything else below is connected to God and I am truly happy on a deeper level than ever before. It took me many years to get over my attachment to money, but in my case

Jesus was speaking to me in his parable of the rich man. Like him, I needed to sell everything and give it to the poor in order to be happy. Now I am free from that burden."

"Do you think everyone needs to do that? That is, give their worldly possessions away?"

"Actually, no. In that parable, the rich man comes to Jesus and he is miserable and Jesus sees that the source of his misery is indeed his attachment to his wealth. I don't think it is like this for everyone. Maybe everyone has to figure out what it is that stands between them and God and give up *that* attachment."

"Attachments… that sounds a little Buddhist to me."

"Well, I don't know. Many paths lead to the same mountain peak. I just happen to be living here where most of those paths are Christian-based. I'm not so sure I'd be Christian if I were living in Saudi Arabia, but I'd like to think I'd still be walking a path to God."

"You know, Edwin, I have to say that you're quite an interesting man. Have you thought about being a preacher yourself?"

"Yes, but that is one of my failings too. I like to talk too much, as I have done just now. Whenever I've preached in my church community I find I lose a bit of my humility. So, until I've given up *that* attachment I suppose I will have to stay in the background. We all have our own hills to climb and pits to avoid. I seem to find new ones every day." He said this with a slight chuckle.

As we stood up, Mark and Sarah said goodbyes to their colleague and then gradually approached us. They seemed to be keeping a safe physical distance from one another, something I noticed the day we met at the Center and a contrast to back in Mongolia where they often appeared attached at the hip. I wondered if the Christian community had rules around the behavior of unmarried couples, though I still wasn't sure whether they had coupled up in the traditional sense. Unlike Elena, who was filled with fire and constantly setting and resetting boundaries based on the forces competing inside her, Sarah's savoir faire spoke of unconditional love. She seemed to be brimming with love for all life, and Mark's proximity meant he felt the same light, just a little brighter. Who knows, perhaps they walked the line during the day and found ways to sneak out of their gender-separated dormitories for late-night trysts. I thought it interesting that all the junior staff lived in these dormitories, where meals and prayers took place in a communal setting. I could never see myself getting roped into a situation like that.

A few minutes later, we bid farewell to the crew, meeting a few of them, who shook our hands and hung their heads in peace and humility. Being surrounded by such politeness and respect, both in Mongolia and the Philippines, at first unnerved me as my cynical side kept expecting the other shoe to drop, but it never did. Was this niceness a third-world thing or had I just stumbled upon good people?

I endured a bumpy 45-minute drive down to the orphanage over an older road weaving through a less affluent area, most of it thick jungle and with the occasional wooden shack tucked back off the road. The orphanage itself covered a few acres of palm and other tropical plants, with several clearings that housed pigs, chickens, and other livestock roaming about within a tall bamboo fence surrounding the perimeter. The grounds contained two buildings: an open-air school and a small dormitory, both constructed from local bamboo and looking worn out. The compound drew a sharp contrast to the modern construction we'd just come from, and I wondered how the Center could have done a better job keeping families together.

As soon as we climbed out of the minivan, a pile of children came tumbling out of the school and leapt onto us, laughing with joy. They drowned Edwin in little hugs, and the smile on his face left me with the impression that every one of those children was in some way his own. He said a few things to them in a language I didn't understand, arms fanning out to touch as many of their heads as possible. I caught Sarah out of the corner of my eye, laughing, smiling, and integrated. Mark seemed engaged too, though from his usual silent distance. I felt awkward as usual, always magnified in the company of children.

"They want to sing us a song," Edwin said to Sarah, and she pumped her arms like an overzealous cheerleader.

"That would be wonderful. Let's hear it!"

The children fell silent, falling into a square of six rows of six. One of the teachers, a young woman who herself looked to be just out of high school, stood in front of them, faces gazing up at her and little eyes darting back and forth to watch us as she gave them a serious look and clapped her hands to start them off. I did not recognize the song, but its tune hung in the air and over us like sweet honey. The youngest child looked to be about four and the oldest somewhere around eleven. They were dressed in clean kid clothes and not the uniforms I'd seen on the many schoolchildren since I landed. They sang with smiles, looking up at the teacher's conducting hands, struggling to concentrate despite the four distractions in front of them. A brood of hens trotted by and skittered through the kids' legs and I caught sight of one of the boys, about eight years old, in the back staring at me, mouthing the words and looking as if this were the last place he'd like to be. When they were finished singing, we burst into applause, and I saw a flash of pride on Edwin's face as he searched my own for a reaction.

"Just lovely," I said, following Sarah into the children, who leapt and climbed all over us. All of them except for the boy in the back I'd seen before, who slid out away from the pack and planted himself next to the fence, sitting down with one knee jutting up into the sky. He watched on with curiosity, but there was no mistaking the sadness in his eyes. It hurt to look at him, yet I could not peel my eyes away, like watching some grim accident on the side of the road. Even when I cast my glances down to the other kids, I continued to observe him through my peripheral vision. I'm not sure how I knew it, but I grasped that among this group of orphans and non-orphans he was of the former group. When this hit me, I put all other thoughts aside, and my body shifted to face him. The rest of the children fell away in my mind, as he sat there regarding me. Underneath the slight curiosity was a look of sorrow, complete resignation. True or not, his story flashed into my mind. It didn't matter where his life would go from that point onward; he had lost his family, and along with it a deep connection to the world. I knew that look quite well and my heart went out to him. A van full of happy people could not bring his life back to normal, nor could the love of others close to him. No, he was adrift for life, and would always have that hole that could only ever be filled by something else–and so young to feel that!

"We have to go. Need to head back to Manila before the end-of-day traffic," Edwin said to us and we bid our goodbyes. I fell asleep on the ride back, my head leaning against the window, exhausted. I dreamt part of the day again:

We arrived at the orphanage in the minivan. Only I came with other people, people with an evil streak. They rushed out of the car, and like ogres began scooping up children. I could hear their cries of pain and anxiety. I slid out of the car, heavy feet pulling through thick mud as I made my way to the school. Once inside, I recognized that same little boy, whose face looked odd, but it was still him. He hid in the corner, and I reached out to help him, but he pushed me away. The more I tried to convince him I was good, the more he cried and covered his face. He suddenly screamed the kind of scream that breaks windows, and in the dream, some of them did break, glass shattered across the floor in fragments. One of my companions heard the screams and ducked his head into the room, telling me to forget about him. "Leave him, he's of no use to us!" he shouted, pulling me out of the room. When I looked back, I noticed the boy vomiting green bile and then morphing into an old man dressed in rags, clutching gold coins. He was dying, and I was leaving him.

I awoke with a startle, the dream still tugging me down into a shameful depression. I could hear the others chatting in the back, so kept my eyes on the outside scenery, trying to regain my sense of reality. It took several minutes to shake the phantoms away. Nevertheless, I faked sleep for most of the ride back to Manila, still feeling occasional shudders.

CHAPTER 4 | SHANGRI-LA

Edwin declined my offer for dinner at the Shangri-La, but Mark and Sarah's eyes lit up when I mentioned it. God knows what they'd been eating the past few months, and the three of us waved goodbye to Edwin and within minutes slid into a comfortable booth at the grill restaurant, underdressed, but tired and famished after a long day and not caring much what we looked like. Mark seemed to be in a chipper mood, and I ordered an expensive bottle of wine, treating this as a cut-loose party compared to the subdued comportment needed for the previous dinner we shared with Ms. Luisa. I started the conversation off by talking about the Center and the day's events, but Sarah's eyes twinkled, and she quickly took it in another direction.

"Harry... do you have someone special back home?"

"Why do you ask?"

"Careful, Sarah, Harry is a sneak. Before you know it, he'll steer the conversation back to you," Mark said with a smile, lifting his wine glass to his lips.

"That's not fair!" I shouted in mock anger, "Besides, my life is boring compared to yours."

"Oh, I don't believe that." Sarah flashed an incredulous look. "Our lives always seem boring to us, but almost never to other people."

"That's true. Look at you and Mark, surviving Mongolian winters and now down here helping slum dwellers. I should say that you're leading extraordinary lives indeed."

"See what I mean, he's turning it back..."

"Oh, shut up, Mark." It was the most playful I'd ever seen Mark, and I think we were all turning giddy off our second glass of wine, empty stomachs awaiting their due. The attentive waiter brought a second bottle at my nod, along with some bread. Sarah raised an inquisitive eyebrow, staring me down until I spoke again. "Well, as you young people say these days, it's complicated. That's most relationships, right?"

"Oh, I wouldn't know," Mark said with a smirk, and I heard a sudden thwap under the table as he let out a soft wail followed by a laugh, keeping his eyes buried in his glass.

"You're not *so old*, Harry. Besides, you do look pretty darned good for your age. Is that wrong of me to say?"

"Of course not, I need all the validation I can get–and to answer your question, her name is Elena."

"And, how long has this complicated relationship been going on?"

"Since last fall. I met her the same day Mark did."

"No way!" Mark broke in. "She's not the meditation lady, is she?"

"That's the one." I felt my face redden. "She also runs a yoga studio and does some kind of energy work."

"That's *so* San Francisco," Mark muttered.

"Wait." She shot an incredulous, almost jealous look at Mark. "What meditation lady?"

"Remember how I told you I worked with Harry at the bank? Elena came in one day to do a guided meditation. Harry sat next to me."

"Get out of town, really? How postmodern!" She gave a screech that turned a few heads over to us. "So, she came into the bank? And then what happened? What did you say, Harry? Did you turn on the charm or what?" She leaned in and fixed intense eyes on me as if telling a secret, lowering her voice, "You know what I think? I think God plans all these beautiful little chance happenings for us, and as long as we're walking our path, it all works out."

"You sound like her, now."

"You know, I still do that meditation she taught us," Mark said, leaning back with his glass to his lips.

"Oh yeah? She sounds marvelous already."

"I'm trying to convince her to come for a vacation in September, so maybe you'll get to meet her then."

"Cool! We should go to one of the islands."

"Sounds good to me." I wanted to change the subject and avoid having to talk about Elena or my personal life in general. "So, what do you think of this country so far? Besides hot and humid?"

"I'm in love with it," Sarah responded, without batting an eye. "Yes, it's hot and humid, and a little maddening at times, but the people here are so darn sweet. Our friends at the Center–they are made of gold."

"I agree. Speaking of the Center, what do you think about all this Christianity stuff at the Center? I didn't ask that right. I mean, you know… about it being so front and center?"

"Well, I *am* a preacher's daughter, so I'm used to it. In fact, some of it gives me a feeling of comfort. Some of it doesn't."

"What do you mean?" I asked.

"Well, it's basically the prosperity gospel in action."

"Oh? I never heard that expression."

"Health and wealth," Mark chimed in with a wry expression plastered on his face.

"Yeah, some people call it that too," Sarah said, glancing his way and resting a loving hand on his forearm. "The general idea is that if a person has the right amount of faith *and* displays that faith in the right way, God will send that person riches and good health."

"Like a cosmic Santa Claus?"

"Never thought of it that way, but maybe." She wrinkled her brow, pondering my flippant comment as though it were serious. Mark chuckled. "You ever read Max Weber?"

"No, but I think Mark has. Isn't that the guy you were talking about that night at the Fairmont?"

"Good memory. Yeah, the *Protestant Ethic*. Great book. America stripped down naked," Mark responded, drinking the last of the second bottle of wine and forcing a third to be brought to the table.

"I'll have to put it on my reading list, then."

"Definitely! It's a real page turner, which is saying *a lot* for a sociology book. Most of my professors saw nothing but holes in his arguments—but I couldn't help seeing a lot of truth in what he says," Sarah cut back in, her eyes blazing, "I'll give you the abridged version unless you want to go back to talking about your love life?"

"No, let's stick with stripping down America. That sounds *way* more interesting."

The three of us laughed and I settled back into my seat, belly satisfied and full glass in hand, feeling the ease of friendship developing between the three of us. Sarah leaned forward, while Mark rested an arm on his cheek, head tilted with his left ear remaining in the conversation. It dawned on me I had succeeded in pushing a button connected to a deep passion inside her, and she barreled forward with a long treatise on a subject that both entranced and startled me.

"Remember the Puritans?"

"Sure, people who wore boring clothes and didn't smile much."

"Something like that. Not a bad description, come to think of it. Well, they were Protestants, doing their best in England and Holland and a few other places to *purify* religion, particularly from Catholic influences."

"I'm guessing that's why they got booted out and sent to America," I cut in, and she nodded in agreement.

"They were most concerned with the salvation of their own souls rather than anything else. The focus was on the individual and his connection to the God, not on priests or indulgences, etcetera. For these guys, idle hands *were* the devil's hands. So, working hard was a big deal. Not just working hard, but also saving money and not spending it frivolously. Of course, doing all that work and living a Spartan lifestyle invariably meant saving lots of money. This took root in America, and became part of our early culture. That is, to be a pious individualist, you gotta work hard, and you gotta save your money. If you know his story, John D. Rockefeller epitomized the Protestant ethic. The American dream is built on these same ideals he followed of pulling oneself up by the bootstraps, being self-reliant, and striking out on one's own."

"Good ole' fashion individualism. Nothing wrong with that," I responded.

"Unless individualism becomes the new God," Mark muttered, without looking up.

"I wouldn't go that far, but America definitely has an ethos of individualism raised up high and wrapped up in the accumulation of wealth," Sarah responded.

"Isn't that accumulation of wealth the opposite of Puritanism, at least the way you've portrayed it?" I asked.

"Not exactly. Everyone has a calling, and as long as he works hard in that calling, he's following a divine path. If God makes him rich in the process, that's just a blessing from God, and not bad as long as it doesn't lead to idleness."

"But is that true of America today?"

"Religion's long flown the coop for most of America, but it doesn't matter. But as Weber said, we're still stuck in an iron cage of materialism rooted in these unconscious patterns that might no longer fit."

I shot Mark a knowing look and he returned it with a sheepish grin. "I guess you found the right girl for you, Marko." Then I turned to Sarah. "Look, I don't see the problem with a little individualism. Isn't it part of what makes America so great?"

"Maybe so, but great in what way? We hear a lot about how people are feeling more and more alienated and isolated. Where's the community there? Could individualism be at the root of the general malaise we see in America?"

"I'll tell you what the real problem is. It's *too much* freedom. That's what I say."

"Really?" She cast an inquisitive eye on me and cocked her head back.

"Well, it's like this. I don't know much about children, but from what I hear, they need lots of boundaries to feel safe and happy. Ever go to a house where the kids are in charge, running around like wild beasts?"

"Oh yeah."

"Those kids might be in charge, but they're anxious because nobody's setting limits on their behavior. Many of them are just acting out to get those boundaries set—though they may not be aware that's what they're doing."

"Interesting. Okay, how does that relate?"

"Every time I hear about a mass shooting or people doing crazy things, I think of the chaos of my cousin's household with his kids staying up late and pulling crazy stunts. Only, now it's older kids and society not setting boundaries."

"Restricting freedoms?"

"Yep. The whole country's going crazy because we have too much freedom, and maybe, as you say, a bit of individualism thrown in there."

"Everybody wants to be special," Mark slipped in. "Killing a bunch of people and winding up with your picture on the front page is an expedient way of doing that." There were several moments of silence after he said this, each of us sensing how little time it took for the conversation to veer into the macabre.

"Well, it seems we have it all figured out," I laughed. "But I'm not sure what the solution is, and I'm certainly not advocating for drastic measures like taking away people's guns or sending in the brown shirts."

"Yeah, that never works," Sarah muttered, refusing another glass of wine and leaving Mark and I to the third bottle as we took a break to ponder the dessert menu. Once the waiter came around and we ordered a few things to share, I couldn't help keeping the conversation going. It had been a long time since I'd had a real intellectual discussion, and we had struck upon that sweet spot thanks to Sarah's knowledge and passion, made fluid by the wine.

"But other countries seem to have similar freedoms and guns, etc., and those people are not crazy. What's that all about?"

"Most of those places have a strong social safety net. Our lack of one cultivates individualism and even accentuates it," she retorted in a sharp tone.

"Sorry, but that sounds like a liberal sales pitch to me."

"Which part?" she asked, sensing a twinge of anger rising in me.

"Well, I just don't see the connection between some guy wasting a bunch of people with a rifle and whether or not he has health insurance."

"When you put it that way, I don't either, but when people are struggling to survive and living a few paychecks away from sinking below the surface *and* they're told they must do it all on their own and nobody is going to help them if they hit hard times, that's a recipe for disaster. Worse, they're being told that nobody *should* help them because they must learn to do everything on their own. That strips them away from their communities and puts them in a different frame of mind."

"A kill or be killed mindset," Mark added.

"Quiet over there in the nickel seats," I thundered with a wink. "I'm planning to win this debate."

"Are we debating? I thought we were just sharing ideas." Sarah feigned a hurt expression before turning a frown into a welcome smile. "Listen, Harry. I get that handouts can enable people, and in some cases, keep them from *self-actualization*, to use a loaded term. It would be a shame to take away a system that helps so many others and one that gives them the opportunity to survive and potentially contribute to society."

"Is that the government's job, though? Why can't churches and NGOs like the Center do that kind of work instead of taking my hard-earned money and doling it out to the masses? I'd much rather have a say in who gets my money than have it taxed away into the ether."

"That's a fair argument. I'm not advocating for government to overstep its role, but I still think as a country, as a world community even, we're all trying figure out how to make sure people get the help they need in the way they need it. Many people just need a leg up. My big concern in shifting everything over to churches and nonprofits is that some people might fall through the cracks—people who are not on the radar of those organizations. So, I think the government's role is to make sure everyone has a fair shake in the world they live in."

"Well spoken." I could have quibbled with a few points she made, but it was getting late and I didn't want us to spend the rest of the evening hashing out details on something we weren't going to resolve anyway. As a bartender once told me, two drunks are not going to solve the world's problems on barstools, and the three of us had long since crossed the Rubicon into Tipsyland. We ate our desserts in silence, punctuated by subdued talk about where they were living. I found out that due to overcrowding, they were not living in the dormitories, but in a rented apartment near the Center. They still showed up at 7:00 a.m. for morning devotion, and stayed for dinner each night, but were free to leave afterward to cohabitate in sin. I was a bit shocked at this revelation given how regimented and structured the Center and its people seemed. Who knows, maybe they made allowances for depraved foreigners who drank and fornicated, marking them for eventual salvation precipitated through modeling consistent behavior. At the end of it all I hugged both goodnight and put them in a taxi home.

I spent the next two weeks following Edwin around metro Manila and learning more about the work of the Center and its pain points. Of course, funding was an issue. His image of microfinance as a locomotive pulling boxcars of various services stuck out in my mind; and that locomotive requires fuel to keep it moving—in this case, money. As head of operations, Edwin made certain each program ran as smoothly as possible. For him, that meant keeping his finger on the pulse of activity. From an outsider's perspective it might seem like he accomplished little by bouncing from one location to another, often spending less than a half hour in each place. I knew enough about effective management to see the wisdom in his method. Each office, branch, meeting, or group of people had at least one person in a leadership role: *The Peer Servant*. He spent a few minutes with each peer servant to listen to them. He never said much, spending most of the time listening. He also jotted down notes on a tiny pad he kept in his shirt front pocket, which I'm sure made the peer servants feel supported. At the end of every discussion he would take their hands in his and bow his head, uttering the same prayer to each: "May God bless you and your family and the work that you are doing to help His children."

I attended several weekly hour-long meetings set up by the Center. These were groups of fifteen or twenty people living in the same neighborhood that knew one another and decided to band together in solidarity. I noticed more than one group at most meetings, recalling one meeting with five groups present—close to a hundred people. People met in an open lot filled with rubble, surrounded by low-rise cement buildings in an area close to the port. Compared to the location where I met Edwin on that first day, it looked more run down and reminded me of a post-apocalyptic wasteland—dusty paths strewn with garbage and a pile of rusting bicycles and other scrap metal. Edwin seemed at ease while strolling through each community, as if he belonged there. I was amazed at how he could make five minutes with a person seem like he was spending all day with them, relaxed and present. I wish I had that in me, always feeling like I've got to run off somewhere when I have nowhere to go. I suppose I've never been all that comfortable talking with other people unless it's a business transaction, and even those were hit and miss.

I fell into a rhythm of spending the early part of my days shadowing Edwin and the afternoons reading, and talking to Elena. Our calls started from every few days to just about every day throughout that August. It was a good way to spend my evenings since between daily downpours and the seedy nightlife culture around the hotel, wandering around after dark was inadvisable. The one time I went out after dinner looking to stock up on bottled water I was propositioned twice. Edwin told me the area used to be popular with American servicemen before forces pulled out over a decade prior.

CHAPTER 5 | THE CITY OF GENTLE PEOPLE

Elena flew into Manila the third week of September. By then I was volunteering at the Center, concentrating on a review of their credit processes and reporting my findings back to Edwin. Since the bank's sale was set to go through in October, I took the last chunk of liquid cash I had and turned it over to the Center as a term loan to fund their microfinance program. It felt strange having a few thousand left in my account, but I wasn't worried since I'd just received the projected payout of my equity share from Don. By the following month I would have enough cash to buy my own MFI if I wanted to.

I was surprised when Elena capitulated to my regular appeals to come out for a week. I wasted no time buying her a first-class ticket from San Francisco before she had a chance to reconsider. Mark and Sarah were planning to peel away for a long weekend and join us, and I had my heart set on one of the lush islands I'd heard about from others I met at the Shangri-La. The top recommendations were Palawan for the natural beauty and Boracay for fun. When I mentioned this to Sarah she had another idea. Seems a friend of hers was down on the island of Negros studying cockfighting culture, and she discovered a place there to scuba dive with sea turtles. When I mentioned the turtles to Elena, she was hooked. I was pretty sure they sold her more than the thought of spending time with me, but it didn't matter. I missed her warm touch.

It was strange to see Elena outside of her environment, and I sensed that stepping out of her world of yoga studios and offbeat friends, she struggled to gain her footing. Natural, I suppose, and something I could relate to. But everything went sideways from the moment she walked off the plane. Whenever she looked at me, her sunny face fell overcast. It was as if I had done her wrong, and nothing I said or did could make up for it. We shared a bed, but she only agreed to come on the trip if I promised to keep things cool between us. I figured I could keep my self-control for nine days, holding out the hope that a few glasses of wine might loosen her up enough to cause that agreement to be revisited ad-hoc. Either way, I was happy to see her and intent on not screwing things up too early. Yet I knew the minute I saw her at the airport I was in for a rough time with her.

I took her around the Center, introducing her to Edwin, Sarah, Mark, and everyone else. I couldn't take my eyes off her, watching as she connected with everyone else with a gracious smile. She looked like a magnanimous queen and the people I'd been working with treated her with a warmth I wished I got from them (and her). They were kind to me, of course, but she seemed to bring out a side in people that lay hidden from the rest of the world, especially other women. It was as if she were giving them permission to shout out, "I am lioness, hear me roar!" Of course, whenever heads were turned, or we were alone, she would cast a cool glance or a hurtful barb to try to knock me down a notch. I mentioned my observations to her a few times, but she acted like I was delusional and labeled me annoying. I stopped bringing it up after a couple days. My ex-wife pulled the same crap with me, so I assumed I just brought out the worst in women once they were caught up in my romantic orbit.

I was glad that Elena and Sarah hit it off well; I somehow knew they would. A day later the four of us, including Mark, were on a short flight out of Manila. We landed at Dumaguete airport on the tip of the boot-shaped island of Negros—one of the larger islands of the Philippine archipelago. The airport was a tiny strip with a single building and one lone gate, and much of the little city struck a similar vein. I was pleased that despite its diminutive size, it had a grand old hotel overlooking a beautiful beach promenade. We booked two rooms facing the water, and I wasted no time booking our scuba tour to a place called Apo Island out of a shop down the street. The shop promised us turtles.

A Catholic University town, Dumaguete offered a healthy blend of student liveliness and scant non-native tourists. Though, I didn't expect to see so many lascivious old ex-pats with arms draped around tiny girls that should have been in school. It was a sad sight, especially in our hotel lobby, which we avoided most of the time. Sometimes, I would look at one of the girls and try to picture myself with her, but the brief thought sent a shudder down my spine. These men had given up on their own kind, both country and people, and taken refuge in a place where their pensions afforded them an affection absent in their previous life. A sorry sight and I considered myself lucky not to have devolved to that state.

The next morning the four of us went diving, though Elena and Sarah decided to snorkel instead of opting for the certification needed for diving with tanks. The dive shop owner was a crusty-looking man in his sixties from Northern California. Nate had sold the family winery and decided to make a go of it in the tropics, buying up the shop and purchasing a motorized wooden trimaran for ferrying people over to Apo Island, just a few miles off the main island. His grisly white beard, shark's tooth necklace and sour looks belied an affable person who welcomed his new environment. He treated his crew and guests with courtesy and expressed an obvious joy for island life. While Sarah and Elena found plenty of things to talk about, Elena's insatiable curiosity about life in the Philippines for Sarah took up most of the weekend's conversations. I spent a majority of the time talking with Nate. Mark, as usual, remained in the background, taking photographs of most everything.

For a man who'd risked most of his savings on this new venture, Nate's insecurity at keeping it afloat was natural. Although, with each minute I spent with him, I sensed the decision still vexed him, and he remained mired in anxiety. It came out not just in the many references to the stock market back home, but also for his disdain of the expat culture. While he claimed they were a bunch of lecherous old men preying on young girls, later, I couldn't help noticing that his girlfriend was local and quite young herself. At dinner, Sarah mentioned that this seedy side of expat culture ran rife throughout Southeast Asia—lonely old men buying their way into families. On the flip side, they were also signing up to contribute to the household income of the immediate family, and sometimes the extended family of their girlfriends. Seemed like a high price to pay for what I overheard mentioned as a "good piece of ass."

We saw more turtles than I expected at Apo Island. They glided by in such shallow water we didn't really need air tanks to see them. At one point, I caught Elena's arm and pulled her down from the surface, feeding her my second regulator mouthpiece so we could hover and watch them together. I couldn't help noticing her red hair swirling through the brine and remembering the wall dive dream months earlier. At one point she gazed over at me and I could see her eyes smiling as she slowly moved close enough that I could wrap my arms around her while we watched turtles the size of manhole covers drift past us. It was one of the few times she let me get close to her on that trip, and I reveled in it. In fact, I made a mistake in thinking she was no longer peeved with me for whatever mysterious slight I'd caused. But once we were on the surface I saw her gaze warp back to angry reproach. I shrugged it off and swam away from her.

The island itself was a bit of a rocky crag with villagers coming over to sell us t-shirts with turtles emblazoned on them. We all bought one, posing for a few silly pictures. Sarah made a kind remark about the Irish accent of the young man who'd taken the pictures. This was not uncommon for her, and I'm sure Mark never took it as flirting. If he did, he never let on.

The Irishman struck me as very approachable and I recall a welcoming grin from the back of the jeep when we were leaving the dive shop. He was stout, with large biceps, short reddish hair and fun-loving mischief in his eyes. He was so stereotypically Irish and like many of his countrymen I couldn't tell if his smile and gestures were leading up to a brawl or friendly repartee. It didn't surprise me when Sarah asked him to join us for dinner later that evening. She wanted to try the new pizza place in town and that sounded pretty good after a day of sun and wind and swimming with sea turtles.

After bidding farewell to Nate and his tribe of locals, we all showered up and met back at the pizza place later. Patrick made a fun addition to our little group and sitting there at a table overlooking the beach, swilling cold beer and waiting for our pizza, I felt the magic in our conversation light up as we shared stories of Nate and the turtles. Elena wore a see-through long white sun dress, and she caught me staring at her too long and winked at me. She liked knowing that I desired her. All I wanted to do was to be alone with her, though I was glad to have the additional company. I hadn't been listening to the conversation, but it wasn't surprising that the main participants were Sarah and Patrick.

"Well, yeah… I'm on an around-the-world trip, so it adds up after a while," I heard Patrick say as I faded back in.

"That sounds like fun," she responded with her usual gusto.

"Yeah, I left my job back in Ireland eight months ago and I have about three months before I go back. My boss said I could come back, but after what I've seen and done I just don't know if I'll go back to doing what I was doing. Just a bunch of spreadsheets."

"I know what you mean," Mark piped in. "By the way, where all have you been so far?"

"Oh, well. I spent some time in Africa, the Middle East, then India. I was planning to do more of Southeast Asia, but I got stuck down in Indonesia."

"Oh yeah? What happened there?" Sarah asked.

"It was like this. I was on my way to Bali for a little scuba diving and sightseeing, but then a friend of mine who works for the BBC was finishing up a documentary on an Irish priest down on the island of Java. So, I stopped there first to visit and to check things out and wound up spending two months volunteering."

"What kept you there?"

"Father Jack. The man's amazing. He's been down there forty years and has completely transformed a forgotten little slice of the jungle."

"Really?" Elena raised an eyebrow and shot me a curious look.

"Yeah. He's built roads, schools, buildings, and loads of other stuff. He's helping the poor in ways I've never seen before."

"Fascinating!" Sarah said.

"Yeah, if you all have time I can show you some footage from the documentary. It's not coming out for another few months, but my friend sent me a rough cut. Most entrepreneurial priest I've ever seen and all of it devoted to helping the poor. Very inspirational."

So, after pizza and more beers, I found myself hunched over a laptop on the couch in the lobby of our hotel with everyone else, watching the documentary of Father Jack. The lechers were there, but they merely glanced at us with passing interest in between unsavory kisses.

At first, I was only interested in getting through the documentary so that I could be rid of everyone else and get Elena alone and take advantage of the good mood she was in. Although, every time I *was* alone with her I felt like someone else had wrestled control over her being and my Elena was inside there somewhere, locked away in a dungeon. Of course, I kept all these thoughts a secret and feigned enthusiasm on the outside. Within minutes I couldn't help getting sucked into the story of an old man with a thick brogue doing amazing things deep in the tropics. I was enthralled by the priest's singsong Irish voice, wit and charm and the moving scenes of his determination and work to accomplish great things in what seemed like a far-flung patch of jungle long forgotten by everyone else, including its own government. He seemed like a normal guy in many ways, and I felt the force of his charm through the screen like a cobra swaying to his master's rhythms.

During one of the pauses between clips, I tilted my head to Elena and her eyes narrowed at mine, a slight twinkle in them. I couldn't say for sure then that she knew what I was thinking, but later after everyone left and we were together in the room, she gave me a searching look as we both gazed out from the veranda onto the beach. The old men selling fish were packing things up, leaving small groups of young people walking up and down the promenade. Many of them were laughing with a giddiness that reminded me of the early fall in Annapolis–young women coming down from Baltimore dressed in their best in hopes of snagging a naval officer husband.

"You know, that was *some* documentary," Elena said finally, turning to me. I kept my eyes out over the water, trying to make out whether the single white light out there came from a ship.

"Yeah," I muttered, slapping a mosquito on my leg. "Damn these mosquitoes!"

"Father Jack seems like an inspirational guy. I bet he'll inspire others to put their entrepreneurial talents to work helping the poor." I knew what she was doing, but I didn't want to let on. "Might be fun to check him out in person."

"I guess so. I hear Indonesia is hotter than here. I pity the man that has to live there."

"People can get used to just about anything–especially if it's integral to their path."

"Well, speaking for myself, I'd say I'm still not getting used to us not having sex."

She paused for a moment, and I felt my stomach drop. I'd crossed the line with her, realizing all those dirty looks and attempts to avoid me held simmering rage. She shook her head and took a deep breath. "I knew this was going to happen. I knew it I knew I knew it!" She lifted her face up and I saw the devil in them. "I told you I wasn't ready for that, and now all this pressure. I'm sick of it, Harry!"

"I'm sick of it, too!" I felt the lid come off my own pot. "Next week marks a year since we first met. Most people in loving relationships are having sex by now."

"Well, I'm not most people!"

"I don't even know who you are!" I shot back. "I feel like I've been watching Jekyll and Hyde in action this past week. One minute you're Mother Theresa to a bunch of villagers and then you turn around and call me a loser for liking my eggs boiled instead of fried. Do you not like me or something?"

"Sometimes I do, sometimes I don't. I don't know why. And I *never* called you a loser."

"I was there, Elena. You saying I don't hear with my ears?"

"I'm saying you're delusional. You hear what you want to hear and see what you want to see."

"Well, right now I'm not sure *who* I'm seeing."

"That's what I'm talking about. You see me on some pedestal. You tell me how beautiful I am. I am beautiful. I'm also ugly. I'm kind. But I'm also a real *bitch*. You don't see me. You don't see anyone for who they are. A *real* man would see me and know how to handle me. You're just too sensitive. Fucking baby!"

"Fuck you, cunt!"

I'm not sure I'd ever said those words to woman. But she found a way to get to me on a level not even my ex-wife could manage. The rest of the conversation spun down into dark tumult, and I wound up sleeping on the hardwood floor–self banishment. Usually calm and cool, I let my anger get the best of me and so did she. It was bound to happen, anyway, and in retrospect probably a good thing. The next morning, she crawled down on the floor next to me and lay against my back. I was dead tired after a fitful night of tossing around on what felt like sleeping on stainless steel. She took a deep breath and began whispering into my ear that she was still recovering from her last relationship and that he had done things to her that she wasn't ready to talk about, but that hurt her in a way that made it difficult to take that step with me or anyone else. I listened without turning to her, taking it all in. The fog of exhaustion cast the whole situation into a surreal field and I felt like I was in a dream. She never talked in that tone before–like a scared little girl. I said nothing, just listened to her. When she was done, she collapsed onto me and I rolled over and took her in my arms. I held her in that way for what seemed like hours.

We didn't talk about it again the rest of her visit, but she had introduced something new into our relationship. It felt like starting over but with a different version of someone I already knew–someone vulnerable in a way that scared me too. I understood in my heart that I had to decide on whether I could live with this new person–and for once didn't have a quick answer for myself. A year earlier and I would have given her the boot right then without a second thought. Something had already shifted in me. Not just about her, but about the whole world. It made me hesitate and catch that sharp mind and tongue before they charged the battlefield.

We made the most of our time together, though. Patrick stuck around for one more day and then he was gone to dive with thresher sharks off Cebu. I envied his freedom to float around wherever he wanted whenever it suited him. Mark and Sarah stayed until Monday afternoon, and we managed to squeeze as much fun as we could from their company before they headed back to Manila. It didn't matter if we went to the beach, explored the local college, or just sat around chatting about the Center, I felt something special in the dynamic of the four of us all together. I can't explain it beyond recognizing a form of individuation achieved through the company of just the right mix of people. Perhaps like when the sails are trimmed just right, and the sailboat is hitting its sweet spot. Like sailing, it didn't last long without careful maintenance.

Once everyone had left and I had Elena to myself, I wasn't sure what to do. I knew the door to sex was shut tight and the sudden slamming of it had undermined the sensuality in our relationship. We still slept in the same bed–after that night on the floor I don't think my body could have handled another like it. I thought we were doing our best to repair whatever was broken by not addressing anything head on, tenderness still rubbed raw. Internally, part of me kept shouting out to pull the plug as a big waste of energy. Too much work! While another part would catch a glimpse of the way her shoulder gleamed in the morning sun as she stabbed little potatoes with her fork at the breakfast table, feeling a deep love well inside me, or was it lust? All relationships have their issues to navigate. She had a scary monster living in her closet, that's for sure. Maybe I also had one just as scary. I guess the fate of our relationship came down to whether we could accept one another and all despite the baggage we each brought to the table.

Our original plan of hopping to another island that next week fell by the wayside as we both confessed that neither one of us wanted to leave Dumaguete, aptly nicknamed the *City of Gentle People*. We made it out to Apo Island a few more times with Nate and his crew. The rest of the time we took long strolls along the promenade and enjoyed doing nothing but resting in one another's presence. While my initial expectations, especially around sex, had crashed and burned, I wasn't disappointed in how things went most of that week. She always talked of our need to cultivate a quiet stillness in our relationship–and I suppose we were doing just that.

She also mentioned Fr. Jack a few times, and I knew she was hinting at me getting in touch with him. She may have had a point, as my time with the Center was coming to an end whether I believed it or not. Soon, I would be a burden to them no matter how much money I chipped in to ameliorate the drain on resources my presence there was having on them. I also felt an attraction to Fr. Jack's story, and my curiosity began to grow each day. Before he left, Patrick had written the email address down in case we wanted to go out there ("he loves visitors", I heard him say more than once), and I kept noticing it on the little table next to the hotel room door, edges of the paper curled up.

One morning I woke up and without thinking too much about it I grabbed the paper, went downstairs to the hotel's computer and fired off a message to Fr. Jack. In my email I told him about my background and all that I'd been doing, as well as meeting Patrick. I suggested that if he were interested I could make a visit out there to see if I could "help" in any way. I had a few other emails to go through, one from Don out to shareholders that notwithstanding the market turmoil, we should expect the sale to go through by October 20th, less than a month away.

Unlike the Shangri-La, which had a Wi-Fi connection in each room, the best the Dumaguete hotel could offer was a single computer in the lobby for guests to use. I only saw foreigners on it that seemed to use it as their sole means of staying connected to home. With Elena around, I didn't need so much of that. After I cleaned out my inbox, I was about to close out and get up, when I saw a bolded message come through. It was a reply from Fr. Jack. At first, I thought it had bounced back, and was about to check the paper again to make sure I had the correct email address. After I opened the message, I realized he had responded. It was curt, but welcoming: *Sure, pop on over whenever you can. We'd love to have you!*

My cynical side suggested he was most interested in me as a social investor, and that's what drove his hasty, welcoming reply. It didn't matter, I was already hooked and ready to go. I wasted no time in booking a flight out there, making sure I was on the same flight to Hong Kong with Elena later in the week. I also sent emails off to Sarah and Edwin, letting them know of my change of plans and that I wouldn't be coming back to Manila just yet. This new adventure felt like the right thing to do. When I told Elena about it later she smiled and gave me a hug. It was as if she was several steps ahead of me and reveling in my catching up. Our relationship seemed to improve after that, and we spent the next few days in sweet seclusion from the outside world.

Of course, our last morning together we had another fight, much worse than the previous blowout. It stunned me into confusion watching her morph from pussycat to raging monster because I left a wet towel on the bathroom floor rather than on the rack. At the drop of a hat, all my words were turned against me and instead of a sweet face I stared at a gloomy iron fortress. Just when I thought we had found serenity down a path of intimacy, she found a way to destroy it all in minutes. It was as if I had stumbled into a maze and couldn't find my way out. I had lost her.

PART IV | JAVA

CHAPTER 1 | ONE NIGHT IN HONG KONG

Elena had a short connection in Hong Kong, so we had little time for more than a quick embrace before she flew off again. As I watched her red hair bounce away and through the gate, it dawned on me that we'd had the best and worst week of our relationship. We'd made the most of rocky patches, made difficult through seeing each other at our worst. Something sinister seemed to be working to undermine the foundation of our tender connection. I could blame it on her, or even us. Once she was out of sight, I wondered how much of the problem lay with me—with my mind—monkey mind as she called it. Through her influence I noticed the little beast hell bent on analyzing everything into a negative slant until it had cast even the purest light into darkness—always at odds with my higher self. Perhaps it was the way she said *good luck* with an ominous air instead of goodbye, as though I was off to slay a dragon that just might kill me. I wasn't sure what to make of it, but she did ask at one point during the week how the crumbling tower was going. That made me angry, and I shot her a snide remark. Ultimately, we were headed in opposite directions. I let out a deep sigh, conceding that I might not ever see her again.

On the off chance I could catch him during my four-hour layover in Hong Kong, I had emailed Kyle, a former colleague of mine who'd taken a job there decades earlier. We managed to keep in touch over the years and met up whenever we were in the same city for a conference or something. Lucky for me, he was available and recommended I take the MTR train to Hong Kong Station for dinner in Soho. I'd made the route once before around mountains and water, reveling in the picturesque landscape made better by a brilliant sunset. I always liked Kyle, someone who shared my gallows humor, something I usually kept to myself but couldn't help unfurling in his company. I met him at Société Générale, where I worked for two years right out of Wharton. He was an expert on telecommunications and foreign markets, particularly in Asia, and he had stayed on with that bank to make his own fortune while I'd rolled the dice with Don. Kyle was one of the quickest thinkers I'd ever met—a mind like a laser and a wiry body that burned through a few thousand calories a day just thinking.

When I saw him approaching me later at the station, I noticed his thin frame and flowing gait passing through people and couldn't help thinking how God must have slipped up and sent his soul to the wrong birth country. It took him a while, but he'd found his way back to his true people like a homing pigeon. Even his face had the same angular features of the Orient, and if it hadn't been for his bright green eyes and sandy brown hair he could have passed for a local no problem.

"What's it been, fifteen years, Harry? Great to see you!" He stood opposite me, shaking my hand, an incredulous look passing over his features. "What the hell you doing out here? On your way to Bangkok for a little boom boom with a *mamasan*?"

"Hadn't thought of that, but now that you bring it up, maybe I'll change my plans. Can you recommend any good places?"

Kyle shook his head and laughed, realizing that the conversation could too easily get dragged down into the gutter, "It's really great to see you, Harry. I have to say I don't miss many people from the old days, but you were one of them for sure. He motioned for me to follow and we talked during the short trip to Soho. "Seriously, what *are* you doing out here?"

"Why so surprised?"

"Well, of all the people I know you're the last I'd expect to leave the creature comforts of the free world and venture out into the unknown. Of course, Hong Kong isn't all that different from San Francisco. You said you had a layover, but didn't tell me where you're headed."

"Java."

"Definitely *not* like San Francisco… or even Hong Kong. You really *are* stretching your comfort zone! I'd recommend Bali if you're doing the white man's vacation thing."

"Maybe after this next stop, but I'm not here for a vacation. I retired, actually."

"Hmmm…." His eyes softened into a curious smile. "Moving out here?"

"Nah." I hesitated to tell him my real reasons, but I knew he wouldn't stop prodding until he was satisfied he'd plumbed the depths of my soul. So, I figured I would lay my cards on the table to save the trouble. "You ever hear of microfinance?"

"What's that, just dealing in ones and fives?" he rattled off without missing a beat.

I chuckled at the jibe, "Something like that."

"Interesting that you mention that. I read a few years back about that guy winning the Nobel Peace Prize for *microcredit*. Something about loaning small amounts of money to villagers, right? I'm guessing that microfinance means more than just microcredit loans."

"Yeah, savings, insurance, et cetera."

"Somebody's making a buck somewhere," he said with a cynical glance as we made our way up a long set of stairs that passed dozens of restaurants and shops more western than eastern. Lots of bistros. I waited until we'd settled into a table at an Italian place before responding to his remark.

"I prefer to call it social investing."

"Jesus, Harry. I knew you were a barefaced opportunist," he said in a mocking tone. "But isn't this going a little too far? Making money off the backs of the poor? You should be ashamed of yourself!"

"Laugh all you want, but it's doing some good."

"Oh, I see... making up for a few decades of sharking, eh?"

"Maybe."

"Well, I'm all for bringing capitalism to the edges of the world. Why not? But I'm not sure this microcredit or microfinance stuff is going to be their ticket out of poverty."

"How so?"

"White man came out here centuries ago and screwed up island life, made a mess of it. Imagine, for a few millennia all people had to do was simply reach up and pick their food right off the tree. Colonialists changed that paradigm. First, they stripped 'em of their natural resources, then taught 'em how to fight over what's left; but they couldn't teach something that is still so ingrained in the western mind and can't really be taught to people who don't have the same agricultural history. There's a big reason why savings rates are so high in places like Norway. Saving money is a natural progression for people used to storing up salted cod and canning fruits and vegetables to survive a long winter. Savings cultures make it over the long haul because they know how to manage money wisely. It's fine to roll the dice and make a few loans, but these people will be hard-pressed to learn to save in a way that's going to build true wealth. Very few people rise out of poverty taking on debt."

"That's a pretty bleak picture."

"It's worse. As soon as someone makes a bit of money, their circle of friends and family come out of the woodwork expecting to be helped. Social capital is *way* more important out here than anything else. You don't help those around you, and well... you're not gettin' very far. So, it's just not possible for most people to climb out of poverty as they keep gettin' pulled back down off the ladder. Of course, the Chinese don't have that problem as much."

"Well, they've got those harsh winters, right?"

"Maybe a bit of that or even Confucianism. Could also be the one-child policy–smaller families with not as many mouths to feed. They're called the Jews of Southeast Asia for a reason. Most of them live by two rules: invest wisely and don't commit the cardinal sin of letting your child marry outside the tribe. The minute a Chinese man marries a Malay, it's all over. Whole new family wants a piece of him."

"Gee Kyle, that doesn't sound politically correct now, does it?" I couldn't resist taking him to task.

"Yeah, well. While you champagne liberals over on the Left Coast are arguing about what to say and how not to offend people, the rest of the world just keeps moving the way it does–the way it always has. Besides, there's always going to be poor in the world."

"Yeah, maybe you're right. I guess after seeing a few of their faces up close I can't help but try to give a few of them a leg up."

"That's fair. So, how you going about it?"

"Stumbling, mostly. I was in Mongolia and the Philippines. Found a few of these small banks that are helping the poor. Did a little bit of due diligence on them, though they're a lot different than regular banks, as you might suspect. Same setup with branches and loan officers, but the whole atmosphere is different than your average bank. Hell, one of them has branch pastors who go out and pray with delinquent clients for the money to come from God. At the end of the day I'm just going with my gut. As you know, it always comes down to people and whether or not we have faith that we'll get our investment back plus the interest."

"And what's that?"

"Around seven percent."

"Wow–can I have a piece of that action?"

"You want to invest?"

"Hell no! That's not a bad *borrowing* rate!"

"But you're a poor credit risk, Kyle. Remember the poker game where I had to front you a few hundred? Come to think of it, I'm not sure I ever got paid back."

"I have no idea what you're talking about. Why don't I cover this dinner and we'll call it even?" He shot me a sheepish grin and stuffed his face with a piece of buttered bread.

"By the way, how are things going for you? How d'you like it out here?"

"Couldn't be better. I feel at home in Asia. Better living, better food, better women, for sure."

"Yeah, Hong Kong is nice, came here once several years ago. I can't say Manila or Ulaanbaatar knocked my socks off. They both have their charms, I suppose."

"Well, you've got to get out of the big cities. Hong Kong, Singapore, Bangkok. They're okay, but most of the others are cesspools. Manila and

Jakarta are the worst. Great people, but traffic and trash everywhere. Once you get out a bit, it's a different kettle of fish."

"Yeah, that was my experience as well in Mongolia and the Philippines. What places do you recommend out this way?"

"Well, pretty much anywhere in Thailand. Dalat and Halong Bay in Vietnam. If you're a scuba diver, Indonesia has some great dive spots. Not much on Java, where you're going. I recommend Sulawesi and Komodo for that. Of course, there's always Bali. Stay out of Kuta, though."

"Why so?"

"Too many Bogans."

"Bogans?"

"Yeah, just imagine fat, tattooed rednecks with mullets and Australian accents walking down the street drinking Bintang beer out of the bottle. They must have some cheap flights from over there, because the whole place is overrun with these characters. Sadly, Kuta's become the Faliraki of Southeast Asia. So, if you get to Bali, just stay away from the area around the airport. Then again, that's pretty much true for any city."

"I'm intrigued by Indonesia."

"It's a very interesting part of the world. Pretty crowded. I think it's like the fourth largest country in the world. Like the Philippines, it's spread out over several islands. The most fascinating part to me is the vast religious spectrum. The western half, Sumatra and such, are hard-core Muslim. Java is Muslim too, but not so intense. In fact, as you work your way eastward it becomes more and more moderate. Bali is on its own as it's Hindu. Lots of interesting statues there. After that, it starts to become Christian. Timor Island. That place is a trip! The western half belongs to Indonesia and the eastern half is its own country. Indonesia controlled it for a few decades, and before that the Portuguese ran it for centuries. The Portuguese didn't leave much except traces of their language and last names. When the Indonesians let them have their independence, at least they gave 'em a massive status of Jesus. Cristo Rei—you can't miss it as it's sitting on top of a mountain overlooking the capital."

"Did the Portuguese control Indonesia?" True to his form, Kyle espoused an encyclopedic grasp of the region vis-à-vis my own lack of knowledge in colonial history.

"No, the Dutch. The Dutch East India Company ran the country for about few hundred years. After it folded the Dutch government took over for the next hundred and fifty, before handing it back to the locals at the end of World War II."

"Are they on good terms these days?"

"Could be worse. After the Dutch Foreign Minister attended the sixtieth anniversary of Indonesia's independence, it seems to have improved relations a little. Foreign direct investment has picked up a bit."

"You seem to know a lot about Indonesia."

"Well, a quarter of a billion people and nearly everyone has or wants a cell phone. So, it's in my interest to know a bit about the place. Like most countries, it's controlled by a few powerful families. Rural Java can be quite beautiful if you know where to go. Where exactly are you headed to?"

"Adipala. South part of the island."

"Hmm… never heard of it."

"I think it's somewhere in the middle," I said, searching my brain for the location on the map I had glanced at after Patrick first pointed it out to me.

"Might be tricky getting there."

"I'll probably take a local flight or something. Maybe I'll stay in Jakarta for a day or two. What do you think?"

"Well, if you think Manila traffic was bad, wait until you experience Jakarta. Though your flight this evening should get in early enough tomorrow to avoid some of it. I suggest getting out of Jakarta as quickly as possible."

We ordered our food; I had the lasagna and he a light pasta dish and salad. It tasted like heaven as I hadn't had Italian food since San Francisco. The Barolo went down like an elixir, and I felt a wave of comfort hit me, not realizing how much I missed the tastes of home which only Hong Kong seemed able to replicate. I could see how a foreigner might live a comfortable life in these surroundings, and Kyle smiled at my enthusiasm.

"Must taste good after the places you've been to, eh?" I nodded my head, and he stopped and tilted his with a searching look. "I'm curious, Harry, why all this microfinance stuff? I never really pegged you…." He trailed off, and I read his mind. I swallowed, took another drink, and answered for him.

"Kyle. You're a smart guy and have obviously done well for yourself. The truth is, and maybe you didn't know this about me before, I grew up without much and spent my whole professional life making sure I was comfortable enough not to have to worry about things the way my father did. Maybe I overshot a little, because at this point I have enough money not to have to worry for a few lifetimes. But that's just it. I don't have a ton of time left on this earth. I've got at most thirty years left in me. Since I also don't have children or anyone else to pass it along to, it doesn't make sense to hold on to more than I need. I don't know, even if I did have kids, not sure I would be handing it over to them either. I'd rather people earned their money instead of a handout, no matter who they are. I suppose that's why I find these small loans to the poor so appealing. It's not charity. Even if it doesn't move the needle much on poverty, at least it's a little money going a long way for a family that really needs it."

"I guess there are worse ways to spend your golden years. Actually, I envy you a bit." He pulled the napkin across his mouth and let out a sigh, continuing in a slower and more deliberate manner. "At this point your only boss is some faceless deity who probably doesn't even exist. Instead of frittering away an early retirement on a golf course you're trying to do something good in this world and in a way that's more sustainable than some pet charity project–some sinkhole. That sounds noble to me."

"Well, thank you, Kyle. That means a lot to me."

"Let me know if you ever need a hand in what you're doing. It's a different kind of banking, but it's still banking and only a matter of time before the two worlds collide. High finance and low finance–at the end of the day it's still finance, right? Besides, with the way the economy's going these days, we might all wind up needing these micro-loans."

"Hmmm, I guess I haven't been reading much lately. I know we had a correction in March and the housing market is cooling off."

"Oh, it's worse. Haven't you heard?" He gave me dark glance and his face took on an ominous expression. "The feds just took over Fannie and Freddie earlier in the month. Lehman Brothers collapsed a week and a half ago. Merrill Lynch bit the dust. AIG got a bailout. Personally, I think it was a huge mistake for Paulson to let Lehman Brothers go under, but the whole financial landscape is changing. In fact, yesterday the FBI said they were investigating the whole lot of them for fraud. Probably a good thing."

"Shit, really? I haven't heard any of this. I guess I've been under a rock for the past several weeks."

"Yeah, big changes going on. You'd better check your positions, make sure you're protected."

"Definitely, thanks for the heads up."

We chatted away for a few more minutes before we finished up and he walked me back to the MTR and saw me off. Kyle's endorsement surprised me, and I thought about his words on the ride back. I might have posed as a banker for thirty years, but he was a *real* banker with a shrewd grasp of the future and the winds of economics. Kyle might have been right that seeking to eradicate poverty was a pie-in-the-sky notion that failed to factor in crucial aspects of human nature and culture. I would later recall that conversation many times when pondering the opportunities for big players to participate in these efforts to alleviate the effects of poverty. People are always going to suffer, that's just the human condition. Giving them a hand up might ease things a bit. That was true of Bold up in Ulaanbaatar, who I wondered about over the past few months. How was that little girl of his? Did he ever get his clean cook-stove?

CHAPTER 2 | FATHER JACK

Jakarta was a mess. Kyle was right. I was glad that I looked into flights down to Adipala once I stepped off the plane, which couldn't be had from the international airport. The closest one was Yogyakarta, a few hours' drive from where I was headed, but there was a small airport a town over on the map from Fr. Jack. The one problem was connecting flights went out of the old military airport on the other side of Jakarta and I landed just in time for morning rush hour. I assumed four hours would be enough cushion to get there and avoid staying in Jakarta any longer than I needed to—judging by the plethora of traffic and people everywhere I wanted to avoid—but I nearly missed my flight.

I'm not sure what I expected, but the airport looked like a dilapidated bus station. I had just enough time to telephone Fr. Jack's office and give his secretary my flight details before hopping on my flight. The plane was smaller than I imagined—a slight step up from a Cessna—a twelve-seater single prop plane with no bathrooms and two fresh young New Zealand pilots sitting up front like bus drivers. I was exhausted from the overnight flight from Hong Kong, and so I dozed off after take-off, tucked into a window with no one sitting next to me—the plane half-full. When I woke up, forty minutes later, we were descending over a misty jungle canopy and so low I thought we were going to plow through the trees. Those pilots earned their stripes on that flight, struggling to keep her steady like wrangling an angry bull to the ground. With a rough bounce we zipped along the concrete runway strewn with weeds like some derelict parking lot. I thought Dumaguete's airport was small, but this one seemed like an old converted highway, the little red roofed terminal house resembling an oversized toll booth. I suppose it didn't get much air traffic, and after the 24-hour journey, I was glad not to be greeted by yet another desperate horde asking if I needed a taxi.

I picked up my suitcase straight off the plane and wheeled it up to the little house, where I could see Fr. Jack's face through the glass window, his shining smile covering a face structurally designed for scowling. The warm weather, his blue floral print shirt and relaxed manner, everyone moving at half-speed; the whole scene made me wonder if I'd spent the past half century living the wrong life. As I passed through the doorway, Fr. Jack lifted himself from a half-seated position against a wooden railing, exuding the same charm I'd seen in the footage Patrick had shown me. His eyes were a blazing blue burning with intelligence and a hint of childlike vulnerability.

"Good to meet you, Harry." His powerful hand gripped mine while the other snatched my suitcase before I could even consider shrugging him off. His singsong Irish brogue seemed both out of place and befitting an already strange environment causing me to feel like I was on the edge of the world again. "How was your journey?"

"Oh, fine."

"A bit long from Manila. You must be tired, yeah." He said "yeah" as a half-question, but meant it more as a way of keeping the human connection. At least that's what I took it for. I suppose it was his version of "you know what I mean?" that I heard sometimes back home. I would come to hear that little word of his so often that it grew to give me more comfort than annoyance.

"A little bit tired, but I'm alright."

"Well, we'll drop you at the hotel to give you a few hours' rest before dinner." Once he'd deposited my suitcase in the back of his Isuzu, he passed me a cold sweaty bottle. "Here, take this. You've got to drink plenty of water in this humidity. It'll bloody well sap the life out of you, yeah."

"You've been here a while," I said to him more as a question as we both sat in the front seat. I took his form in after noticing the comfortable gait and his rapport with the locals.

"Oh, yes," he bellowed and gave me a shrewd glance through thick glasses, tossing the Isuzu into reverse and stomping on the gas, lurching us out of the parking spot and on our way along a narrow road cut through the jungle. "Nearly forty years."

"Wow, that's a long time."

"Well, it's like this, you see." I heard his tone change to storytelling mode. "When I finished seminary back in Ireland, the superiors told me I wasn't a gentleman. That's their code for not acting like an Englishman, yeah. Well, I told them if that's what passes for a gentleman, I don't want any part of it. Rubbish! I was a bad student anyways, so they didn't know what to do with me."

"So, you came here?"

"Not at first, no."

"They sent me to the Missionary Oblates of Mary Immaculate in Australia, exiled me."

"Oblates?"

"The Oblates is a Catholic order to which I belong, yeah. I lasted a few years in Australia and didn't fit in there either. I think the Bishop thought I was a rabble-rouser and perhaps a bit of a heretic. So, he exiled me over here. Perhaps he hoped that sending me deep into the jungle would cure me of my crooked ways."

"Did it?"

"Hell no! I'm a bit arrogant and I know it. A bit of a crook, too—and I think the fella upstairs thinks that too, yeah. He mustn't mind it so much because I keep doing the things I'm doing and receiving blessings on my path. I believe in getting things done and helping the poor, that's my path. I also believe in gay marriage and that women should be priests and loads of other things that get the Church fathers back in the Vatican in a tangle. So, I'm here on my own… a blissful exile."

His words stunned me. I don't have a lot of experience around Catholic priests aside from being bored by their Sunday masses throughout my childhood. From what little I know, Fr. Jack didn't espouse the usual party line. In fact, I've never even heard of a priest advocating for gay rights or women in the priesthood. What shocked me even more was how candid he'd been with a man he'd just met. Was he a fool or a very wise judge of character? Perhaps he said all those things just to provoke a reaction. As usual, I tried to put on my poker face, with limited success. One thing I could tell right away from Fr. Jack was his ability to read people. All the while he spouted his opinions he held one eye on the road and the other searching the contours of my face. It's fair to say I was instantly captivated by this man content with no other role save striving to grow larger than life.

The trip to the hotel took less than ten minutes in a tiny town with few other cars on the road. Once we pulled into the driveway, I could tell from the décor and smartly-dressed porters that someone had put a lot of money into it. The whole scene seemed out of place amidst a neighborhood adorned with rows of run-down shacks made of plywood and corrugated steel-roofs all set up to do business. Tired and desiring as much luxury as possible, I wasn't about to complain. I noticed a vendor across the street with a pyramid of coconuts stacked on an old wooden pushcart, making a mental note that I'd visit her at some point. Once we arrived, Fr. Jack grabbed my suitcase and strutted into the lobby, waving off the two young porters and saying something in Javanese that made them laugh. The petite front desk clerk stood behind a sleek new desk gleaming in white, her smile radiating warmth.

"Good afternoon, sir. Welcome to the Orchid. We are pleased to have you." She tipped her head like an aristocrat while a colleague beside her beamed at me. I couldn't help but feel like their first guest, noticing a few workmen installing a chandelier in the distance. I turned to Fr. Jack.

"New hotel?"

"Yes. We are getting more and more foreign visitors this way. If you'd come two months ago you'd have had to stay with me in the parsonage. Trust me, the atmosphere here is a lot more pleasant and the food in the restaurant is much, much better, yeah." He turned away from me and said a few words to the clerk before shooting me an inquisitive look, "How long are you planning to stay?"

I turned to address the front desk clerk, scanning her name tag first. "Lia, I will probably stay for a week, maybe longer. Is there a room available?"

"Of course, sir. Everything will be taken care of." She said this as a short boy who looked all of fifteen edged up to me carrying a tray with a drink on it that looked like iced coffee.

"Sir, a welcome drink? It is made with fresh coconut milk." he said to me with a soft smile.

"*Terima kasih.*" I tried out a phrase from the little dictionary I picked up at the airport, glancing down at the book like a rookie traveler.

"You are most welcome."

Fr. Jack and I exchanged a few more words before he left, promising to pick me up later for dinner. As excited as I was to jump right in and learn more about this intriguing man and his work, I was exhausted and desperate to keep my eyes open. After the porter showed me to my room and apologized that the Internet was not yet hooked up to the hotel, I fell straightaway to my bed and didn't wake up again until the phone rang several hours later. When I answered it, I heard a female voice on the other end tell me I had a visitor. So disoriented was I that I had trouble remembering what country I was in—thinking through a mental list: Mongolia, the Philippines, Hong Kong... before settling on Indonesia. After hanging up I looked around the room at the furnishings as if waking from a nightmare and talking myself back into reality. With a groggy head and stooping body, I willed myself to push my legs over the bed and slump into a sitting position. Then I stood up. After changing shirts and splashing water on my face, I bolted out the door and down to the lobby, where Fr. Jack stood there as though he'd never left. Sensing my incoherency, he gave me a simple nod and led me back to his car. At least he knew when to keep his mouth shut.

We drove out to the beach, a barren scene save a few sandy restaurants. No promenade or even a sign of the kind of beach life that attracts tourists. A shame since I was used to any beach with a half-way romantic view already developed to generate as much money as possible. How could anyone squander the natural beauty of the landscape, even obscure spectacular sunset views with rundown shacks? Of course, even the crumbling boardwalks back home suffered under the weight of slow dereliction. At least someone slapped a coat of paint on them every few years to keep them going. I mentioned the untapped value of the beach to Fr. Jack as we sat down to a meal of fresh fish he'd selected from an old ice case missing a leg. We were the sole patrons in the restaurant, not to mention the only ones in any of the other half-dozen nearby shacks.

"Well, southern Java has a long way to go. That flight you took is not for everyone. The airport in Yogyakarta is roughly two hours away, yeah, which is where most people fly into. So, not much tourist traffic here and the locals are so used to the beach that they don't really see its value–yet."

"Too bad. Developers would give their right arm for a piece of a place like this back home."

"Well, it's all about location. We'll get there, yeah. Businesses are starting to move in, which accounts for the hotel. By the by, where in the States are you from? Where's home for you?" he said, taking a long swig from a bottle of local beer.

"I was born and raised in Baltimore, but I've been living in San Francisco for decades. Have you been?"

"To San Francisco? No, never enough time to see the places I want to see, but I seen the pictures, yeah. Beautiful pictures."

"Yeah, you must have your hands full here."

"Always something to do. In fact, tomorrow I'm going knocking about. Need to check up on the vocational schools and so forth to make sure everyone's still minding the store if you know what I mean. You're welcome to join me if that sort of thing interests you."

"Sure, would love to. As I mentioned in my email, Patrick told me about your operations and I am interested in seeing whatever I can."

"Some of them are quite a distance away, so I'll come around in the morning and we can make our way up to them. After we return I'll take you round the maritime academy here in town." He took the last sip of many bottles of beer the both of us had before he dropped me back at my hotel to collapse for a long Benadryl-induced sleep.

Fr. Jack rolled up promptly at 7:00 a.m. and we set out to the vocational schools. After an hour of driving along a patchy paved road and past several villages, we stopped at an enormous compound surrounded on two sides by white three-story buildings. A large administration building stood in the front, and on the other side of the main gate I noticed square-shaped pools covered with lily pads, a few small fields, and a rudimentary playground. Several people wandered about in bright blue school uniforms, and I caught sight of a few of them erecting posts for what seemed to be a volleyball net. Everything was connected by interlocking stone pathways, and much care had gone into making sure the grounds were kept tidy and clear of dirt. This seemed like a Sisyphean task given the outcroppings of vegetation that filled every available break in the concrete. Even the sides of the buildings traced streaks of mold so ubiquitous in this part of the world that it seemed futile to fight the scourge. Aside from the Shangri-La in Manila, I'd seen virtually no buildings without some blemish created by an environment determined to regain the upper hand over man-made edifices. It led me to wonder whether it might be easier to just give in and use a green-brown paint color for all exterior buildings.

We strode into the administration building and though I sensed the Catholic vibe throughout, I saw very few symbols to suggest that, save a small cross hung above a furled-up calendar on the wall next to the front desk. Everyone flashed a genuine smile to Fr. Jack, who smiled back with his twinkling eyes and garrulous bounce. His demeanor had shifted to boss mode. Nevertheless, he shot out funny quips in Javanese to each person who went by, touching them some way: on the arm, shoulder, or even pats to the head. Most of the staff looked young enough to have been recent graduates of the school, and in a way, it seemed like he treated everyone he met as a special child of his. The way of a Catholic priest, I suppose.

One of the women approached us with a graceful step in her manner, who Fr. Jack introduced as Aulia, the head of the school. She was young, and her beauty struck me down. With a graceful poise and a serious face, she gave me a magnanimous nod, though more of a long blink, but she did not offer her hand. She wore a brilliant white scarf around her head, so I could not see her hair–what I found most attractive in a woman. Yet without that distraction, her soft copper face was on full display, lips gleaming. Her eyes spread wisdom and strength and determination, and a touch of restrained sensuousness. It was as if stoical self-control had won the struggle for her soul, hinting at the possibility of a lapse into passion at any moment. How many men had fallen under her spell, I wondered. I smiled the best I could, trying to hide scandalous thoughts and reminding myself I was in my fifties and no longer nineteen.

"Is there something you would like to ask me?" Aulia asked with a confident air and curious eyes as she caught me gazing at her just a little too long.

I stumbled with my words at first, but soon found a good rhythm of questions around the various schools she ran. She provided quick and direct answers with a seriousness reminiscent of courtroom testimony, and I took her words down in my little notepad. They served over eleven hundred students at any given time through one of three schools: primary, secondary, and vocational. Some of the students lived in dormitories on campus, though most lived in the nearby community, and many from very poor families. The vocational school was designed to provide older children and young adults with valuable skills they needed to survive and thrive in their communities. The large pools were filled with fish, and the students learned how to farm and sell them. She also took me through the light automotive training shop. I was impressed with that shop, as young men in blue coveralls were busy dismantling and reassembling old Toyota pickup trucks and other vehicles that used to belong to Fr. Jack, as he pointed out. I also spotted a few small motors hooked up to wiring meant for testing electrical systems. The teacher, dressed in a black and red tracksuit, stood underneath a large Yamaha banner, relaxed pride spreading along the counters of his face.

We passed by a few other rooms, some filled with older computers (the kind I hadn't seen in years) and others with sewing machines. A student sat at each station deep in thought. I wasn't sure if they were putting on a show for the guest passing through, but they seemed to know what they were doing. Fr. Jack's jovial behavior struck a sharp contrast to Aulia's reserved manner, but I noticed a casual deference to him as he seemed a pleasant whirlwind to all he stumbled upon, showing a paternal love for everyone crossing his path.

From the vocational school grounds, we made our way past smaller buildings filled with children of all ages, each of them dressed in the same blue and white uniform—a symbol of equalization it was pointed out to me. At one point, we spotted four girls giggling in a corridor and wearing shy faces. They must have been around nine years old. Fr. Jack made a sudden stop, shooting them a stern look. He called out to one of them, who smiled, then quivered in slight fear before approaching him. He curled his hand over her shoulder and asked her something, at which she then smiled and straightened her spine as tall as she could. Though his hulking back obscured part of her, I could still make out her face. With each questioning remark he made in her language, she nodded her head in eagerness. He finished with a sing-song shout and she cried out in joy. It was then that he spun his body back toward me.

"I was just asking her about her goat," he said with satisfaction and one eye cast down on her.

"Goat?"

"Yes, she is part of a program we have here where she's responsible for looking after a nanny goat, yeah. She comes in before school every morning and makes sure the goat has enough food and water and so forth. In a few weeks, she'll give birth and the net proceeds will go toward her education. So, she's reporting her diligence in looking after the goat, yeah. Can you see the pride on her wee face?"

"Of course—and yours too," I answered, and he twinkled at my remark.

"I have no children of my own—that I know about, at least. So, these are my children, as it were. These girls will one day have kids of their own, so the program teaches them a bit about responsibility, yeah. You might be surprised at how early some of these girls have children of their own. The hope is that this gives them a little perspective and a chance to reflect on the work that goes into caring for another of God's creatures."

When it came time to finish the tour and my questions that all seemed rather dry, we said goodbye and jumped back into the Isuzu. I watched Aulia's angelic face stare back at me as we drove away, Fr. Jack honking his horn at the throng of children waving goodbye–an apt extension of his personality. It dawned on me looking at her that I found all the women I encountered on Java to be beautiful in their own way, and the men just as gentle in nature. I broached the subject with Fr. Jack on the ride back.

"This is my first time on Java. The people here seem very peaceful."

"Oh yes, that is their nature. Gentle souls, the whole lot of them. You took a shine to Aulia, I see. Difficult to avoid, yeah."

"Something about the scarf, I suppose." I assumed it would be futile to dodge Fr. Jack's poignant remark.

"She wears the *hijab*, the headdress for Muslim women. Some people think it hides a woman's face, but I believe it only accentuates her beauty. What do I know? I'm supposed to be celibate and not think of such things...."

"I couldn't agree more. One question I have: if it's a Catholic school why do you have a Muslim woman running it?"

He chuckled at my question. "You expected a nun? Not many in these parts. It's like this, yeah. First off, she's the smartest student ever to have gone through that school. I watched her grow up and always viewed her as a standout, someone special. One of the most even-keeled persons I've ever encountered, yeah. Essential personality trait for a headmistress."

"I can see that."

"And the other reason is perhaps more political. This is a Muslim country and we must respect that, yeah. No question that having a Muslim running the school, not to mention a young woman, sends a strong message to the community. Now, I catch a bit of flak for this sort of thing. When the assistant general came out and we went up by boat to see the villages he said to me, 'Jack, when are you going to start converting people?' I said, I'm not. He said, 'you're a missionary.' Yes, I said. I'm a missionary, but a missionary is witnessing. So, I'm here to witness. If I have an agenda–if I want these people to become Catholics–that's not really the loving Jesus wants. It's got to be unconditional."

"I heard that you've won a few interfaith awards."

"A few of 'em over the years."

"What do you attribute that to?"

"As you can see, I have no trouble picking the best person for a job. Also, in our schools we teach the children about Christianity, Islam, other religions and such. In my experience, the more somebody knows about somebody else's religion, the less they fear that *other* person, yeah. I have great relations with the Imams, and so far, they've been in support of me as long as I stick to humanitarian work—helping people and such."

"How did you get started with the schools?"

"My first day here they put me in a boat and took me over to villages along the sea. That was over forty years ago. People had no healthcare and most of them were illiterate, and so on and so forth. This one fella came to the door and he was real hungry. He looked like a skeleton. All the villagers looked like skeletons and it was like stumbling upon a concentration camp, yeah. My first thought was to just get food for them, but I saw another thing wrong there, the real problem. They didn't have a road, and the village wasn't that far away from the main road. We were just going there by boat because we had no other way, yeah. So, I came upon an idea to build a road." As he spoke, particularly after he said the word *idea*, I could tell that the subject had turned to something dear to his heart, like flipping the switch from priest to entrepreneur. Perhaps it was his true talent slipping out. "Well the problem back then, and still today if you know what I mean, was when you wanted to do anything out there people were trying to rip you off. So, the only way I could make it work was to have trucks of my own. I borrowed some money and bought a truck, yeah. That meant we could do what we needed to do without getting ripped off. I rented that one out and with the proceeds and a little more borrowing got more trucks and more trucks and more trucks. To build the road, there's an old quarry up a ways that wasn't being used. So, I used it, yeah. Got the rocks from there and dumped them. The villagers come out and done the rest of the work themselves, but that wasn't the last of the roads."

"How many roads have you built?"

"I've lost count over the years. All I know is we still have hundreds of villages looking for more roads. So, we still got a lot of work to do, yeah."

"That must have cost a lot of money just in fuel and upkeep for the trucks."

"Yeah, but we started charging the local governments, so most of the costs are covered. When you're coming from a developed country you forget the value of the road. It's only when you don't have one that you see how important they are, yeah. You see, the further you go into the jungle, the poorer the people are. There's no electricity out in some of these places." He waved his hand towards a dense thicket of jungle. "When you bring the roads in, people get electricity. You can upgrade the houses little by little, and haul in materials to build schools, clinics. Some of the roads even serve as dikes to keep the sea at bay and the river from flooding. We've been able to reclaim thousands of hectares of land, so families can plant rice. The road is the building block to bringing about economic development."

"So that's how you also got started building schools?"

"Oh yes, even this road we're on now." We had turned off the main road and onto a narrow one paved with the types of stone that seemed like they were taken from a quarry, fitted together to form an eight-foot-wide path through the jungle. "This is one of our roads, yeah. In all we've built about thirty schools so far, like the one we just visited and the one we're headed to now."

CHAPTER 3 | AKADEMI MARITIM

Fr. Jack and I "knocked about" that next school and another one, as he liked to say in his thick brogue and swagger exaggerated from what appeared to be a slight bowlegged limp brought about either through injury or age. Both schools were much smaller than the first, and one of them was a one-room concrete building for primary school students. I was touched by how polite the kids were, and how they sang to us and smiled and giggled at everything he said. His love brimmed for each child, and I don't think I've ever witnessed the level of adoration they had for him in someone else. It was beyond paternal, and almost took on a mystical quality. All this despite a playful clowning around that would never have flown in the schools where I grew up. I chalked it up to cultural differences, but also the sly way he was able to skirt the edge of silliness without engendering contempt. Perhaps it all came down to how much they knew he fought to make their lives and communities a better place, but I also saw him as just a big kid having a lot of fun as they tapped into his jovial personality.

Before heading back to Adipala, we stopped at a roadside restaurant. Not much of a restaurant, but rather a simple bamboo hut where a skinny old woman stirred a large cauldron of stew she served out into small bowls for pedicabs and other passers-by. As we sat down to a small table, I watched the slow and deliberate way he ate, like the way he'd eaten the previous night. This was all in sharp contrast to the speed at which he drove the Isuzu, walked on foot, and generally got from point A to B. It was only when he stopped and spoke to people–looked them in the eye–that the world began to slow down, and he seemed to have all the time in the world. I suppose he made time for people and food, but not much else. We ate in silence, enjoying the sounds of everything else around us.

Thirty minutes later and we were on the road again and he was back to his usual, convivial self. As we approached Adipala, he grew more animated. When I caught sight of the building we were headed to, a flash of Superman returning to the fortress of solitude blazed through my mind. In a land where no building stood more than a few stories high, I was not prepared for the monstrous edifice that was taking him the better part of a decade to build. It was as large as a ship. I counted nine stories in all.

"This is it," he said with an impish grin, turning the wheel with his massive arms and braking so hard in front of a set of glass doors I wasn't sure we would stop in time. A hefty young man in khaki pants and a red floral print shirt emerged from the backdraft of dust, pulling my door open for me and offering a hand to help me out.

"It is my pleasure to welcome you to the Academy, Pak Harry," he said in a congenial tone and a warm smile. He couldn't have been more than twenty-five, but then again, I often underestimated the age of men in this part of the world, who seemed to retain their youthful appearance much longer than in other places. "I am Father Michael. At your service."

"Nice to meet you, Father Michael."

"Did you enjoy visiting the schools with Romo?"

"Who?"

"That's just their nickname for me," Fr. Jack shouted out as the three of us went through the glass doors inside the building. I wasn't sure what Fr. Michael's role was, but he seemed to dress like Fr. Jack and did a fair job emulating his gregarious personality, though he had his own gentle way and seemed more eager to please rather than evoking the same devil-may-care coarseness of Fr. Jack.

The lower two floors of the building housed a maritime academy, which Fr. Jack had set up to train cadets. The academy provided merchant vessels around the world with talented crew, and thus perpetuated Indonesia's long history as a maritime people. The building had been a decades-long goal of his, and every time he got a little bit of money he would erect another story. The topmost story contained an exact replica of a ship's bridge, enveloped in windows and equipped with the same controls found on real ships, along with electronic simulators. The bridge looked out over the sea, and when I asked Fr. Jack why he hadn't just bought an old ship he responded that ships in the water needed maintenance to prevent rust and so forth. So, keeping everything on land made sense. We stood at a railing around the seventh story inside the building, looking down three floors into a huge atrium—ready for banquets and whatever else a thousand people could do together. While the construction looked local, complete with shiny white tiles fastened over concrete floors and pillars, the overall design smacked of an overt attempt to replicate Roman architecture. I was astounded at the scale of everything—as if Fr. Jack had built a monument to either himself or to the Indonesian people that might last several lifetimes.

"What do you plan to do with this part of the building?" I asked.

"Once it's completed, we can hold our graduations and other ceremonies here. We're a bit short of funds on it, so it's a work in progress, yeah," he said while Fr. Michael's servile smile brightened the air between us.

"This has been Fr. Jack's dream for many years now. It is slowly coming into fruition," Fr. Michael said in a smooth voice, adding, "you will dine with us at the parsonage this evening, yes?"

"Absolutely, that would be great."

On our way back down the stairwell, we stopped off on one of the lower levels that contained several open-air offices. Fr. Jack introduced me to his gang of lieutenants, friendly locals who cleansed me with warm smiles and gentle bows. Each person headed some tentacle of Fr. Jack's extensive network of community development programs. One of them, an old man, had been working for Fr. Jack for thirty-five years, now managing a program dedicated to helping people obtain artificial limbs. A younger man with an obvious spitfire temperament and a quick mind to go along with it oversaw all the computer systems. All but one of them was local, and he looked like an American in his early thirties. As I passed through each person, I took a special interest in him.

"You look like you're from my neck of the woods," I said as he beamed kindness at me. "I'm Harry. Where are you from?"

"Monterey, California. I'm Zach."

"That's pretty close to me. I'm in San Francisco. Now, is that Zack with a 'K' or with a 'CH'?" I asked.

"Actually, this man's full name is Zacchaeus and not Zachary, if that's what you're after, yeah." Fr. Jack said with pride as he laid a hand on the younger man's shoulder. "He's named after a biblical character—the chief tax collector who gave away half his possessions to feed the poor. An astute father giving you that name knowing you was to someday help the poor. Blessed are the pure of heart, for they shall see God."

Sometimes people with an odd-sounding first name had a certain look to suit the name. Even ordinary names fit so well that it was hard to imagine them having any other, as Fr. Jack alluded to the instincts of some parents knowing how their children would turn out. Back in the day, I met a lot of guys named Earl with greasy slicked-back hair, tattoos, and a pack of smokes rolled up in their shirtsleeve. In fact, I never met an Earl in a suit. I also learned that Mitches tended to pick fights. Walters were uptight. Graces were the nice ones. Jessicas, Nancies and Colettes almost always had a sexy quality to them.

Zach looked about as normal as anyone. Average height, brown hair, brown eyes, and a winning smile, he looked like an all-American with a cheerful glow. Italian roots, maybe. He had a trustworthy air about him as though he had no secrets other than a name cut short. No shameful family history to hide or personality defect repressed below the surface like the rest of us. It was obvious the first time I met Zach that what you saw was what you got. He got all the hugs and love from his parents growing up that the rest of us didn't get. I only spoke with Zach that brief moment before we finished meeting everyone and left the office, but I knew right away I wanted to spend more time with him.

As impressive as the building and its maritime school was, with its students, both male and female, crisp uniforms and flashing broad smiles wherever we went, I could not help but feel how out of place it all was. Fr. Jack was attempting to disrupt the natural order of life, at least an invisible, but entrenched status quo that mandated the servility of a poor population. I asked him about this later during dinner at the parsonage–that is, why he was enduring such a Herculean task. He responded after careful thought, "When Jesus said that we will always have the poor with us, he did not mean that we should turn a blind eye to their plight or even blame them for being poor, as many people do. People forget that in the very same passage, he went on to say that you can help the poor any time you want. See, you must look at these things in context in which they happened, yeah. In that story, Christ was protecting a woman who was pouring an expensive ointment on him while he was sitting round a table in a leper's home. Remember, this was just days before he was to be crucified. The disciples criticized her for wasting money on the ointment, instead of spending that money on the poor. Yet, Christ was reminding them that the mission of helping the poor is ongoing, and that people can still be generous with the poor yet extravagant in their worship of God. So, to those people who go on and on about the poor having to put up with their lot in life, I say they've got it all backwards, yeah."

"I'm sorry, Fr. Jack. Theology is lost on me, but I think I get your meaning."

"You do? How so?" I detected a slight, bothered tone to his voice, as though he were challenging me. He must have read something on my face that betrayed my words. I hesitated a moment, wondering if I should let it go, but perhaps it was the sweltering heat or the bottle of wine he, Fr. Michael, and I had just finished, but I grew more curious about his aims.

"I think it's true that some poor you can help. Sometimes I wonder which ones you should help and which ones you shouldn't. Who are we to decide who gets help and who doesn't? I mean, are we not then interrupting their path and assuming we know better than God? That sounds a bit warped, I know."

"Well… this was precisely Nietzsche's argument against Christianity–that we are imposing ourselves on others by helping them." As he said these words, I saw a dark wave wash over Fr. Michael's face, deep fear, as though the fate of his own existence and everything he stood for lay in the path of a giant wrecking ball. Fr. Jack started up again. "I'll take that risk, though. I'd rather be overly officious and help someone than second-guessing the ways of God and passing by a sick man lying in the ditch, reaching out for my help. If Nietzsche's right, I'll find out soon enough when I'm six feet under and have to answer for all the sins I've committed–spoiling people's lives and such. I've gone toe-to-toe with the devil several times already and anyone else who messes with me can go and fuck off with the devil, too."

Fr. Michael raised his glass in admiration, and I couldn't help but chuckle as well, though Fr. Jack was all at once stirred into a passion, face boiling red and eyes popping out of his skull. He didn't seem to understand why I found his remarks humorous, and I knew I'd inadvertently crossed a line with him. Up until then I couldn't tell if he was out for glory and recognition to satisfy himself, but his face revealed he was knee deep in a war against complacency. One of the few lines I recall from the Bible was Jesus remarking that he did not come to bring peace, but rather the sword–a line that never quite squared with everything else I heard about the guy. This was until I met Fr. Jack. If ever there were a dark angel out there, he had stiff competition from this man. Fr. Jack was up there in years and by the looks of Fr. Michael, who did his best to follow in his hulking master's footsteps, he would never be able to strap on those boots. Even Fr. Jack knew this, as I saw the way he teased the other Father without a shred of mercy.

The room lay in an eerie quiet save the humming of an overhead fan. After a few moments Fr. Jack faded back into the room and in a softened voice offered me a glass of Irish whiskey. I nodded and the three of us stood up and I was led out a door onto a balcony overlooking a large courtyard bathed in overhead lights that highlighted five of the large mustard colored trucks he had talked about earlier. Fr. Jack followed us out with a bottle and two large shot glasses, pouring a hefty amount in each and offering me one from the tray. I waited until Fr. Jack took his, and we chinked, and he bellowed out the Irish word for cheers, *sláinte,* before downing his, placing the empty glass on the rail and proceeding to the other end of the balcony to a cage that I hadn't noticed before. He messed about with a few locks and at first, I couldn't make out what was in the cage, but something was moving around and screeching like a large beast. It was black and hairy, and jumped into his arms. When Fr. Jack turned around, I realized it was a kind of monkey, all black with white fur surrounding its face. It looked at me and gave an alarming howl.

"This is Magda, my gibbon." He wore her in his arms like a sling, and I could sense protectiveness emanating from her as I inched closer, hesitated, then stopped. "You're wise to keep back a bit. She takes me for her mate,

128

yeah. I found her out in the bush when she was just a wee one, her mother had died and there was no one to look after her. So, now I belong to her forever."

I thought the scene sweet and a welcome change after such an awkward moment back at the table, with Fr. Jack holding his gibbon, stern face looking out over the courtyard, and Fr. Michael still standing there holding the tray like a patient servant. A wave of tingling energy passed through my body, and I felt the long day catching up to me. I still wasn't quite over the redeye flight either, and I felt an itchy heat rash around my hips. So, I asked Fr. Jack if he could ring a taxi for me. Fr. Michael shrugged the suggestion aside and insisted he drive me home himself. It wasn't more than ten minutes to my hotel, so I acquiesced, too tired to argue with him. My head was swimming with wine, whiskey, and such an infernal fire of heat and humidity that I longed for a cold shower, crying out in joy as I stood under its cool drops back at the hotel.

CHAPTER 4 | THE ORCHID

A long night of vivid dreams, some of them quite scary, and I woke up soaked in sweat. My head throbbed, torso pinned to the bed. Shouldn't have had that last whiskey, I thought. It felt more like the flu than a hangover with my body quivering and flashing hot and cold. The rash on my hips had spread to my lower back and felt like it was on fire. It was all mild enough though and I didn't want to miss out on the one day Fr. Jack was planning to visit the prison. Before I left the parsonage, he mentioned he was going there in a way that sounded like he didn't want me to join him, which I wrote off as him being sore from our conversation that ended with such unease. "They call it the Alcatraz of Indonesia... a very grim affair, yeah." But his clever remark couldn't dissuade me, and instead I inserted myself into his plans. I hadn't come all the way to Adipala to go visit a few schools and then call it a day—even if I'd somehow insulted him.

No, it was dawning on me that all this travel, however haphazard it seemed, was beginning to paint a picture to me. Some divine hand was guiding me. Perhaps Fr. Jack's own passion, however self-promoting he was, touched my heart in a way that linked his motives and actions with Edwin back in the Philippines, and everyone else over the previous year. My life was shifting for sure. I had a hand in it as well. A tiny bell in my head seemed to ring louder, even above the swimming headache, to tell me that it was time to wake up from a fifty-year slumber. I stood up in a fervor, unsure if the sickness was a good sign or a bad one, but nonetheless determined to make the most of the day. Life had snapped crystal clear, if only for a brief time.

Fr. Jack did not pick me up. In fact, Fr. Michael came to tell me that a parishioner had died and that they were both on their way to visit the family. He could have telephoned or left a message with the hotel, and I was touched at the gesture given that he was dressed in his vestments. He told me Fr. Jack had already gone out to the family, and Fr. Michael was on his way to pick up a few other people and my hotel was on the way. While he was courteous, I could tell he was in a hurry, so I shook his hand and told him I'd catch up with them in a day or two. He told me to stop by the head office as Zach wanted to meet with me and discuss his programs. Fr. Jack had already told me a little about the financial services he provided to the communities where he served, and I was intrigued to learn more. At that moment standing in the drive of the hotel, after I saw Fr. Michael off, I noticed the stand across the street, with its pyramid of coconuts. It wasn't quite 9:00 a.m., and already sticky hot. So, I walked over to the stand.

The old woman gave me a curious, but warm smile. A half-dozen teeth remained in her wide mouth. I motioned to one of the coconuts, and she held up five fingers, which I took for five thousand Rupiah (about fifty cents around that time). I nodded and handed her a battered old note and she immediately went to work hacking at the coconut with an old rusty machete. She may have been a short, old woman who looked weak, but she could wield that thing with great ease. I was mesmerized at how she spun the coconut to carve its hat off, then bashing it again and again to cut out the inner layer. She plucked a straw from a plastic bag and absent ceremony plopped it in the exposed hole, not realizing that for me it was still a novelty to watch. She'd probably performed this act thousands of times. I nodded and smiled and took a drink, which to my weakening body felt like nourishment flowing to every part of me that needed it.

With the hot sun on my face, she motioned for me to sit down on an empty white plastic chair beside her, beneath the shade of a tattered striped umbrella. I looked around, trying to come up with a reason to say no, but I was too tired and the cool shadow on the chair invited me. So, I sat down, straw still in my mouth. That coconut went down in a few gulps, and I let out a long slow exhale, feeling its elixir going to work on me, but also knowing that this was no hangover and might not pass as soon as I'd suspected. Without missing a beat, she reached over and took the coconut from my hand and in one rapid movement, brought the machete down on it and split it in two. I laughed. I'm not sure why, but the whole scene tickled me.

I sensed a maternal kindness about the old woman, along with a no-nonsense approach to life. *Just get it done,* her facial expression seemed to say. She handed the halves to me with a low grunt, along with a thin flat metal spoon. When she caught me hesitating, she grabbed one of the halves and dragged the spoon through it, curling up a bit of white fruit, grinning and offering it back to me. I laughed at this too. How come I'd never seen this done before? So natural, it was like I'd just been born, and everything was fascinating and new. I scraped every bit of whiteness away from that coconut, and when I'd chewed it up she unceremoniously chucked the nuts over her shoulder onto a heap of other discarded ones mixed with garbage. I handed her another five thousand and we repeated the process again, only this time much slower.

I felt my body pinned to the chair, the same as in the bed earlier, and I sat with her for what seemed like hours. For some reason, just resting and looking out from her stand at cars and bicycles and rickshaws and people passing by on foot, some of which she sold coconuts and other fruit to, I felt almost local. Many of them noticed me and said something to her. Other women her age flung a lot of jokes her way, and she gave it right back to them. She and I didn't talk at all, and I appreciated not having to say anything, yet still feeling her appreciating my company. She seemed to know many of the people who came around, and a few looked like family members, kissing her and then moving on with their day. I sensed she was a happy person, and at one point, I caught her profile gazing along with pride at a little girl in a school uniform who had stopped by, given her a hug, and then trotted off again. Maybe her granddaughter. It was a sweet scene and I lay back in the chair taking deep breaths and letting cool drops of sweat trickle down my spine and sooth the rash that still prickled at me.

I woke in a delirium. A strange-looking man with glasses on a large head and a stethoscope stuck in his ears stood over me. The room was dark, but I could tell from the décor that I was back in my hotel bed. He was wearing a gold watch, gazing at it with the end of the scope to my chest. Why was he examining me? I took him for a phantom at first, just part of the crazy dreams I had been experiencing those days, their intensity at once surreal and disturbing. When he noticed my eyes open, he considered them as if trying to see through me. He had kind eyes with gentle and deliberate movements to go along with them. He said something to me, asked me a question in English. It sounded like gibberish as I was having trouble connecting my brain and my mouth, struggling to understand what was happening. I slipped under again, unconscious.

Next time I woke up, I was a bit more coherent, scanning the room and seeing Lia standing near the door with a tray and what looked like another welcome drink. I was so thirsty, and the slender glass made me wonder if she had more than one of them—I could have used a bucket full of the stuff. She moved closer and cast an awkward smile in my direction.

"Pak Harry, you awake?"

"Yes, Lia." She held the drink out for me and I lifted my head up to a straw she had placed in it to make sipping it easier.

"The doctor was here. He give you a shot to help you feel better. You feel better, Pak Harry?"

"A little bit. What did the doctor say?"

"He say you take rest. You need to take rest."

"Yes, but did he say what's wrong with me? Last I remember I was sitting across the street?"

"He say he don't know, but could be *demam berdarah*, but not sure unless you get a test. Too difficult for you here in Adipala. It's OK, we take care of you here at the Orchid."

"Dema-who? What is that?"

"I'm sorry. I don't know in English. You need take rest. We bring you food and what you need."

I finished the drink and lay my head back. It ached like I'd been knocked around by a linebacker. "Great, I'm stuck in the middle of nowhere Java with a disease I can't even pronounce." I muttered this to myself in desperate resignation, but loud enough for Lia to hear. She grew anxious as though she was failing at her job.

"You no need to worry, sir. We will take care of everything. You in good hands here at the Orchid. You are our number one guest."

"Thank you, Lia. I've not seen anyone else in the lobby or the breakfast buffet. So, I think I might be the only guest."

"Well, lucky for you, right?" She said this with a mischievous edge, and it made me feel better that she wasn't taking too much responsibility for my condition.

"*Terima kasih*, Lia." I placed my hand on her arm and gave her the most serious look I could muster. "You are doing a wonderful job taking care of me. Better than any hotel in America."

She seemed quite pleased by this remark, and with a nod asked me if I needed anything else. I requested another one of those drinks, a few bottles of water, and some soup. I was hungry, though feeling lightheaded and weak with my stomach struggling just to keep the welcome drink down. She said she would do her best to bring something nourishing. I also asked her about the Internet, and she gave me the guilty frown that I had grown used to over the past few days, so I let it go. The world would just have to wait for me to come back to it.

As it turned out, the world had to wait over two weeks. The fever rose so high that first night I considered the possibility of my head exploding, imagining the walls sprayed with brains and blood. At times I wished this would happen. Lia, the boy porter from the first day, and another woman transitioned into nurses who routinely checked on me, supplying water and whatever food I could get down. I refused the maid service until the bed started to smell as if it were growing black mold from my sweat. I'm sure they had to chuck the mattress after my stay. The woman from the coconut stand began delivering coconuts a few times a day, and I would slip the porter purple 10,000 Rupiah notes each time, twice her going rate. She first tried to give them to me for free, and though she herself never came to my room, I wondered if she did it out of guilt or just plain kindness. I resolved to believe the latter. In looking back, I think it was those coconuts that saved me–not just keeping me hydrated, but keeping me from going mad.

The doctor returned each afternoon to check on me and to give me a shot here and there. When I was coherent I would ask him questions, which started occurring around the third day when I gained semi-consciousness. While his bedside manner far surpassed any care I'd received back home, it seemed like he failed to identify my condition at first. That unnerved me because without a solid opinion I soon lost confidence in his ability to treat anything beyond the symptoms. About five days into it when the rash had spread to my entire body he nodded emphatically, touching the itchy sores on my legs, back, and even my groin.

"Ah, yes, it looks like *demam berdarah*," he muttered.

"What is that? Lia said the same thing the other day, but I don't know what that is." I asked, by this time hanging on his every word.

"I believe in English they call it the dengue."

"Dengue fever!" I shouted, my heart sinking. "Isn't that deadly?"

"Perhaps, but only in some rare cases," he said in flawless English, and I could tell that he was well educated. "We can't be sure that you have it without a test. Like most tropical illnesses, it should pass through you without incident."

"This seems like a pretty big incident to me, doc!"

A quick grin passed over his face and he patted my arm, "You should rest and continue to drink fluids and eat as much as you can."

"Don't you think I should be in the hospital?"

"Perhaps, but actually this place is much more comfortable. So, I think it better for you to stay here. For the sores, I recommend an oil massage."

When I turned my head to stretch my neck, throbbing with a pain that traced its way down my spine, I noticed a blue tinted picture of a laughing man propped against the lamp on my nightstand. The man had long hair and flowing robes, radiating joy like he didn't have a care in the world.

"Did you leave that picture?"

"No, it wasn't me," he responded; and he too laughed when he saw it.

Lia and the others became my lifeline. Without their constant visits, I would have surely died. I'm not sure if the two-week episode gave me a glimpse into assisted living, but I lapsed into a regressive state where getting my coconut took primacy over everything else except having my makeshift chamber pot dumped so I wouldn't have to walk the extra fifteen feet to the toilet. I saved that arduous crossing for bowel movements, usually a scary process attempted only after the energy shot from a coconut or welcome drink. Those trips were about every other day given that I wasn't eating much. Around a week into the illness I realized that little bit of extra fat around my waist that I had waged war against for the past twenty years had disappeared. I felt a touch of relief when I noticed it, thinking that at least there was an upside to all of this. If it killed me, that was one thing, but at the very least I was trimming down those last ten pounds that had always eluded me. Of course, I could think of other more effective weight loss regimes that didn't involve semi-consciousness, extreme body aches, a rash covering my body, and wishing I were thrown from a cliff and put out of my misery.

After the doctor's massage remark, I asked Lia the next time I saw her to bring someone around. She adjusted my pillow for me so I could sit up and drink the coconut she had brought. After she left, I began to drift off to sleep again, head pounding and sinking into a whimsical depression that pulled me under whenever it felt like it. The room was dark with the shades drawn tight. This helped to alleviate the throbbing pain behind my eyes. It also turned the room into a dank sarcophagus and sent me into a death spiral of fantasies for how I could end it. Not many options, though, aside from holding the damp pillow against my mouth. I preferred to call out to God to send a lightning bolt through the roof and into my torso, killing me off for good. I remembered the old joke about people being so seasick they offered to buy the gun if someone promised to shoot them. I now knew how close to the truth that joke came. If I'd had the strength, I would have limped out to the street and hurled myself in front of a truck.

These fanciful dreams were cut short by my own fears of failure and humiliation. No, offing oneself needed to be quick and simple, and most of all, foolproof. Even if I had a bathtub for the cliché razor-blade death or even a rope to hang myself, I worried that God might send someone in last minute to save me. Of course, wouldn't anyone who'd had this illness sympathize with my plight? But a fear of divine intervention and then having to answer lots of questions about why I tried to do it stopped me. I also held a lingering fear about cosmic retribution for suicide–violating the will of God, if there was one, might mean purgatory for eternity if I was too quick for the last-minute savior to get to me. In the end, I decided to just let go and let God do the damage.

A knock on my door woke me up, and a young woman swept into the room carrying a basket. After the first day of my illness, I had asked the staff to leave my door unlocked so I wouldn't have to get up to answer it, half hoping that a crazed lunatic would come in and lop my head off and take me out of my misery. In Java, I'd be hard pressed to find any willing participants among those gentle souls even if I paid one of them to do it. Instead, the woman set candles about the room, lighting each of them, along with an incense stick in a simple bamboo holder. Either she must have been told beforehand the room needed a little sprucing up or simply deduced it from her first step into the room. Her oil massage soothed the aching mess my body had turned into, and she left me dozing off to sleep after temporary relief of my pain and itching.

CHAPTER 5 | CRUMBLING TOWER

I had a dream so vivid and dramatic that it startled me awake, where I lay looking at the shadows caused by the sinking of the sun at the end of a day. Normally, my dreams contained warped versions of reality, but this one tapped into subterranean fear from the mere fact that it spoke the truth to me. It was the summer before my second year at the Academy, and I spent it in three chapters. The first chapter consisted of staying on in Annapolis for a week to drink myself into oblivion with the help of the other Midshipmen who hadn't yet headed off to their homes for the summer. Then it was off to spend most of the summer on a training rotation aboard an amphibious assault ship. This was all great fun and much more pleasure filled than that first intensive summer where for seven weeks the upperclassmen did their best to turn us from civilians to midshipmen. Despite the long days of grueling physical exercise and near constant yelling and bullying, I appreciated the structure that gave me a life-long sense of durability and resilience. Nothing could ever be as hopeless as that feeling of being ground down and not knowing if I could keep going and become a member of the Brigade.

After stepping off the ship and catching a bus back home to Baltimore, I headed for a backpacking trip through the Monongahela Forest in West Virginia—one of the most beautiful places I've ever known. My childhood best friend Thomas joined me on that trip, someone whom I'd spent my teen years with, ambling the Appalachian Trail on various Boy Scout trips and other occasions where we could get out of our drab neighborhood on the wrong side of Fells Point. Thomas and I found each other at the cusp of puberty, and he was one of the few people at my school with a home life worse than mine. While I knew some of the kids pitied my own condition, having more than once seen my disheveled father still in his rubber overalls filthy with fish guts trudging up our crumbling stoop each afternoon with a sour look on his face, *everyone* felt sorry for Thomas. Compared to Thomas' household, where he lived with a crusty old uncle stuck in a wheelchair who shouted profanities at anyone who so much as looked at him sideways, mine was a picture of bliss. At least I had a father and he made sure we had food on the table, even if it was the worst culling of the day's catch. Thomas had no idea who his father was, and his mother had long since dropped him off at her half-brother's house, saying she would be back to get him in a week, which never happened. The old timers said she was a whore, and we all knew the story, though no one ever said anything. Over the years, she would sometimes send the odd letter or Christmas present with a promise to visit soon. She never did.

On top of everything else, Thomas seemed to draw a black cloud around him wherever he went. He was run over and all but killed on his bicycle in the ninth grade, and then had one of his testicles removed after a short bout with cancer in the eleventh grade. These were just a few markers in a life filled with accidents and just plain being in the wrong place at the wrong time. Nothing bad ever happened to him when he was around me. My instinct always revealed the safer path. We had a lot of fun hiking and camping together, and I like to think the Boy Scouts and our friendship were his saving grace. They were also *my* escape during a time when neither of us wanted to go home. All this changed once I went off to the Academy.

After that first year where I had set out on a path of great promise of eventual financial freedom and comfort, I came home to find Thomas barely holding his life together. Still living with his uncle, he had just been fired from the auto shop where he'd worked the last year of school and then stayed on to complete a few classes he'd flunked, classes he never wound up passing. He always struggled in his courses, and it was only later in life that I wondered if his slow reading and inability to digest the material pointed towards a learning disability—something so often overlooked in those days where both teachers and students seem to operate a little slower due to overindulgence in recreational drugs. So, I was never quite sure if Thomas' failure to finish high school was the result of one too many joints, a crazy mixed-up brain, or a household devoid of love and healthy parental modeling. For my part, I figured I made it by skipping out on the drug scene and working my ass off to get as far away from Baltimore as possible.

As soon as the bus dropped me off downtown, I headed over to the auto shop, where the owner broke the news that Thomas had been fired the week before for coming in late just one too many times. My heart surged as I raced to his house, wondering if he'd already left town for good, but he hadn't, having nowhere else to go. I saw him out back lounging on an old dusty couch parked in a patch of weeds. He was looking up at the sky and hadn't noticed me creeping up and standing against the chain link fence out back, watching him without making a sound. I stood there for a few minutes, studying and noting how little he had going for him, not even good looks or charm to win over the people where those qualities mattered. He did have a generous heart, although where we grew up that didn't get you very far. In fact, it often worked against Thomas since he was always being taken advantage of and manipulated into doing things that wound up getting him into trouble. He was far from feeble–very smart, actually–but his forgiving and subservient nature had done him in every time.

As much as I loved Thomas and respected his durability in the face of poor odds, over the years my exasperation with him grew from acorn to oak. For whatever reason, he seemed to attract the worst people and events; no matter how many times he'd been wronged he still assumed everyone had good intentions. Yet his resentment took shape as a child of Cain donning the mantle of victimhood. The world owed him something, and when that something never came he continued to stumble and blame others.

I suppose that had I walked in his shoes for a little while, I might have lapsed into the same vicious pattern that led to alienation and a slow descent into permanent misery, but that's what disturbed me most. Both of us stumbled upon more obstacles than most. Why couldn't he see the paths around them with the clarity in which I saw them? Furthermore, why had he failed to see the beauty and optimism at having come of age just out of reach of the draft? That was a death sentence our senior class avoided by a razor-thin few months. I loved him like a brother, but hated his pessimism. He also served as a grim reminder of what could happen to me if I didn't keep pushing myself so hard. That's what angered me most about him–that he was still around and not moving upward.

Thomas eventually turned his head toward the fence, unsurprised to see me and flashing his devilish grin and throwing out a smart-ass remark about my military haircut (his dark hair was down to his shoulders, which accentuated his nose in a comical fashion–warped from being broken back in the eighth grade). A few seconds later I hopped the fence and was wrestling him to the ground. He was stronger than me, but I had greater skill. I simply had to endure his bear growls before cinching him into a head lock. He almost never beat me at wrestling, but could go faster on the hiking trails, which we wound up on several hours later after packing our gear into his beat-up old blue Ford.

We were never sure how long we'd go out, packing enough food for a week and running out by the third or fourth day. That trip wasn't unusual in this respect, and after stopping for provisions, including a bottle of Southern Comfort, we had our packs on and made our way to Bear Rocks Preserve through the Dolly Sods Wilderness. We'd hiked these trails several times over, both with the Scouts and on our own. We knew the place almost as well as our own neighborhood back home.

My dream in Adipala picked up on this trail, and though the colors were more of late autumn, with its bright yellows and reds than the time of year on that fateful trip, I recognized the day right away. We had camped overnight in a clearing a few hundred yards off the main trail. We found the spot several years prior during our stealth days—where we did our best to hide from everyone else, acting like renegade commandos and even carrying around machetes. On our first few trips, we brought along the machetes because we thought we were cool and didn't have to play by everyone else's rules. In high school I'd read James Dickey's novel *Deliverance* about a few city boys who ran afoul of some mountain men and one of them winds up raped. The movie version had come out the previous summer, and its horrors were still fresh in the minds of most Americans seeking a little respite in nature. I remember Thomas half-joking on the drive up that we should try to find a gun before setting out in case we run into any hillbillies. Ironically, soon after we started on the trail we passed a crusty old man in overalls carrying a pitch fork who flashed us a rotten-teeth smile. Thomas gave me a queer, self-righteous glance, which I waved off with a grumbled laugh as he thumped out the banjo tune from the movie with his tongue.

That second morning we set out for Bear Rocks, and right away I knew I wanted to race Thomas to the top. He could sense my pace increase, and let out a little chuckle as he matched it. At that point the trail wound up a ridge that emptied out at the bottom of a steep slope up to the rocks. Most people took the *kids' trail* around, as we called it. Always looking for ways to test ourselves, we instead went straight up and over the rocks. This required climbing on massive boulders and needing gear we didn't own, but we always managed to do it, even if it meant lots of scrapes and bruises. It was all part of being better than everyone else by setting ourselves apart. Now I realize the Bear Rocks trip that summer was my last day of doing anything against the grain once I found refuge in the predictable and safe confines of the Academy, and later, the world of commercial banking.

At the base of the rocks, Thomas overtook me, and we each did our best to ward off attempts to knock the other one down. Thomas tried a different route each time, finding new footholds, some that worked out and some that didn't. Meanwhile, I clung to a tried-and-true sequence that for the most part stayed fresh in my memory over the few dozen times I'd done it. I remember him once telling me how boring I was for always doing the same thing over and over. Like the rest of my life, I wanted to minimize risk and control outcomes, while still taking small leaps towards a goal of winning, whatever that might be.

About half way to the top, hundreds of feet of boulders the size of buses lay below us. Thomas' new chosen path crossed mine and I spotted him ahead, pulling himself up with the help of one of the few small spruce trees growing up out of the rocks. He had the physical strength I envied,

140

which I could never match. My best chance of winning any competition was to plod along at a steady pace and give it my all, hoping for the best. I'm not even sure why we felt the need to compete to get to the top of the rocks, but that's the sort of thing a nineteen-year-old does to prove himself.

Thomas's tree gave way, uprooted. I heard it tear free, then stopped to look up and see dirt and dust flying from the roots and hearing a curse escaping my friend's mouth as he tumbled backwards, still clutching the little tree like an oversized root vegetable. I stood twenty feet below, watching him scrambling in a fury to catch hold of something to halt his momentum. That something wound up being my left arm, which I hadn't planned on throwing out to catch him, which happened out of instinct. It all happened so fast that before I could gather my thoughts he was clawing at my arm as he slipped, clutching two of my fingers and the cuff of my shirt. As my shirt stretched, I could hear the stitching tear at the shoulder and the feeling as if my entire arm was being dragged under a strong wake.

The dream brought back a long-buried realization: despite the universal belief that I had done the best I could to save Thomas, I was lying. The truth—the thing I've not shared with another soul before now and which only Elena herself might have come closest to recognizing in the dark streak she once mentioned—is that I could have tried harder. On that warm sweaty August morning, looking down at Thomas struggling with eyes gushing with fear, I realized that it was indeed within my power to try to save him. I wasn't sure then, or even now, if giving all my strength would have helped or perhaps worse, resulted in us both falling to our deaths. In that moment I thought of Thomas and his miserable life and how he'd hinted the night before after too much Southern Comfort that in his depression he often thought of doing the unthinkable.

Oh, what a miserable life he had, and I was sick of seeing its slow train wreck. It sounds cruel, but as he struggled to catch hold of my wrist my mind set off to questioning whether it was the right thing to even try to save him. Perhaps his life had run his course and it would end in a way he would have wanted—out in nature, out in one of his favorite spots, but his gripping fingers and fear-crossed face held no hint of an internal struggle. He wanted to live, but that was not in the cards, thanks to my abandoning the lessons of valor that were so drilled into me that first year at the Academy. My final memory of him was a look of surprise and terror from holding merely my left sleeve, torn free and with it, shedding our final connection.

That specific yellow flannel pattern still haunts me whenever I notice it on a random scarf or pleated skirt, reminding me that I could have done more if my mind had gone in that direction during those half-dozen seconds that sometimes feel like someone else's memory. Sometimes fantasy takes me to a place where I rise to the challenge and pull him up and then all is well, and we laugh at the near miss. Those thoughts bring back the shadow of shame, so I no longer entertain them as I did in earlier years.

Sometimes I miss Thomas' friendship, the kind of eternal bond I would never experience again, neither in companions nor in loving relationships. We had passed through adolescence together, sharing laughter, strife, and the perpetual sorrow of living under the jackboots of home and school. He knew me better than anyone–knew my ambition to crawl out of that miserable neighborhood, my dreams of security and success, and the black side of my heart that I keep hidden from everyone. I wonder if that's the last thing he saw before signing off for good and falling from that tower of rocks. Over the years I expected his voice to come out in those dreams, either reassuring or condemning. Isn't that how it works in the movies? But that never happens. Only silence and the truth shining its incriminating beacon, reminding me that no matter where I go in life, whatever my achievements, that stain continues its rot in the core of my being.

I heard a soft knock at my door, and sitting up, I yelled out, thinking it was Lia or one of the others. I didn't expect to see Zach's face, but in he came, shining light. He was carrying something under his arm, and approached my bed with a soft step. I wiped my face and let out an embarrassed laugh. I'm sure I looked a mess.

"I heard you were sick, so thought I'd stop by and drop off a home cooked meal." He laid a covered basket on the side table. "I hope you like it."

"You make it?"

"No, my wife, actually."

"Wife? I didn't know you were married."

"Yeah, I came here two years ago. Wasn't planning on staying long, but you know what Lennon said about life happening while you're busy making other plans?"

"You can say that again." He startled me with a quote I hadn't heard in a while. "I appreciate it. A home-cooked meal sounds *really* good right about now. Do you have time to stay a little while?"

"Unfortunately, I can't stay long today. I'm sorry. You're probably bored stiff cooped up here all this time." He sat down on the corner of the bed as I lifted the cloth from the basket, looking at several bowls of local rice and fish dishes. He sat down, not as someone uncomfortable and looking to head out at the first opportunity, but rather as if he had all the time in the world.

"Well, thank you for bringing this food–and please thank your wife. I haven't eaten much, mostly coconuts. My fever seems to have broken, so your timing is perfect. Do you mind if I eat it now?"

"Please, go ahead! That's why it's here, Harry."

He had a pleasant way about him, both wholesome and strong, and I couldn't help asking how he came to Adipala–amused pride on his face as he watched me devouring the bowls of food. "You say you got here two years ago? Where were you coming from?"

"West Africa."

"Really? What were you doing there?"

"Similar kind of stuff as here – financial inclusion."

"I guess you've been to a lot of places."

"A few." He gave me a modest smile and for some reason I got the feeling he'd been all over the world.

"By the way, this stuff is *really* good. Some of the best food I've eaten in Southeast Asia."

"Now you know one of the reasons I stayed here."

"And the other reasons?"

"Oh, that's for another time, maybe. I've gotta run. Father Jack let me believe you were on your deathbed, but you seem to be getting your energy back. That's great. Dengue is rough going, but usually passes by the end of a week or two. So, maybe when you're up and around you can stop by the office, and even come out to the villages with me?"

"Sure, I would love that. You mentioned Father Jack? But he wasn't here."

"Of course he was." Zach pointed to the picture beside my bed. "That's his calling card. Laughing Jesus. He always complains that the pictures of Jesus don't show his fun side. So, he gives those out. He even gave one to the bishop when he was here. I think it pissed the guy off."

"Figures."

CHAPTER 6 | UNDER THE RUBBLE

I devoured the entire meal before Zach left. It gave me enough strength to stand up and wash the past few days off me in the shower. I felt a layer of slime sliding off me under the hot water, dousing myself with enough soap in hopes of killing off the still itchy blisters covering my backside. My body continued its fight and I lasted ten minutes before collapsing back onto my bed in a heap of exhaustion, but I felt lighter, like a new man. I had been scared, more scared than I'd ever been, in fact. Maybe it was because I wasn't sure whether the dengue would kill me off or not. I thought about being stuck in a strange place with people I didn't know. The more they cared for me, Lia and her crew and then Zach and even Fr. Jack leaving his calling card, the more I felt loved in a way that I hadn't in a long time. I can't imagine too many of the folks back at the bank even stopping by to say hello–everyone was always too busy. Perhaps Mark would have come, though I thought of him less as a former colleague and more a friend. I wondered how he was doing in his own little jungle on that other island chain. I fell asleep thinking of Mark and Sarah and that dinner we had at the Shangri-La and the weekend in Dumaguete. I woke up the next morning to a flood of light into my room.

"So nice to see you, Mr. Harry," Lia said to me, as I approached her desk in the lobby. She came around when she saw me wobble a bit, trying to hide a look of concern. "You are feeling better? You are almost smiling, no?"

"Yes, much better, but I do need some breakfast this morning."

"Of course, please come with me. I will take you to your table."

As on the first morning, I was the only guest in the breakfast room. I had a small buffet of local fare all to myself. "Lia?"

"Yes sir?" She helped me sit down as if I were an invalid, sliding a cloth napkin into my lap.

"I've been here about a week now, albeit mostly in my room. Tell me, have there been any other guests here?"

"Sir, only one. But he is gone now. So, it is just you."

"Nice! I have the place all to myself."

"Yes, but a conference is coming next week, so the hotel is getting booked up. You will stay another week?"

"Why not? You've been so hospitable. I was planning to go to Bali, but Bali can wait. Besides, Adipala is growing on me."

"You're welcome, sir."

"By the way, I brought my laptop. Is your Wi-Fi working now?"

"Yes sir. It is a bit slow, but it should be working now."

After a breakfast of chicken, porridge, eggs, and fried bananas, I opened my laptop feeling a deep energetic anticipation akin to Christmas morning. The Internet connection chugged away as I watched my home page trying to load. I had been thinking of Elena, missing her and hoping to see a message in my inbox, though I doubted it. Maybe I'd get some news from Mark or Sarah or even Edwin, to whom I didn't get a chance to say a proper good-bye. Who knows, perhaps my friends in Mongolia had something to share about how my investment was doing. All those thoughts took a back seat to the stunning front-page story of the *New York Times*: "For Stocks, Worst Single-Day Drop in Two Decades." What the hell was happening? As I read through the story, I recalled the crash of '87 earlier in my career, which rattled many of the old timers. This felt different. This crash was tied into the housing market and its underlying property values, homes. So, losses seemed *real* instead of just on paper. The more I read about a trillion dollars vanishing into thin air, the more I felt dread at my own financial position. I should have paid more attention to Kyle's warning, but what could I have done?

With shaking fingers, I forced them to override the urges from a little voice, perhaps a scared one, begging me to bury my head in the sand and forget about my accounts. It took a few minutes to open and access my brokerage website where I kept my retirement account. I cursed the slowness of the Internet, gazing at pages struggling to open and warding off my own concerns of accessing my financial data over an unsecured network. I looked around the room. There was nobody else there. Who could possibly access my account out there in a jungle town with few people owning a computer, much less possessing the capability of using one? Heck, the front desk still did everything through paper and those old sliding credit card machines that made carbon copy impressions of the card. I was lucky to have a connection out there, much less needing to worry about people accessing my account. When I saw my balance, that didn't matter anymore. Nothing mattered. It looked like a mistake at first. My retirement had shrunk to less than a tenth of its value.

I scanned my emails for anything from Don. The sale of the bank was supposed to happen within days. With trepidation, I opened a single email with the subject line: *Notice to Investors*. The message was to the point. The bank was under pressure to *mark to market* their loan assets. I'd already read about this in the *Times* article, that banks both large and small were fighting for their lives and needed to report the actual value of their assets rather than the inflated ones before the crisis—or risk having them set to zero. So, it wasn't surprising that the sale was on hold. What surprised me was that Don had finished his email with an ominous warning about the potential of having to wind down operations. "I will send regular updates where appropriate." I thought about responding to him with questions, but I knew him well enough to step back and let him do his job and not waste time answering anxious pleas for reassurance. Besides, something told me that the bank was doomed and nothing I could do would change that. Time would prove my intuition accurate.

I looked around the room again. This time not as Harry Stone the retired, wealthy philanthropist traveling the world doing good. No, I felt like Job, the one person in the Bible who seemed real and to whom I felt more akin to than at any other time in my life. In ten short minutes I was transformed into Harry Stone the aging, unemployed man who'd slept through the financial crisis and lost everything. He was broke, and I was him. *Damn! Damn! Damn! Damn!* I took a deep breath and looked up for some god who could help me, my energy sagging and mind circling down to the bottom of an abyss. I closed the laptop and wiped my face. How could this be happening? What was I going to do? That bachelor pad I rented on Telegraph Hill would be too expensive to go back to. I'd have to give that up. Besides a few thousand in my checking account, I had nothing else save a baseball card collection worth maybe five thousand, a motorcycle, and a summer home in once desirable, but now crime-infested Acapulco. *Nice going, Harry! Loser!* My life was over.

Monkey mind then went to work on me. I couldn't seem to shake off the self-criticism that reached a fever pitch, browbeating me without mercy over how I'd bungled my life. I should have fought harder in the divorce instead of rolling over and giving up so much just to get it over with. I should have taken my own risk-averse investment advice and not been so bold in putting my retirement savings into such risky positions. I should have heeded Kyle's advice sooner, should have called the brokerage and transferred everything into gold. Isn't that what smart bankers do? I should have done a lot of things. Now, I'd lost the nest egg I spent a lifetime amassing. Perhaps it would have been easier had I just gone the way of Thomas, fallen with him. The hotel didn't have a second story, or that instant I would have jumped off it to break my neck.

But Fr. Jack *did* have a nine-story building—tall enough to do the trick.

No one would miss me. While my appetite had returned, I was still too tired and achy to leave the hotel. No way I'd make it up all those flights of stairs. So, I slunk off to my room and lay in my bed, staring up at the ceiling and plotting out when I could muster the energy to head over to the Academy and get it over with. After a few hours of shock and boredom, I called Lia to send for a massage. A strapping bodybuilder came in and worked me over like he was finishing his daily workout.

As lethargic as I felt, I tried to get out of my room for meals and to walk around a bit for the rest of the day. I had begun to detest my room and its isolation long before I was feeling better. So, now that I could mobilize the energy to leave it, I did as much as I could. Later in the day I made my way over to the coconut lady, who greeted me with a concerned, but pleasant smile. I tried to give her several thousand Rupiah to show my appreciation for bringing over the coconuts, but she would have none of it. She only took five thousand and handed me a fresh one, letting me sit back down again in the same chair as the last time. When I sat down, I shot her an expectant look, and she caught my joke and laughed, patting me on the arm as if I were seven years old. Fortunately, I did't pass out again before saying goodbye and heading back to the hotel. After a few refreshing coconuts in my system and plenty of food at dinner I went to bed early and woke up feeling ready to go to the Academy to kill myself.

After breakfast, I asked Lia if she could set me up with a motorbike. As it turned out, Lia's cousin had a 150cc Kawasaki *Moto Baki* he rented to me for a "good price" of around seven dollars a day. It was a dirt bike without a lot of power, but enough to have some fun. An hour later I was zooming away from the hotel and splashing through mud puddles on my way to the Academy. The wind whipping through my shirt soothed the still-itching sores on my sides and back, though many of those sores were starting to heal and recede a bit. In fact, my body felt much better, though my psychological pain had shifted the focus away from corporeal concerns.

Along the way, I passed by a fisherman casting his circular net into a small waterway. He was about my age. I'd seen him before when I was riding with Fr. Jack, who stopped to show me a small dam above the road that he'd been responsible for building. I remember feeling a pang of guilt at tuning him out while entranced by the slow steady motions of the fisherman. He would gather up the netting material and in a grand motion send it spinning out fifty feet in front of him. Then, with steady hands he pulled the net in, emptying his meager catch into a large plastic bucket beside him. He wore one of those traditional conical hats made of bamboo that one often sees in rural pictures of Southeast Asia.

In fact, I stopped this time and took a picture of him, laughing at myself for wanting to retain a memory at this late stage of my life—in less than an hour I'd be dead. He seemed so content out there, despite working hard. Surrounded by green fields and lush forests, standing out over water, I envied his life even though I knew little of it. I sat down on the bridge, my legs dangling over the side, entranced by his graceful movements that seemed to transform me from an anxiety-ridden curmudgeon to a ball of peace. Every few minutes, he'd yell back and forth to a friend of his, another fisherman further down the riverbank. Sometimes they'd both laugh, and then continue casting and pulling in their white nets. I wondered what they were talking about—perhaps something mundane or maybe even swapping jokes about the creepy old white guy lurking around up at the bridge.

I got back on the bike, and just before I zoomed away I noticed the man I'd been watching nod to me and I nodded back to him. The road led straight to the Academy building, and I pulled up to the side, around the corner from the entrance. Fr. Jack's Isuzu was nowhere around, and I sighed in relief. I didn't want to see him. I eased myself off the bike and nudged out the kickstand, leaving her resting on an angle. Like a cat burglar, my movements were measured so as not to draw any attention to myself as I made my way to the open stairwell and up the levels. I was forced to stop and rest after the first flight, feeling lightheaded and achy. I had to continue at a slow pace if I were going to be able to make it to the top.

At one point I had an excuse to sit down, feeling the painful twinge of a pebble stuck in one of my sandals, or so I thought. The leather around the outside edge had come loose and when I pulled it off the entire shoe disintegrated. So much for expensive sandals! No wonder the locals wore rubber as it held up better against the humidity. I tore off the other sandal and in a flash of anger threw them both out one of the openings that led to the bottom of the building.

A gruff voice inside my head lashed out at me—reminding me how I'd long lost the ability to make wise choices with so many signs that I had become a useless void taking up space. I could no longer walk my path. My abandonment of prudence bore the symptoms of a larger theme at play. If there was a God, he, she or it was pulling me in and punishing me for decades of transgressions dating back to the fateful day with Thomas. Luck had carried me far, but I tried flying too close to the sun for sure. I remembered that voice, more like a dark force: the same one at the cliff's edge, the sinister hand reaching up in my dream, pulling me into the abyss. I knew that voice quite well. It has always been in me, lurking about in the shadows, always waiting to pounce when my mood turned sour. I drew comfort from the fantasy it spun in my mind of a quick death to seek out and wrestle my maker, forcing him to pay for the miseries he caused me. I wanted to punch God in the face.

CHAPTER 7 | ZACH

"Harry! What are you doing here?" I heard Zach's cheery voice from behind me. It startled my core. He'd been coming down the stairs and had it not been for the broken sandal, I might have just missed him on the way up. *Damn!* I stood up in my bare feet as he passed by and looked up at me from a few steps below, carrying what looked like a metal shoeshine box. "You're looking a bit better than last time I saw you, I must say."

"I came to, uh…"

"To see me? Your timing's great. I'm just headed out to a few communities. It would be awesome if you could join me. That is, if you're up for it."

"Sure." I let out a deep breath and Zach instinctively grabbed my elbow to steady me. *I guess I could always die tomorrow.*

"You didn't have to go up all these stairs, Harry. You could have called me or told the people downstairs and I'd have come down."

I didn't say much on the way back down, just glanced at Zach a few times. He seemed excited to have me join him. He had a *moto* too, and hesitated as we approached it. I noticed the concern washing over his face.

"Don't worry, I rented a bike. It's over there."

"Great. You'll need shoes, by the way."

"Oh yeah, I just had a sandal strap break. Damn thing fell apart. Any ideas?"

"There's a little shop around the corner. Let's head over there and get you fixed up."

Zach strapped the box he'd been carrying to a small rack on the back of his bike using a bungee cord. He waited for me as I walked over to my own bike and started her up. I followed him out of the lot and we made our way over to a small store, shoes lining the walls and spilling out into the street in small heaps. A thin young woman saw us pull up and spit out what she was eating, making her way from the back of the small plywood store to the street. I pointed to a cheap pair of flip flops, and watched her frown at my choice, guessing she was hoping I would buy a pair of shiny expensive dress shoes. Zach seemed impressed at my negotiating skills as I haggled her down several thousand less than her initial price. Of course, I knew I was still paying over the local price, as usual.

Before once again asking if I was feeling up for it, Zach gave me a rough idea of where we were headed, and I followed him as he snaked his way through streets, alleys, dirt roads, mud puddles, creaky bridges, and eventually to a remote village that seemed so far out I wondered why people even wanted to live there. Nevertheless, the scenery was beautiful with its lush green fields and tall palm trees straddling a straight dirt road terminating at the village. The community itself, with its dozens of bamboo houses on thick hardwood stilts, seemed to be a throwback in time. I spotted an ancient man plowing in a field, trying to keep the water buffalo from veering off course. We approached a tiny building that resembled a toll booth rather than a variety store. The young woman behind the counter shot me a cool smile and I stopped to buy a few bottles of water, handing one to Zach. We pressed on a little further and parked our bikes on the edge of a flat open courtyard that served as the village's main square.

I rested on my bike, swigging the water and waiting with a stitch of nervousness as Zach dismounted and said hello to three older women who approached him with broad grins. He moved as a carefree spirit, a man comfortable in his body and radiating warmth, a man who knew the world and how to treat people. While I watched him, it began to dawn on me that underneath my stiff militancy and occasional lapses of kindness, perhaps the latter was my authentic self-trying to slip past old, decaying barriers and show itself.

Zach waved me over and I swung my leg around and walked over to him. I still felt a lingering fever flashing through me as I walked over to him and the three women, but it could have been the heat. With their proud, strong faces, I found them intimidating at first, especially the oldest-looking one who scrutinized me up and down as though I'd come to collect taxes. A few more approached and encircled us. Zach had a quick interchange with one of them and then pointed to his bike, and she nodded. He moved over to his bike and removed the metal box, bringing it back to her. Another woman approached us with a smaller wooden box that looked to be on its last leg. It was then that I noticed that both the wooden box and the larger metal one had small padlocks on three of the sides.

Before I had a chance to ask about the boxes, the old woman turned and shouted something to the group. It must have been a call to assemble as they now began to form a small circle, covering the flat ground with tiny colorful mats. A few other women joined until they were about fifteen strong. The old woman bowed her head to me and said something in Javanese, which Zach translated as a request to join them. We then all sat down on the overlapping mats, a young woman bringing out a large pot of tea and pouring it out into little metal cups, passing them around.

The old woman muttered something, and soon three women sitting in different parts of the circle produced keys, which were given to another woman in the center kneeling beside the wooden box. She slipped a key into each of the three padlocks, unlocked them, and set the opened locks to the side, pulling the lid open. It was then that I realized one of the reasons for the larger metal one: the wooden box was way too small for the pile of Rupiah notes that tumbled out of it. The box also contained a notebook, pen, and solar calculator, which the woman lifted out and placed next to her. All her movements were slow and methodical, as though she were handling plutonium.

I sat beside Zach, and he did his best to interpret what was happening, though much of it needed little of that. The box was used for collecting and storing the savings, with the group of sixteen women meeting weekly for a year and agreeing to put ten thousand Rupiah each into the box every week–around a dollar. Anyone who didn't chip in that amount was fined a thousand, which would have to be paid the next week. That seemed to be enough incentive for most of them to find a way to scrounge up the money each week. One woman fell short and we heard a rumbling wave of playful jeering in the circle. It was enough to cause her to lower her head in shame, like a child who'd just struck out at bat and cost the team a win. Sensing her anxiety, the woman next to her poked an elbow into her ribs and said something that made her laugh and leave the shame behind.

These transactions were captured in little notebooks each woman brought with her. Once they'd contributed their ten thousand, the group's secretary would stamp her book with an ornate blue flower. I could see blue flowers all over the pages of the open books. One person even threw in thirty thousand and received a commensurate three stamps. As Zach explained, members could contribute up to fifty thousand per meeting. When I asked why there was a limit, he pointed out that without a limit these groups could be at risk of what's called *elite capture*, whereby a wealthier person might seek to control the group or use it for their own financial or political advantage. This was because members could borrow from the group savings at abnormally high interest rates, which encouraged saving and discouraged borrowing. At the end of the year, members received a portion of the accumulated interest based on how many stamps were in their books. So, members who saved and never borrowed, and who also saved a lot, had the potential to earn a lot of money. The group also needed to be protected from any one person trying to dilute that through large savings contributions. Zach said this was uncommon, but the system included limits on savings based on past experiences where it had happened.

The treasurer would record all these transactions, including loans to the members into a ledger book kept inside the box. Each member reconciled their own book with the ledger at every meeting. This all seemed like a lot of work, but the members didn't seem to mind the time it took since it gave them an opportunity to chit-chat with one another. Given all the laughing and side conversations going on, I sensed the members looked forward to this social hour as opposed to the type of resentful anguish I saw on the faces of people back home forced to sit through regular staff meetings.

Zach said he attended the first few meetings to teach the process and shepherd the group. He came around periodically to check up on them and find out if the original process was still being followed. He also performed other tasks like arranging for guest speakers on relevant topics like addressing domestic violence or proper sanitation, or even just logistical things like swapping out the wooden box for a metal one. He explained that after a year of using the wooden boxes, he was finding that the humidity was causing them to warp and fail, so he was transitioning groups over to steel ones. One of Fr. Jack's vocational school workshops produced the boxes using scrap metal from a merchant ship retired earlier in the year. Since steel could rust, he primed and painted the boxes a bright yellow, almost gold color. From the admiring glances and the way the women touched it, they were thrilled with the new box: bigger, sturdier and the color of gold.

I asked Zach the typical amount the groups raised in a year, and his response shocked me. It seemed that in some groups most members earned double what they put in, generating enough to pay for their kids' school fees and still have enough left over for household needs. Sometimes these groups, either part or whole, would pool together the amassed savings and build a community hall or buy commodities in bulk and resell them at a profit. As he put it, once these women realized the power of their collective savings, there was no stopping them from realizing and even overshooting their dreams. It was a system based on homegrown savings clubs that have been around for over half a century, springing up all over the world. So, the whole thing was nothing new to Zach as he'd spent the past decade traveling around the world spreading it to new communities. For me, having just learned of it, it was revolutionary.

As I watched these women passing money around and placing it all in the box, locking it up, and giving the keys to three random members to secure the box from prying fingers, I felt my whole world shift into sharper focus. Small loans to poor people were great, but this was *phenomenal*. These women didn't need money from outside investors or to be told that an entrepreneur living deep inside them was struggling to climb out. Even the box and materials they manage to pay for out of their collective savings once it reached critical mass. All they required was some upfront help and a little guidance. Zach mentioned that half his week was spent training locals in the model, so they could go out and replicate it in other communities. So, one day he might no longer be needed. As he put it, that's the beauty of these groups–they are self-managing, self-regulating, and self-reliant. Moreover, by design they modify behavior away from taking on debt and reward those who choose to save their money. *If only we had something like that in America!* Zach reminded me that many credit unions in the western world were initially set up to help people in a similar way.

We left for another community after wrapping up the hour-long meeting. By the time we were on our bikes, I had a few women who'd warmed up to me, though I hadn't spoken a word. They surrounded me, asking questions as Zach did his best to translate their words. Most of their questions were about my marital status, where I came from, etc. I laughed them off. Just before I brought my *moto* to a rumbling start, he said that the old woman, the one with the stern face, had asked me why I'd come to their village. She fixed me with her gaze and I turned to her, unsure how to respond. Was I there out of curiosity? Was it a better way to spend my day than hurling myself off a nine-story building? Or was it that I had no idea, but was doing my best to put one foot in front of the other and this is where it led me? I took a deep breath and felt her penetrating my mask with an advanced bullshit detector.

"Not sure. Suppose I came here to meet *you*," I said with a cheery tone. Once Zach translated it to her, I saw her face turn into a deep smile–the first time I'd seen one on her face, disrupting her physiology. She was tickled by my cheekiness, though I detected more amusement than being won over. I waved goodbye to her and she nodded back like a magnanimous chieftain, her face having drifted back to normal.

Zach and I rode away and I followed him over a few bridges and into an area that seemed different than the others, more remote. He told me his home wasn't far, and we could stop there for lunch. I was feeling tired and sweating more than normal–feeling the fever trying to come back. I started to grow angry at Zach as he should have known I was not feeling up to the trek. Yet, I had a blossoming thought, which I didn't acknowledge until days later. He knew what he was doing. There was something guileless about him, but underneath a spirit at work who hovered just over him and used that knowledge to drive his internal ship. I'd seen flashes of this phenomenon over the course of my life, times when the world just clicked, and a responsible figure stood in the center. Often, these were just subtle displays of power, such as the man who'd grabbed my shoulder on Market Street just as I was *thinking* of stepping off the curb into oncoming traffic. I never saw his face or who he was, perhaps a phantom, but whoever or whatever it was, it read my thoughts, and sensing an unconscious one leading me off my path, took decisive and appropriate action without fanfare. No ego waiting around for a pat on the back. Just one mind looking down on thousands of others, and seeing one of them out of tune, reaching down for a gentle twist to bring it back into harmony.

He slowed his *moto* down and turned left down a dirt path no wider than a car's wheels. We followed this for a few hundred feet, where it ended onto a large circular drive in front of a small house nestled behind a grove of palm trees. I stopped my *moto*, took off my helmet, and collapsed.

CHAPTER 8 | RATU THE DUKUN

When I came to I was lying on a thin bamboo mat, looking up. A bright fabric tarpaulin hung over me, and turning my head I noticed it was suspended between a few trees, the sun doing its best to burn through it. I was outside. An old Javanese lady knelt next to me, old as dirt. She looked deep into my eyes. I turned my head to avoid her stare and noticed Zach sitting on a small stool in the corner. He didn't see me looking at him at first, but then his face brightened and he sprung to my side. The woman placed protective arms around my shoulders, preventing me from sitting up. She then slid a damp washcloth from my forehead and moistened it in a bucket, wrapping and laying it back on my head. I wore nothing but my boxer shorts. They must have stripped me before lying me down.

"You gave us quite a scare, Harry."

I didn't say anything, disoriented as I had snapped awake during the climax of a dream.

"I'm really sorry. I should have known better that the trip was too much for you. Listen, this is Ratu, my wife's grandmother. She lives with us. She's a *dukun*. It's kind of like a shaman. She's able to heal people. I told her you are just getting over dengue, but she's saying that's not why you passed out earlier." As he told me, I sensed he was neither comfortable sharing this nor was he sure I would receive it well, much less believe him.

"What do you mean?" I managed to squeak out.

"*Nandhang sangsara kien!*" she belted out, nodding with an intense gaze burning into my eyes the way I suppose witch doctors do—though she was my first.

"What's she saying?"

She repeated the phrase several times, continuing to nod, her look darkening. Zach gave a sheepish smile, his head bobbing back and forth, and I could tell he was trying to put a diplomatic slant on her words.

"Don't worry. At this point I can handle the news."

"Well, she says you are suffering from... money."

"Money?" He shrugged at my question.

She stroked my hair with a pitiful look, then lifted my head so I could sip water from the corner of a small plastic bag she pricked open. A tiny stream flowed into my mouth and the coolness filled my throat, giving me temporary relief from a throat made sore from thirst.

"*Dhuwit iku master*," she said in a hushed tone.

"Now what did she say?"

"Only that money is your master."

"Well, maybe it used to be. Now I have nothing. So, tell her it's a waste of time."

He spoke to her in Javanese, and she glanced at me and then held up a dirty old coin, whispering "*Kerokan....*" Zach pursed his lips and gave me a more serious look.

"Listen, Harry. She wants to do something. It may seem strange, but she says it will help you. It's an alternative treatment. She says there are spirits inside your body, and she wants to send in a wind to cast them away."

"With that coin? What's she going to do with it, stick it up my ass?"

He laughed. "*Kerokan* is a common practice for people who are sick. Mothers here do it for their children. Many people swear by it, but she does everything a bit differently. Chanting and stuff. Listen, I've seen some crazy shit in my life, but trust me, she's legit."

I hesitated, and the old woman gave me a pathetic smile. "They already try kill you this morning, *Dimas*," she said in tattered English I struggled to understand. At first, I thought I heard her wrong until I caught her grave face. Indeed, she had unmasked me, and I felt my eyeballs tilt down to her bosom, catching sight of an intricate necklace dangling from her neck. She was as big as a ten-year-old back home, but I felt her power take me in and I let out a long slow breath. Nowhere else to hide. I nodded to her and without catching anyone's eyes, I closed my own, tired beyond belief.

"If it will help. I'm already dead, though," I heard myself mumble, shuddering at the delirious resignation in my own voice. "She called me *Dimas*. What does that mean?"

"Indonesian has many forms of address based on age and gender. It means 'golden younger brother'," he said as if it were a meaningless form of address. Nevertheless, I was touched by it. "We need to turn you over on your stomach. It's going to feel a bit painful at first. Some people say it kind of feels good. Though maybe those are just masochists."

I was useless to help them, chortling under my breath as they pulled my arms over my head and worked my sweaty body into a roll. After years of indulging in massages, I knew the position quite well, and lay there not sure what to expect, my cheek resting on a floral print pillow hard as a rock.

She went about the small area under the tarpaulin, lighting little candles and something on a large gold platter that began to smoke. I kept my eyes fixed on the smoking log, with Zach's hazy image sitting back down on the stool behind it. The smoke gave off a pleasant scent that made me think of the massage in my room several days earlier. She began to chant, though it sounded more like a song. I asked Zach what she was singing, but he said it was in a dialect from another part of Java. Something the older folks managed to keep alive.

After a few quick wipes of my back, she went to work on it with the coin. She scraped the same short path from spine outwards until the sensation changed from a relieving scratch to mounting pain. The opposite hand stroked my shoulder blade, and I felt hot energy coursing through my insides. I began to dread each swipe as I would footfalls aggravating an exposed blister on my heel. I recalled an eerie little Kafka story about a sadistic man who'd invented a torture machine that would slowly etch the words of a crime on a prisoner's back with a needle until he was dead. After what seemed like hundreds of swipes, she started in on another area with the same sideways motion. Her chanting followed the rhythm of each scrape, and with the pronounced upturn at the end of a motion, it sometimes felt as if she was indeed singing out spirits or demons. I was delusional, so anything seemed possible.

At one point I even laughed, remembering that a year earlier I was sitting in a plush leather chair gazing out the window of my office overlooking the roof of the Pacific Stock Exchange—a majestic building shuttered after online trading rendered it useless—relishing how comfortable I felt, in life and in form. I wanted to regret how far down the drain I had gone, but even in that moment of anguish I felt freer than ever. Although, at the time I didn't notice it. I felt good even though it all seemed so bad. In fact, I began to berate myself for believing that my life had improved. There I was, hot, sweaty, tired, racked with pain. I was in the presence of two people caring for me even though I had nothing to give them in return. The people in the hotel, the woman with the coconuts, they had shown the face of altruism—something I had long dismissed as a quaint philosophical belief impossible to prove and perhaps rooted in concealed self-interest. I wondered if I'd been wrong all those years. Face down and vulnerable to the scrapings of an old woman, I felt more connected to her than I had to most people throughout my life.

She must have worked on me for hours because by the time she made her way down my back and then rolled me over and made the bright red tiger stripes on my belly, the sun was beginning to go down. Zach had disappeared early on, and while I wondered where he'd gone, I lost myself in the rhythm and pain of the therapy. I felt each swath burning and she began to move her hands all over me with a touch so light I barely sensed her fingertips. I'm not sure why, but I felt cool waves of energy wherever her hands moved and the inexplicable sensation that each stripe set something free. Of course, this could have been the delirium. She finished with a loud clap of the hands that gave me a rough jolt. Not what I expected since the final few minutes left me relaxed and drifting off. She lifted my head and trickled another bag of water down my throat, and with a quick bow she disappeared without saying anything.

I lay prone for several minutes, a tingling feeling throughout my body and a mind gliding through thoughts of what to do next. Then I gave up thinking about anything and drifted off to sleep. When I woke up, it was dark, and Zach was sitting in the corner again, his face illuminated from the candle next to his foot. I was so hungry I wanted to eat the stool he was sitting on. The woman returned and spooned something white and mushy and sweet into my mouth, which I ate up like an underfed dog. Three more of those and I began to feel human again.

"*Terima kasih,*" I said to her, and she shook her head as if I didn't need to say thank you.

"By the way," Zach said with a sideways glance, "she knows Bahasa. Everyone does because it's the official language, but Javanese is more prevalent around here. So, you can also say *matur nuwun* if you want to sound local."

"Good to know."

Two young men approached me with short bamboo poles, and Zach said something to them that set them to the task of shoving the poles under my mat. They each flashed subservient smiles before throwing their heads down to the poles. "My wife's brothers," Zach said, "they'll lift you inside. Ratu says you cannot be near wind for a while. So, no fans or air conditioning. I'm afraid it's going to be a hot night for you, but she says in the morning you will feel better."

"I hope so. Feel like shit now."

Ratu folded a wet cloth over my eyes and the two brothers-in-law carried me into the house and set me down on a soft mattress on the floor of a little room. It felt like a shrine, covered with candles and religious-looking paraphernalia. Ratu followed and stayed close to me, watching my eyes as though she were searching for something in them. Maybe she was trying to see if the spirits were still lingering around inside me. I didn't know what to make of it, and part of me wanted to play the game while another still considered it a bunch of foolish rubbish. I thought they would all leave the room, but I noticed a woman young enough to still be in school appear at the door and lay a pile of blankets and a pillow in the corner.

"What's that for?" I asked Zach.

"Ratu says she needs to stay with you."

"In case the evil spirits come back?"

"Listen. I know this all seems a little hocus pocus, but I will say I've seen her do some amazing things. So, try to keep an open mind."

"No worries. I've got nothing to lose. Besides, I kind of like her."

Zach chuckled at that. "She said you would."

"Really?" I was a little taken aback at his comment.

"I'll tell you more about it tomorrow. For now, rest up." And with that, he was gone, and I was left alone with the woman who hadn't taken her eyes off me since the first time I saw her.

Indeed, it was a long night. Not too dissimilar from the crazy dreams I'd been experiencing, but these dreams seemed more vivid, and Ratu appeared in each of them. Not some warped version that looked like her but also looked a bit like someone else. No–it was *her* in those dreams, standing in front of me as a silent protector. Once it was a huge grey beetle trying to attack me, and she fought it off with something that looked like a long spear. Another dream had me stuck in dark mud that tried to pull me under. Ratu stood on the shore, pulling me out through a vine she'd tossed to me. There were dozens of these different episodes that increased in intensity, some of which I don't remember beyond a feeling, but I would then wake up and see her either curled up next to me or offering me water. Once I went to the bathroom all over myself, and before I had a chance to let the embarrassment set in, she cleaned me up without batting an eye.

The final dream fragment remains clear in my mind even years later–its intensity and ferocity outweighed all others. I was home, on Pine Street, looking up at a building that resembled my bank, but it was out of focus, almost like it was sweating or dripping. I tried to open the door, but it wouldn't open. A fat security guard smiled at me and kept motioning to me, but I couldn't understand him. Finally, he shouted, 'closed!' and waved me away. I looked at my watch. Two o'clock in the afternoon in the middle of the week. It couldn't be closed. It took me a little while, but I realized that the security guard was Mr. Stuard, my economics professor at the Academy. A jolly man both in the dream and in real life, and one of my inspirations to go into banking after I fulfilled my naval obligation. In fact, he helped me get my first job. What was *he* doing there? I knocked again and pointed to my watch.

CHAPTER 9 | THE WATERCOURSE WAY

It was then that I woke up. It must have been the bleating of a goat outside the window. It sounded like a baby crying. There was no sign of Ratu at first, but when I craned my head around to look at the door, I noticed her sitting in the corner in a cross-legged meditation pose. When I turned over onto my back, she opened her eyes, a soft frown on her face. I could feel the striped wounds along my entire backside, though they seemed to be on the healing side of pain.

"You awake now, *Dimas*. You safe now."

I heard a thumping on the other side of the doorway, which didn't have a door save a thick cut of striped cloth bathed in dark colors. A toddler dressed in a diaper and nothing else peeked through the doorway. Her eyes were big and brown, and I could tell from her facial features that she was a product of Zach and a local woman. She had his twinkle, standing there studying me as if I were a strange creature come down from another planet.

"Lily!" I heard Zach shout from another part of the house, and then he himself appeared, hand gripping her shoulder as she leaned into him for security. "Sorry, Harry. Did she wake you?"

"No, the evil spirits leaving my body woke me. I feel lighter now." This was a half-joke, and I suppose it was meant to acknowledge that I was not quite sure I believed in all the hocus-pocus he and Ratu had introduced into my life, but nevertheless grateful for their help. "Is she your daughter?"

"Yes, this is Lily." He looked down at her with an arc of love.

"She's beautiful."

"Takes after her mother. By the way, you haven't met my wife yet. She's just gone to get us some fruit for breakfast. Maybe you'd like to take a swim this morning. We have a small pool out back and I'm sure it'll feel good after sitting in a hot box all night."

"If I can stand up."

"Here, let me help you." He got me to my feet. I wobbled, and we both looked to Ratu for her blessing, who tossed a few fingers in the air and bent down to pick up her bedding. We took this as assent, and he all but carried me through the room and out the back door. Along the way I caught a glimpse of his living room, sparsely decorated, containing a rattan couch and small flat screen television. Outside we passed the place where I lay the day before, under the suspended tarp. The candles still sat in each corner. I hadn't realized I had been a few feet from an in-ground pool. It looked new and pristine, so inviting, with a large patch of cut grass and carved wooden chairs in the backdrop.

"Nice setup, Zach!" I remarked as he helped me sit down at the shallow end.

"Yeah, the pool was a present from my parents. They said it's cuz they know how much I like to swim, but I think it's so they have a place to cool off whenever they come visit. This place is too hot for my father. All he does is complain about the heat and the constant sweating."

"Well, right now it's the best thing in the world," I said, slipping underwater and letting all my air out, descending to the bottom of the pool. The coolness peeled away the sweaty slime that had encased me. It felt like layers of life melting away and I gazed up, seeing Zach's wavy image standing next to the pool. Before I knew it, he'd launched himself into the deep end in a full cannonball. I felt the shockwaves and bubbles as a tumble of flesh crashed down next to me. When I surfaced a few moments later, we both took one look at each other and slipped into deep belly laughs. I hadn't laughed liked that in years–at least while I was sober.

For a moment, I forgot about everything. Zach looked over at me and something about his face and the way his eyes shone made me realize it was the first time I'd seen anyone truly happy to his core. Not just having a good time or thrilled that a deal went through or even content with his lot in life. No, he had a joy that ran deep, making each day worth getting up for. Where did it come from? Had he carried this joy into life from some faraway place? It was as if through him shone a shimmering light that I saw traces of in Mark, who sought it, or Elena, who brushed up against it in the right environment, or Sarah who gave it away freely. I thought about this while his little girl toppled into his arms and giggled in the beautiful way only little ones her age can do.

"How did you ever wind up in this place?" I asked without considering that my question might sound insulting.

"You mean here… Java? Indonesia?"

"Yeah, I guess so. But really, how did you get involved in this whole line of work? I mean, I never knew about this kind of stuff before. I've heard about the Peace Corps. Is that where you got started, one of those outfits?"

"No. I wish I had–probably would have saved me lots of trouble. No, I got out of school with a classics degree, which meant I wasn't prepared for anything beyond working for the parks department."

"Where d'you study?" I asked him.

"A little school in Maryland... St. John's College."

"Really? I went to the Naval Academy. Across the street!"

"Wow! Small world. Did you ever make it out to the croquet matches?"

"Between St. John's and the Academy? No. Sadly, all that stuff came after I was commissioned."

"For the best. We beat you guys every year. Still do." His face sparkled and I realized how connecting it was to know we went to schools who couldn't be more different, resembling Athens and Sparta. "Anyway, I knew a little Spanish, so I spent the summer after I graduated down in Guatemala, taking language classes. This was at the tail end of the civil war, so it was cheaper to do than to live back in Monterey. I stayed in Antigua for the first few months, living with a family."

"That must have been an *experience*."

"Oh yeah. It was a great way to get immersed in the language and the culture. Whole extended families live in the same house. Makes it so much easier to take care of children as everyone pitches in to help. There's always the odd aunt hanging around the house cooking or doing something. I thoroughly enjoyed my time there, and the city is beautiful with its cobblestoned streets and all. After a few months I met a guy that was working with the Mayan women in the highlands, trying to help them get back on their feet. Mayans had it the worst during the war."

"How so?"

"May sound a bit strange, but the pecking order in that neck of the woods seems to be based on height. At least that's what I gathered from my short time there. Lots of people with German and Spanish backgrounds–those with European descent–they're at the top of the food chain. That's why you'll often see the Miss Guatemala beauty queens barely look Latin American. At the other end of the spectrum, you've got the indigenous Mayans themselves–several different tribes who you can often identify by their colorful dress. Then you've got the *mestizos*. They're a mix of European and indigenous people and make up the bulk of the population. While the Mayans still get crapped on because they're shorter and often don't speak Spanish as well as the others, power is slowly shifting to include the *mestizos*. Half a century ago the entire country was controlled by the United Fruit Company, which had strong ties to the U.S.

"Anyway, I befriended one of the teachers at the Spanish school I was attending. Juan was helping the rural villages where indigenous women were forming cooperatives to try to keep their families and communities intact. Since Juan's mother was *K'iche'*, one of the indigenous groups from the highlands, he knew their language and culture. I started by going out with him on the weekends. I learned about farming, food production, and alternative ways of financing. Some NGOs were also trying to get a toehold in there to move beyond just helping people with basic services like food, shelter, and clothing. So, I started to meet some of them and soon began working for them. It was fun stuff and I have to say, I loved the food. Simple, but good. You're probably finding this boring, Harry."

"Quite the opposite. For one thing, I've been lying down in a pool of sweat for the past two weeks. Even so, I find your story fascinating."

"Anyway, Guatemala's a great place and if you ever go there, you have to visit a little city by the name of Esquipulas. It's near the border with El Salvador and Honduras. There's a white church there with a big black Jesus hanging on the cross. People come from all around to see it. Makes you wonder what color that guy was. I'm pretty sure he wasn't German like most iconography makes him out to look like."

"Maybe I'll check it out someday. How long were you in Guatemala for?"

"Two years. I came home after that, fluent in Spanish and bursting with ideas, but still trying to figure out what to do with my life. I thought about joining the military. My father taught at the Naval Postgraduate School in Monterey where I grew up. So, it was something that had sway with me. In retrospect, I wish I'd have joined the Peace Corps, but around *my* dinner table growing up that sort of thing was looked down on. Peaceniks. Didn't even seem like an option."

"Believe me, I know what you mean. What did your father teach?"

"Meteorology."

"Very interesting."

"Sure, I guess; but growing up, whenever I asked him what the weather was going to be like that day he'd just tell me to look out the window. So, I couldn't take it all that seriously. In fact, when I got back home I got a lot of pressure to do the kinds of things he wanted to do. Being an officer wasn't for me. I knew that even before Guatemala. After what I'd seen and done over there, all I could think about was getting back out there."

"To Guatemala?"

"Any developing country. You know what it's like, I'm sure. The minute you get outside of the U.S. and the so-called developed world, it gets raw. Nothing seems to work the way it's supposed to, but there's beauty in that. There's also incredible beauty in the hospitality. Fifteen years of traveling the world and that's my big take-away: the rest of the world is just plain nicer. Besides, I have the wanderlust gene in me. Family lore has it that my great-great grandfather wanted to go to the World's Fair around the turn of the century and hopped on trains all the way from upstate New York. He was only eight years old. Not sure if it's true, but it sure left an impression on me when I heard that story growing up."

"Maybe you're right about the beauty outside America, but these places are not very efficient, are they?"

"Depends on who's holding the wheel, I guess."

"So, where did you wind up going to?"

"Originally, I was planning to go back to Latin America. Just loved the culture down there and was itching to get back to it. I only came back home to get some visa stuff straightened out. It wound up taking longer than I expected and one day I was in a café reading and I met this girl. She was reading a guide book on Mongolia and the way she was dressed, hiking boots and all, it looked like she was leaving that day. Turns out, she was just breaking the boots in for a trek she was going on."

"Mongolia, huh?"

"Yeah. One thing led to another and I was sitting next to her on the plane. Her name was Michelle. Had a wild streak in her and a big mass of wild curly hair to match. I spent the next year bumming all over Asia with her. To this day I don't think I've met anyone like her. She had a genuine love for people and just ate life. Without even doing it consciously, she taught me the way of the Tao. The watercourse way, they call it. I only read about it before, but she embodied it."

"Watercourse way?"

"There's a book by Alan Watts that talks about it. In a nutshell, life is like a big river and the way is to go with the flow of that river and follow its natural and supernatural forces wherever it takes us, like a tree branch riding down a mountain stream."

"How does one do that?"

"Well, I'm definitely no expert. I think it has something to do with relying on one's intuition and letting the signs of nature and just plain everyday life lead us where we need to go. Don't overlook the easily overlooked."

"I like that, don't overlook the easily overlooked."

"Yeah, Michelle taught me a lot about that sort of thing, and like a couple of branches, we floated downstream. We went everywhere together: Mongolia, Cambodia, Thailand, India, Turkey, the Middle East. Sometimes I would wake up forgetting what country I was in. Wherever we were, we found some work teaching English, building a well, or doing community development work. Looking back, it was kind of amazing that we didn't get killed or die from some strange disease, though we were close to both several times. She just knew which way to go all the time, even though it often seemed like she was just being flighty. After the first few months I began to sense she was somehow tapped into the rhythm of the Universe. So, I just went with it. Before I knew it, I too was doing the same. One couldn't help feeling the light around her, I suppose."

"What's the secret? How did you know which way to go?" I cut in, eager to learn some secret truth eluding me all these years.

"Oh, I don't know. Part of it is slowing down and letting things happen. Another is in who you meet when you're slowing down and listening. Everyone is here to help each other, and some more than others–like they were sent by some god or something. I'm not sure how it works, but it's like we are all made of a specific color, like a certain frequency. When we're tapped into it, we notice others with the same frequency–like we're unconsciously seeking each other out. Anyway, once you hit that zone life takes on a cadence all its own. Synchronicity takes over. The cool thing is when you realize that *your* purpose is to help others on their path instead of just doing your own thing. It's like their path is your path."

"I like that." There were so many things I wanted to say in response, but I didn't want to derail his story, so I closed my mouth and let him continue.

"Anyway, it was in Jordan where I lost her. She had a crimson scarf that was always either around her neck or holding up that bunch of curls. She'd told me once early on in Mongolia that when it was time for her to go on her own, she'd simply wave the scarf and be gone in a flash. I thought she was talking in her usual fantastical way, and so I forgot all about it. We'd made our way up from Aqaba, a beautiful little town on the Red Sea, up through the desert and into Petra–an ancient city carved deep into the rock. We walked a mile down a narrow corridor that opened into a valley with buildings carved into the stone. Amazing place–and huge. We walked all over, all day long. Towards the end of the day, I was tired, but she still had the energy to walk the thousand steps up to the monastery. I followed her, and we had to dodge donkeys trying to make it up steep stairs carved into the rock. Finally, we made it up there and I thought I was about to die. I lay down across from the entrance to the temple–a stunning façade carved into the rock. I must have dozed off, because when I stirred I felt a bit dizzy and disoriented–no doubt a little dehydrated. I saw Michelle way off in the distance, that huge frizz of hair flowing freely in the wind–it was super windy up there, though still hot as hell. I'll never forget the painful swelling I felt in my gut when I saw her waving that crimson scarf. I could make out here bright smile, and then she turned and was gone. Just like that. Of course, I tried to track her down and discovered that there were no paths down where I'd last seen her. It was almost like she was a phantom that just popped out of reality.

"Well, I made my way back down, cried a few tears and drank a few beers. Those were in the days just before September 11th, so traveling around the Middle East was easy to do. I saw most of it, on my own, all the while missing Michelle–though she'd taught me how to be resourceful and to look for the signs of where to go next. I remember standing in Jerusalem near the Wailing Wall, somewhat oblivious to all the people around me praying in that bouncy sort of way they do, wondering which direction to go. I couldn't decide, and it was such a hot day I thought I was going to keel over. So, I made my way to a stand selling bottles of water. As I was standing there in the shade drinking water, I realized how truly free I was. I didn't have much money. In fact, I was dead broke and barely had enough for a hotel room, much less a plane ticket. Michelle must have rubbed off on me because I didn't care. I'll never forget that feeling of complete freedom. Funny, because moments before as I looked out over the masses of people dressed in very traditional garb, mixed in with tourists wearing silly-looking t-shirts and shorts, it seemed like a vortex of anything but freedom. I was standing in the center of it, initially worried I would be swept up in it myself. Then a soft voice, one I'd heard all my life and I'm still learning to hear, whispered for me to go get some water and just stand there and relax."

"What happened?" I asked after he had paused, still cradling his daughter, who by then had fallen asleep in his arms. He kissed her and in my rapt impatience, I hoped he wouldn't stop.

"I saw Father Jack walking by. I'd met him a few years back when we were passing through Java. Michelle and I spent a month here volunteering for him. I looked over at his big fat belly and floral print shirt and smiling Irish eyes beaming at me. He was by himself, wandering around, and walked up to me and asked if I knew a good place for falafel. I just laughed."

"Really? That's a hoot!"

"Yeah, I took him to a tourist trap around the corner. You know Father Jack. He likes to talk and before I knew it, we were having lunch together and he was telling me his life story. He was a bit standoffish with me when I was first around Adipala. So, I guess he figured God was throwing us back together. Anyway, he knows lots of people and one thing led to another and he brought me back to the friend's house where he was staying–some retired monk. Then, before I knew it, I was on my way again to West Africa and living in the bush in Sierra Leone."

"Really! What's *that place* like?"

"Very remote. Even more than here. In fact, I was the first white man *ever* to have come into some of the villages. That was a little crazy. In one village the headman gave a speech when I arrived saying that he was happy that the prophecy of my arrival had come to pass. When I asked about it he said generations before the elders had predicted that *I* would come to save them. A man fitting my description, anyway. They called me *Papa*, the localized version of father, even though I told them I'd rather be thought of as a brother. The people I didn't know called me *Oporto*, which is their word for white person–something I heard hundreds of times a day as I would pass by huts where half-naked children were bouncing up and down with smiles on their faces shouting 'hey, white person!' over and over again. It never bothered me, seeing that sheer joy in those little faces as I passed by on my motorbike, waving to them."

"Isn't Sierra Leone where they had the child soldiers?"

"That's the one. Very sad story. After the war they had to be assimilated back into society. Many of the boys were given motorbikes as part of their integration into the economy, becoming *okada* drivers, or taxi drivers who give people rides on the back of their bikes."

"Wow. Did you feel safe?"

"Always. Some of the sweetest people in the world. I'll never forget the hard stares I got when I first came through Lunsar, the main town that serves as a hub for the surrounding villages. The *okada* drivers were all boys around fifteen or sixteen, some of them younger. They were sitting on their bikes all lined up looking at me. It scared the hell out of me to have a dozen rough-looking older boys staring at me without a smile. The minute I smiled, though, I saw a transformation flash over their faces—faces shining with brilliant teeth. From that point on, all I did was smile. In the two years I was there, I never once felt unsafe. Though I did make sure my stuff was secure as thievery was rampant, but I chalk that up to simple opportunism. People are pretty poor there."

"What exactly *were* you doing there?"

"Well, initially I went to work for some fly-by-night NGO that Father Jack's monk friend had been in touch with. Some American guy had read some book on giving and decided to start helping people. How he stumbled on Sierra Leone, I don't know, but he needed someone to manage the operations he'd set up over there. I was broke and needed to get out of the Middle East since things were heating up after September 11th."

"I'm sure."

"Yeah, well, having been all over half the world and going to places like India, I thought I'd be ready for West Africa."

"How is it different?"

"Well, people do live in huts there and society and life are quite simple. I think that sort of thing seems very attractive, but I found it very difficult to connect with people, to be honest. I couldn't even relate to the Italian Fathers who'd come over several years prior to run missions. Those missions became places of refuge during the war. The nuns, too. They were the real heroes, hiding out in the bush for days with families and children to ride out village raids. So, most of them were jaded and superstitious of outsiders who were swooping in after the war to try to 'save the savages' by driving around in their white SUVs throwing money out the window and driving off, never even bothering to get out of their vehicles.

"I remember one day when I was supposed to pick up a tractor from one of the villages where the organization was building a school. I hadn't made it to the village yet, so it was weird that I was coming to introduce myself, survey the site for the school, get the tractor, and then leave. I didn't have time to talk to them. It was early on in my time there and I really didn't know what I was doing—even how to relate to the people. So, like a typical American, I came in guns blazing. I said hello to the village headman, then trotted out to do some measurements in the field for the school. I could tell right away something was off—just the way the headman was looking at me. Of course, I didn't help much running from place to place. It was late in the day and I was hungry and just not feeling comfortable in the country, etcetera.

"I remember when I said hello, the headman mentioned something about a *store*, which was their word for a slab of concrete used for drying out rice. Rice is their main crop. Anyway, when I came back and jumped on the tractor, trying to get her started, the headman came up to me, flanked by what looked like the whole village. They were glaring at me. Not like the *okada* drivers, but like people with a deep-welling anger—a rage that had nothing to do with me, yet somehow had *everything* to do with me. Again, he went on about the store and how my boss when he was visiting from America promised them he'd build them a store. There wasn't much I could say, and I can't even recall what I *did* say to placate them just so I could get out of there. I started to get the feeling that they wanted to kick my ass. Who knows, maybe if I'd stuck around longer they would have.

"The whole thing was strange, and as I drove off with them all looking at me, I realized I'd looked at the face of collective resentment. People who'd been treated like objects and who had no say in their future and no real help other than a bunch of so-called experts showing up and telling them what they needed without taking the time to truly listen. Even I caught myself acting like I was listening. I'd merely adopted a persona of empathy and nodding my head and using reflective listening and all that mumbo-jumbo crap that only works if you're doing it for real. I was just faking it. I felt like an idiot—a lackey. I slept like shit that night and woke up realizing that I was going to slow down and listen to them and figure out what they needed rather than simply assuming that I knew best even after everyone around me told me I knew best. Even my boss started to get pissed at me because work slowed down and my reports were all about stuff he hadn't assigned me to do, but I didn't care. That look of resentment has never left my mind and I'm glad it hasn't.

"Anyway, it was obvious that the loan program I was supposed to be administering was a disaster, but I didn't know what else to do, so I still tried to collect monthly repayments, but even then, it was half-hearted. During this time, I was going to the local hospital canteen for meals as there wasn't any place else to eat besides the occasional hut on the roadside with a woman stirring a large pot of rice and river fish stew. I eventually met the canteen cook's husband, a staunch Catholic working with church groups who were saving money on their own through a model developed by Catholic Relief Services. He offered to show me how it worked, so one day I jumped in his truck with him and drove out into the bush to a group of people in a tiny village sitting around a wooden box, talking and putting money into it."

"Oh, so that's where you learned about the savings clubs like the one from yesterday?"

"Yep. That's where I first learned it. It was amazing to see how dirt-poor villagers were working together to pool their savings together. Just a bunch of women meeting once a week. Several months later they had enough to build a community center or buy cooking charcoal in bulk at wholesale prices and then resell it in the market. It completely transformed how I saw the nature of development work."

"And what's that?"

"The power of groups. We Americans think individualism is so great, something to aspire to; but these ladies were teaching me that unless we work together in a collaborative way, especially in times of need, it just doesn't make good economic sense. Not only that, the social value of those groups meeting once a week reminds me why our society is so fractured. Your generation used to go bowling and spend more time together. Now, everyone just sits at home in front of their TVs staring away and isolated from their own communities. Community is pretty much gone–and the kicker about these savings clubs is that they don't really need outside money. No loans or special interests. No social entrepreneurs seeking personal glory or to pad their resume. None of that. Just a need to be taught the method and make sure they follow the rules. After I've taught them the rules, I just stay in the background and fade out when necessary."

"But don't some of them need loans? How do small businesses fit in?"

"I'm no banker. I don't know. Depends on where we're talking about. In Sierra Leone, in the bush, where people are barely surviving off what they can grow, outside capital might disrupt their economy–distort the market. People need someone who can hire them, so supporting a medium-sized business that creates jobs is one thing, but I'm not sure people should be encouraged to start their own business because no one else will hire them. Besides, who wants to be in debt? I've seen entire villages in debt to these small banks. Sure, they get funding, but often they're just using that money to pay school fees or medical bills."

Zach had a good point, and I didn't press him on this even though I had a thousand arguments against it. I felt gratitude that Zach's daughter slept and he spent the time telling me his story. She stayed sleeping, and after a deep breath, he tried to turn the conversation back to me.

"What about you, Harry? What brings you here?"

"I heard about Father Jack. Watched a documentary on him."

"Yeah, he's got charisma. Draws people in like moths to a flame."

"What do you think of him?" I could feel a conspiratorial inflection in my voice. Zach gave me an answer that I wasn't quite prepared for.

"Oh, he's straight out of a Conrad story. Though, unlike Lord Jim, I'd like to think he makes nobler choices. He truly loves people–but enough about him or me. What about you? I heard you were a banker."

"I honestly don't know. Lately, every time someone asks me who I am, I can't seem to get my story straight. Hard to explain, but maybe it's like that tree branch floating down the river you were talking about before. I retired back in January. Got fired, actually. Forced retirement, if you will. Since then I've just been floating through life and in many ways hoping for the best. I'm not seeking enlightenment or anything–I'm too far from it to even try at my age. At first, I was looking for a little adventure and maybe to pat myself on the back for helping people–the secret dream of rich people. I didn't grow up rich. Quite the opposite. So, I've felt like a fraud my whole life. In fact, the job I had, the wife I had, everything, it was all just a way to try to tell myself I was normal. Took me thirty years to realize it was just a thin veneer. So, I guess the past year has been a little like eat pray love, but more like drink stumble hangover."

"Have you read any John Cheever?"

"No, is he any good?"

"Maybe. What you were saying just now reminded me a little of his writing. We see the beautiful suburban house, trimmed roses, perfect lifestyle, but it's merely a façade hiding life's real struggles."

"Sounds like I should read some of him. You seem pretty well read." He shrugged, and I couldn't help asking him about Maugham's book. "Have you read a *Razor's Edge*?"

"Fantastic book!"

"I haven't read it, but a friend of mine has. Does the main character find himself?"

"I believe he does, and if I remember correctly, his friends go broke during the Great Depression, and he's able to help them through it."

I chuckled at the irony in his response and tried to steer the conversation back to him.

"Say, you seem pretty happy, Zach. Do you think it's because of the books you've read or all your adventures or helping people?"

"I don't know. Sometimes, but it's those low points that keep me going. There's a little devil inside all of us that needs to be cared for and fed. Otherwise, we're miserable. There were many times in my life, when I felt alienated from the whole world, where I recognized that *otherness* of myself and learned to accept it for what it is. That's one of the things I learned from Michelle, that life just *is,* and while I'm an active participant, there's something bigger going on and my attitude and actions are the only things I can control. The rest is the river. I get my perspective from remembering how silly it was to stand on that cliff in Petra and be so distressed by Michelle's leaving that I imagined myself leaping off it–and having to physically stop myself." He gave me a vulnerable look, and I knew he'd had enough. Besides, his daughter started to stir in his arms, her sweet face turning up towards his in a gentle smile. "Well, if you're sick of the hotel, I have a room out back if you want to stay there. You could work with us awhile. We could really use an extra hand around here if you're up for it. That is, once you get over this illness." He let that hang in the air as he pulled his daughter up with a kiss to her cheek. I could sense his love for her shrouding the two of them as though they were the only two people on earth in that moment. Her face morphed from sleepy to bright, especially after he blew a raspberry on her belly. She pushed at him with little fingers and giggles.

The next day I moved into the little room out back, which was almost an apartment, with its own shower and toilet across a courtyard. I didn't leave the house, but had the hotel bring over my things on a *tuk tuk*. Zach's family was concerned that if I pushed myself I might relapse with an even worse bout of dengue fever. That scared me enough to heed their advice. I would spend the next five hundred nights in that little room, and my days with Zach and sometimes Fr. Jack and the others. Initially, I helped Zach expand the savings clubs to different villages. It was gratifying to look on a map and see these groups spread like a slow-moving salve.

And little by little, my tenuous friendship with Fr. Jack transformed after he asked me to fill in for a volunteer English teacher that left one of the schools. In fact, it was the same school we went to on that first day, where I met Aulia, the beautiful headmistress. I was reluctant to take on the job as it required a long ride on the *moto* each morning and I was also a bit scared of her beauty, not to mention I had no clue how to teach English. Over time I began to appreciate the ride where I saw the same people in the same places on my route, waving to most of them each time I passed. My infatuation for Aulia faded once I began to get to know her as a person. It shifted to a deep respect for someone who'd struggled her whole life and felt duty bound to pull as many others out of poverty as she could. I chuckle now at how childish I was that first meeting. In many ways, it was the best year of my life. It was the year I began loving people, especially my young students who found me amusing. They brought out a kindness in me I wasn't aware I possessed.

CHAPTER 10 | LEAVING JAVA

That year gave me a chance to reconsider my life. I had many talks with Zach and sometimes with Fr. Jack. Zach held an air of optimism, believing that faith in the rhythm of the Universe, likened to honing one's instrument in life and doing the best to play along with the symphony of life, where God remained an ephemeral conductor, would lead to ultimate happiness. I appreciated his metaphor and he proved its meaning through consistent actions. I could never quite figure out if he was religious or not. For one thing, I knew his wife was Muslim. Although, I never heard him going on about any specific religion. Whenever he did speak of spiritual matters, his language sounded more mystical than anything else. Someone could have told me he was a Muslim, or even a Christian, and I would have believed either, since he seemed to be sitting at the pinnacle of some great mountain gazing down on the paths and recognizing each for its worth. Indeed, he was drawing from a different source, one more pure, than most people I've met in this world.

Fr. Jack was a different story. He spent most of his waking hours defying both man and God. I think he got off on the idea of being a maverick or a hooligan or whatever else he liked to call himself. It was like he got Christ's message and was on His side, but assumed everyone else seemed to have missed the boat entirely, unless they were poor. *Fuck the bastards!* was one of his favorite phrases when referring to any hierarchical policy he disagreed with, or just about anyone who got in his way. He moved about like a whirlwind, although crafting goodness in his path instead of destruction. So, I couldn't fault him for that and tried my best not to drink whiskey with him so as not to rile him up again like that first night. In fact, our paths didn't cross much. I felt as if he always knew my whereabouts but stayed out of my business. Later, I wondered if he saw me not with an eye of disdain or even competition, but rather as another damaged soul drawn into his monastic heart of darkness deep in the jungle. I kept my distance, but like everyone else, I grew to love the scoundrel.

For much of the year, I was broke. The big banks got a bailout, but Don's bank did not, and I saw my equity vanish overnight. I had unwittingly staked my retirement account on the housing market, since my portfolio consisted of high-rated bonds–labeled low-risk, but packed with junky mortgages. I stopped caring after I started living at Zach's place. It was like a haze of oblivion settled in, cleansing the pains of my past.

I still thought of Elena, sometimes. Despite the good times in the beginning, I struggled against the tide of memories toward the end when her monster would slip out of the closet and attack me. I never saw her again. Like Zach's friend Michelle, she came into my life when I needed her and left when we no longer needed each other–raising her own crimson scarf to say goodbye. Now, I have a mountain of exquisite memories to remember her by, all the lessons she taught me–especially how to open my heart.

Stranger still was losing all concern for being broke because I'd spent my entire life worried about money and making sure I was set up for retirement. Life just seemed simpler not worrying about it. In fact, I worried so little that I'd forgotten the loan I made to the Mongolians. By March, they paid it back in full plus the meager interest I tacked onto it. America was defaulting right and left, but poor Mongolian families were coming through without a single one skipping out on their loan. I'd learned to live on so little that I could survive off the interest and I rolled half the loan back over and invested the other half into Zach's program, plus an education loan program I set up so poor kids could afford to attend the Academy or one of the other schools around Adipala. I'd heard too many requests from parents the past six months needing help sending their kids to school. Fr. Jack suggested an outright donation, but I still couldn't see myself going that far when I knew I could recycle that money while holding the trustee accountable.

I was planning a trip home and contemplating leaving Adipala for good. Part of me desired to stay there for the rest of my life–in the jungle and surrounded by good people, but that goodness had already planted a seed in me and I could feel it guiding me towards a new path in life. At first, microfinance had captivated me, and I assumed that my life and investments would follow that course. Though, there was a huge difference between the entrepreneurial loans that seemed to be drawing people into a market that might need something else, and the savings clubs, which seemed more powerful with their grounding in social connections, not to mention the focus on saving money rather than spending it.

But my work in the school made me realize that most of the people I'd met over the past few years were stuck; and while money for a business was a way out, a solid education was a better long-term path out of poverty for most people. So, I was proud when we launched the educational loan program in April and watched as Fr. Jack's schools swelled with new students. Perhaps financing their education proved less sexy than other rags-to-riches stories we Americans so love, but I knew this was the right thing to do, especially after drawing a connection to my own life. I'd spent most of my childhood skirting poverty, and the rest of my life doing my best to overshoot that and provide a solid line of defense against slipping back into it. Even the idea of having children gave me a scare when I figured out how much raising one of them (the right way) would cost. Though, none of my successes came about through my sheer will, but rather because of my education, both formal and informal. The Naval Academy got me off that dreary stoop. The connections I made over those four years propelled me to a life of cushion and protection. Education was my ticket out just as it was for those poor kids on Java.

I'd gotten in the habit of checking my email once a week. Saturday mornings I'd ride up to the same café and open my laptop. I'd kept up with Sarah and Mark. I knew Sarah had finished her website and was headed back to the States to launch her business. Despite the economic downturn that had plunged many people into unemployment and chaos, paradoxically, philanthropic spending in some sectors had skyrocketed. One thing I love about my country is that once that individualism is stripped away, people gravitate towards helping one other. One of the articles I read in praise of American solidarity even referred to a quote from Churchill during the Second World War that likened the country to a pressure cooker that picks up steam the hotter it gets.

I was glad to hear that Sarah's venture might take off, and I even introduced her to the few friends I had in the venture capital community who had the cash left to help during such a rocky time, even though the financial crisis was a year-and-a-half old and most people were still not betting on new horses. It wasn't clear what role Mark would play in all that, but I assumed he was helping on the technical side. In one email a few months prior she'd not mentioned him once, and I guessed they may have parted ways. So, I was somewhat surprised, and delighted, to see a wedding invitation in my inbox. Even more surprising was the location: Jerusalem. A destination wedding. I'd heard of, and even attended, a few of these in semi-tropical places like Costa Rica and Bermuda, but never Jerusalem. Of course, I'd never met two people like Mark or Sarah. So, in a way it made sense. At least they gave us several months to prepare. Late June might be a good time to go. Couldn't be much hotter than Java at any other time of year. Zach's story of Petra stuck with me and I put it on my bucket list. So, I booked a flight to Jordan, with a plan to travel overland to Jerusalem after

Petra and the Dead Sea. First though, I would be making a stop along the way in Baltimore.

I hadn't seen my father in twenty-five years. Like many a father and son, we had a hard time seeing life from the other's perspective. Everything was fine when I was seven years old, helping him drop crab pots in the Bay. Back then, all I wanted to be was him, or at the very least get him to appreciate me. Unfortunately, he wasn't built for the kind of nurturing I needed, and I came to consider myself just a free deck-hand and petty slave criticized for his untalented hands. I couldn't seem to make them work fast enough, and when I did, I wound up cutting myself or dropping a rig overboard by accident. He never said anything, but would just give me that disappointed frown. In fact, I'm not sure my father ever said more than three sentences at a stretch to me. He was not only a quiet man, but wrapped up so tight no one could get in. As time went on I began to realize that his personal prison kept him from getting out to connect with anyone.

When I was a teenager I often wondered what in the world my mother ever saw in him. She was a kind person worn thin from years catering to a somnambulist. She once told me that in his youth he'd been different—optimistic, and at times on fire. He wanted to go to college and study to become an engineer, so he joined the Marine Corps to pay for it with the GI Bill. All that changed as the Korean conflict broke out while he was in boot camp. My mother said he came back from that war a different man, a broken man. She didn't have to tell me that his soul was so damaged that higher education was no longer an option. It was written all over his face. My mother was stuck making meals for this shell of a man, watching him sleepwalk through life, scraping by for his family.

I was a product of this brokenness, born a few years later. I suppose his melancholy drove me to hide in books. I had my sights set on entering the Academy ever since we had an officer come to the school on career day back when I was fifteen years old. In his smart outfit and outgoing, confident manner, he was everything I wanted to be and everything my father was not. I approached him after his session, along with several other boys who were just as drawn to him. This was at a time when the Vietnam War's unpopularity meant naval officers took a risk even coming to a school campus, but this guy was different enough that he got people to see past all the vitriol. It didn't hurt that he was going into a poor neighborhood where we were ready to trade anything for escape. I waited for the throng to thin out and just as he was leaving, I caught his sleeve. He turned and with a smile asked me my name and what my plans in life were.

"I want to be like you. Be an officer."

"That's great, kid. How are your grades?"

"Well, they weren't the best last year, but this year I hope to bring them up."

175

"Bring them up. If you want this life, you must be disciplined in both body and mind. Don't forget that."

"I'll do whatever it takes, sir. You mentioned in your presentation that tuition at the Academy is free. Does that cover food, too?" When I said this, I could see him looking deep into my eyes and for the first time, taking a real interest in me.

"Everything, son." He reached into his pocket and pulled out a card with his name on it. I still remember seeing *Commander Barnes* on the card and wishing I would someday have a card on it that had that title before my name. "Here, take my card. Why don't you put your head down this year and get straight A's and make sure you exercise *every* morning. Do you think you can do that?"

"Yes sir!"

"Send me your report card in June. If you get straight A's, let's talk again. Maybe I'll have some extra-curricular work you can do with us in the summer. I coach the sailing team and if you're interested, we might have a spot open to help with the gear and scrubbing and repainting the hulls."

I often think back to that day and the moment where I hesitated. I almost didn't reach out for his sleeve, wondering if he'd take a messy-looking kid seriously. That fateful day, meeting Commander Barnes, led to three years of straight A's and sit-ups, along with spending my summer helping the sailing team. I would join that team when I became a Midshipman. So, my life turned on a three-minute conversation with Commander Barnes in that old brick high school, giving me the hope and encouragement I needed to chart a course through life that sent me sailing to places I never imagined.

My father never got that. He tried to talk me out of the service, and I knew why, though he never said it. He was worried that I would wind up like him, a broken soul. Of course, we never had a real relationship, so I didn't listen to him. Over the years I managed to avoid contact with him altogether. My mother would write or call every now and again and invite me out to the house, but I was always too busy—even if I wasn't. It was just too painful to think about his sour face and dashed hopes or whatever it was that drove his depression. At least he didn't drink much like Thomas' uncle or some of the other fathers in the neighborhood that made life even more miserable for everyone else around them.

I couldn't place the urge for wanting to go back and see my father. Why now? Maybe it was because I'd just spent over a year watching a few loving fathers in action. It made me nostalgic for what could have been, I suppose. There were times throughout the years I wanted to go and show him how successful I had become—but I knew even if he was proud of me he would never show it. So, it was no use. I had been angry with him all those years, but that anger had morphed into empathy and in a way, I just wanted to go back and thank him for doing the best he could. Even if I couldn't muster the courage myself to say it out loud, I'd think it in his presence and perhaps those brainwaves would be picked up by what was still left of his brain, if he hadn't already degenerated into a vegetative state.

I spent another month with Zach and Fr. Jack and the rest of the people I'd grown so fond of. A week before I left, Aulia told me she'd gotten engaged to "someone nice from her village." I was happy for her. Happy that she'd found someone the way Mark had found someone. It made me think of Elena and what could have been with her had our hearts not soured. Some relationships are just karmic lessons, I suppose. When it came time to say goodbye to everyone, I told Fr. Jack I'd be back and he looked me square in the eye and said dryly, "No you won't. God's got other plans for you." At that everyone laughed, and we passed around a cup of wine to celebrate my departure. Magda the Gibbon was cradled around Fr. Jack's neck, as usual, and she looked at me with what seemed like a triumphant sneer.

The person I had the most difficulty saying goodbye to was Zach's daughter Lily. She loved to storm in my room every morning and get tickled by me. Many people use the trite expression that someone has the face of an angel. Indeed, she had a glow that rivaled the angels and a smile that radiated for miles. I would miss that smile, and I still often look at a picture I snapped of her smiling up at me during one of her morning rampages and I would sing her a song I made up repeating the lines *consider the lilies of the field*. She loved that silly song and cried when I told her I was leaving, asking when I'd be back. I told her I didn't know, but that I would write to her and send her presents on her birthday. It's been over seven years and I still do that, though she may not even remember me anymore and wonder who the guy is that keeps sending her bits of jewelry once a year.

I flew to Washington, DC on the cheapest trip I could find. Fr. Jack insisted on driving me to the airport. "I picks 'em up and drops 'em off," he muttered when someone asked who was taking me. I think he just liked driving that Isuzu of his—knocking about, as he would put it. In fact, we stopped at a school on the short trip out there and I got to see him in action one last time: patting the heads of children as they gathered around him. It was just the two of us on the drive and I was nervous since he and I hadn't been alone or talked more than half a dozen times after that first week. It turned out to be one of the more meaningful conversations I had with him and part of it was that I had learned to listen without butting in with questions or commentary or even restless mind chatter in the background. I chalk that up to keeping up the meditations Elena taught me, along with a few other practices that Zach taught me that were much simpler. More than anything, Fr. Jack wanted to be heard. Which is true of most people, I suppose. When we reached the airport, he went to grab my bag and I beat him to the punch.

"I'll take it this time, Father." He grinned at me like I'd tried to steal his pot of gold.

"Well, young fella. I guess this is where you get off and go on back to your world. May the road rise up to meet you. May the wind be always at your back. May the sun shine warm upon your face; the rains fall soft upon your fields and until we meet again, may God hold you in the palm of His hand."

I thanked him for everything, shook his hand, and I was gone. So was he.

PART V | THE MIDDLE EAST

CHAPTER 1 | BALTIMORE TO AMMAN

Four stops and fifty-two short hours later and I was in DC. Those earlier trips were shorter, though leaving me feeling crushed by the end of them. For some strange reason, this one felt lighter, easier. I felt lighter, easier, I suppose. It helped to catch up on movies I'd missed while down in the jungle. I also found that in Java I had learned to take an interest in others and in life itself. Everything seemed exciting, although for the life of me I couldn't figure out why. If I could go back and talk to myself that first year I would have given some stiff advice about lightening up and going with the flow instead of being worried all the time about pretty much everything. *Oh well.*

I arrived in the late afternoon on a Saturday, renting a car and stopping just outside of Baltimore. I was tired and wired, and checked into a roadside motel before crashing out for fourteen hours. I woke up and went for a run through a lush field of green. It felt good after so many months of either dodging wild dogs or talking myself out of the adventure of being hunted down by confused animals watching a man running past them—something they never habituated to or even tolerated. The air smelled different, a different kind of humid, and it brought me back to my childhood, those smells I couldn't describe but knew right away were of home.

Traffic was light heading into the city—Sunday morning. I passed by the downtown harbor, which had changed as part of Baltimore's redevelopment plan that I'd heard about years before but never seen with my own eyes. I suppose it looked better than the burned-out dreary brick atmosphere I recall—save the massive electric guitar on the side of some building that looked tacky and represented everything wrong with American style. It was still difficult to imagine the whole place being a tourist attraction, but at least the city had tried to do something to bring a few dollars in and turn back a century-long descent into despair. My old neighborhood hadn't changed much though, and it occurred to me as I pulled up in front of the house that I'd not spoken to either of my parents in several years and hadn't even given them a heads up that I was coming. I couldn't be certain they were still alive. I noticed my father's tall foul weather boots beside the door and that put me at ease. I doubt my mother would have kept them out there for nostalgia had he passed on. She would have gotten in touch with me had he croaked. I took a breath, got out of the car, and knocked on the door.

My mother answered the door, squinting at me as she struggled to recognize who it was on her doorstep. After a few moments, her face wrinkled into a smile and without a word, she stepped out and buried her body into mine. I think it was the first time I'd felt the warmth of one of her hugs since I was a child. The other times I waited for it to be over with, rather than taking it all in as I did after so many years. I had forgotten that like my father, she was quiet and didn't speak much. However, unlike him, her eyes and facial expressions communicated more than anything her mouth could say. She pulled back to look into my eyes, and I saw a mixture of joy, pain, sorrow, and a hint of anger all at once floating through her. When a wave of gratitude washed over me, I swore I could see it pass onto her and she lit up like a bright light in a dark room.

"Harry…" she whispered, turning to pull me into the house by the arm. I'm pretty sure I was smiling, even after passing through the musty foyer whose scent never left my memory, and moving to the kitchen where she plopped me down and without a word made me a bacon sandwich. As I watched her back at the stove, moving pans and spatulas and dials around, I sensed that she wanted to wait to let my father know who'd come home. A sensitive person, I bet it was just too much for her to see me out of the blue and without warning. She needed time to let it sink in before bringing my father into the mix. I was in no hurry either. In fact, I had half hoped he was either out or dead, though the latter thought still a remnant of how I used to feel. The air flowing through my nose smelled different this time. Not just in the house or the neighborhood, but everywhere. Indeed, I wanted to see my father.

Half way through eating my sandwich I felt a soft hand on my shoulder. When I gazed across the kitchen table at my mother, I noticed the sparkle in her eyes and her looking up with love at the other end of the hand.

"Hey sailor," I heard my father say with a grunt. I turned around and for one of the rare times in my life, I saw him smile. Time had withered my father. Nevertheless, to see those shining teeth looking down at me I wondered if he was pleased to see me or had somehow found his own peace—perhaps both. I wouldn't find out, spending a single night there, with my flight to Amman, Jordan booked for the following night. That timing was deliberate.

My father and I watched an Oriole's game on television, talking in bits and pieces over a few beers. I enjoyed it, and it *did* appear that he'd mellowed with age, perhaps recognizing his own mortality and so few days left on earth. He said goodnight around nine and let his hand touch my shoulder as he climbed the stairs to his room. The next morning at the crack of dawn, I heard the front door shutting, my father heading off to his old boat for another day on the water. That was the last time I heard him.

I drove by Thomas' old house before I left the neighborhood. It was strange seeing it again after all these years. Had he a grave, I would have visited that too. I even thought about driving back out to the Monongahela Forest. However, there was no time for that, and as I looked at that front door I'd knocked on so many times so many years ago, I realized I had made peace with what I'd done or not done with him. He was part of a memory of a person I used to be who I hardly knew anymore. Perhaps I'd see him in the afterlife and apologize. Something told me that dead people grow wiser and he'd long forgiven me—and forgiving myself was what made it easier to wave goodbye to his door and leave for the airport.

Getting bumped up to first class without warning is one of the best things in life. I was sitting back in economy when the flight attendant approached me just prior to takeoff, calling out my name and handing me a new boarding pass with the seat assignment 4A. After an eventful few days, goodbyes to my mother, and the drive to the airport at the tail end of rush hour, I had pictured a bleak trip across the Atlantic. So, it was with new life that I rose up and sat back down in a seat up front that turned into a bed. I had missed that luxury the past few years. When I arrived in Amman late the next day, I felt rested and refreshed.

It was my first trip to the Middle East. From a lifetime of media reports, I expected to be greeted by hordes of angry, rock-throwing peasants. Instead, I found everything drenched in calm, kind and slow-moving people all around. Maybe it was the heat, for as I walked outside with my hired tour guide I felt as though I'd stepped into a furnace. *People live in this heat?* Tariq, who was also my driver, was an older man who spoke flawless English. Zach had given me his name and I contacted him ahead of time to help with booking hotels and figuring out my sightseeing agenda before heading to Israel for the wedding. As soon as I met Tariq, I knew I was in good hands.

For some reason, I assumed the drive out to Petra would take an hour or so. Instead, it took half a day of long straightaways cut through a barren desert. At least we had air conditioning, which I didn't appreciate as much until we stopped at a roadside coffee shop along the way. Tariq had a wealth of knowledge about his country and the history of Petra, which he described in immense detail. I was fascinated by this city carved out of rock, envied by the Romans who made several attempts to subdue it. After both Tariq's and Zach's descriptions, I was excited to see this place hidden deep in the arid lands. The desert has always made me nervous, having spent most of my life close to a large body of water, but this desert seemed magical in a way. Maybe it had something to do with the few cars and buses going out there, all headed for the same place as if drawn into a vortex. When I asked Tariq about the relative lack of traffic, he said that ten years ago there'd been lots more. Though Jordan was one of the safest countries in the Middle East, it couldn't escape the region's stigma that had shattered the tourist industry after September 11th.

CHAPTER 2 | PETRA

As we entered the area surrounding Petra, I noticed a few large chain hotel buildings rising from the sand, the kinds of places where I used to stay. Traveling on a budget these days, I had Tariq put me in a cheaper place, which turned out to be a quaint little boutique hotel run by a sweet older couple. I suppose it didn't matter where I stayed since the main attraction was the old city and all one needed was a bed for the night. Tariq mentioned that he stayed with a cousin whenever he was in Petra. He asked me if I needed time to relax, but despite being tired from the long trip, I was too excited to stay indoors. It was late in the day, but we still had a few hours of sunlight. So, he showed me some of the areas near the main entrance. I thought about Zach a lot, wondering as I passed each site what he'd thought of the architecture and ruins.

After passing a few street vendors, one of which sold me a bag of dates that I ate while we walked, we descended a large sandy road. Large rocks lined the sides of the road, some rounded by nature, some showing small caves, and a few enormous cube structures. Tariq referred to them as *Djinn Blocks*, or God's blocks. Humans had carved designs around them, though these bruised and faded over time. I noticed one with a tiny doorway. He said scholars think they may have been used as tombs. He also mentioned that the Bedouins steered clear of them, believing they contained evil spirits. A covered two-wheel carriage pulled by a white horse passed to the left of us, going back up the road on an elevated dirt road designed for non-pedestrians. A fat, greasy European-looking man and his haggard wife reclined in the back behind the driver, looking worn out from a long day. The driver stared ahead, steadily whipping the horse to get her to pull them up the hill. The driver's head was wrapped in a headdress, and his clothing and everything else about his carriage appeared camera ready. It struck me as odd that the couple in the back wore shorts and tank tops. Even background characters and extras in movies dressed like Indiana Jones to play the part of world travelers, but in my travels, I saw so few fellow tourists doing the same. Many of them looked like they were on their way to the gym or Disneyland. I suppose it didn't matter, but I wonder if they'll look back on those travel photos and wonder what the hell they were thinking standing in front of an ancient wonder wearing a tank top with the words *Tang* splashed across the front of it.

Although the sun was beginning to go down, the heat still beat everyone down who remained too long underneath it. I had a wide-brimmed hat, so between that and munching on dates I felt fine. To our left we passed what Tariq referred to as the Obelisk Tomb, the burial place for a king and his family. The façade of the tomb spread high over the face of a large rock. It must have taken years to carve its intricate features. The first level reminded me of the entrance to a mausoleum, and the top level had jagged arches that looked like dragon's teeth biting into the sky. We stuck our heads into a few of the cave entrances. Not much to see in there, though. Part of me was hoping to see a few bodies on display, but the chances of that happening were close to nil.

We continued to the entrance of *Al-Siq*, a narrow road a mile long, cut deep into the rock and leading down to the rest of the Petra ruins. Tariq suggested we wait until the morning, when it would be cooler. So, we set off back to the little town, a place dependent on tourists spending their money on food, drink and shelter. I reminded Tariq that I was on a tight budget, and he took me to a small kitchen where we both sat down to fresh-squeezed orange juice and large chicken *shawarmas* filled with hummus and vegetables. The place was packed with tour guides and other men that looked old and local. Everyone was eating, drinking, or smoking. I heard an *oud* playing music in the background, and after a while what sounded like singing. When I asked Tariq about it, he waved his hand, saying it was the call to prayer.

"It sounds beautiful," I said.

"The song of God. But they'd never admit it was singing," he said with a chuckle. "You said earlier this was your first trip to Jordan. Is it also your first time in the Middle East?"

"Yes."

"Ah, well, you picked a good place to start. So far, is it what you imagined?"

"Some of it, but honestly, I didn't expect people to be so nice and polite."

"I hear that every week, you know."

Two young women passed by us wearing bright yellow headscarves, bronze faces gazing forward, looking like they were a hand-carved artist's dream. Shining beauty. Both Tariq and I paused and watched them glide past us. I couldn't make out their figures, but the way they moved suggested they were comely. They radiated class. In fact, their radiance blasted me out of myself and I noticed the entire world taking on a crispness akin to a new set of sharp glasses after years of blurry vision.

"And what do you think of our women?" he asked with a serene smile, raising grey eyebrows.

"They certainly have a way about them. Funny, but back home women show a lot more skin and hair. Many of the women here only show their faces, but somehow, they seem more beautiful. Maybe it's because I'm not used to it. Exotic, mysterious, maybe. The *hijabs* are exquisite. Accentuates their faces. Makes them look more elegant."

"I would have to agree with you. I think the *hijab* makes a woman look sexier."

"Do you have a family, Tariq?" I asked, wondering if that was an appropriate question in this part of the world.

"Yes. I have a wife, two daughters, a son, and five grandchildren," he answered with a prideful grin. He was missing a few teeth on the bottom, but he had the face of someone who'd achieved success and happiness.

"Must be nice."

"My family is everything. This is good, being here with you, taking people to see the sites and explaining various aspects of my cultural heritage. I got into this a long time ago to learn English."

"Which is flawless, by the way. Better than most Americans," I interjected.

"Thank you for that," he said with a casual smile, returning to his thought process. "When I go home to my family, it is *my* Petra, my rock." A skinny young boy brought over two small glasses filled with coffee. Tariq said *shukran* (thank you) in Arabic, and gave him a stately nod. The air outside started to cool, and I listened to the music, drinking my coffee with Tariq, both of us watching tourists and locals passing by, most of them walking away from Petra to hotels and taxis. I felt a giddiness wash over me. It had started when the two women were passing by, but took some time to sink in while I sat there chatting with Tariq. I will never forget that moment.

I can't describe it any other way but that it resembled an absence of anxiety or dread or boredom or whatever else I was used to feeling brewing just underneath the surface. Even at other times in my life when I was experiencing joy this other dark streak loomed in the background, eager to ruin it. That phantom disappeared for a good half hour, maybe longer. The sky had turned twilight, and everything continued to burst into bright color and sharpness. The last time I remember anything close to that feeling was playing stickball in the street on a late summer day in my childhood, me and the other kids screaming in laughter at just being alive. I felt a certain

187

lightness of spirit I recall Zach once trying to explain to me that I couldn't quite grasp. Now it was clear. I had let go and in turn let whatever goodness was out there in the world enter me as though forever knocking on the same door for over half a century, patient as a conscientious chambermaid. Later, I would wonder if I'd been in such a hurry earlier because part of me must have known what was coming. Of course, half an hour of borderline enlightenment, or whatever you choose to call it, might make for a better story on some mountaintop. Instead, I felt it in a dirty roadside kitchen. I glanced over at Tariq, who gave me a warm smile as he took a slow sip of his coffee. *All the time in the world*, I thought.

That night I sunk into a deep sleep, waking up to the call to prayer outside my open window while it was still dark out. The day before I might have responded with a grumpy huff; but I felt new, different. Nothing seemed to bother me. Even the fellow at the hotel who messed up my egg order to-go got a smile from me.

As promised, Tariq came around the hotel at sunrise. I made a slapdash egg sandwich out of the breakfast bag and ate it while we made the walk back down to *Al-Siq*. We didn't talk much, enjoying the quiet and the occasional sounds of horse hoofs on the dirt track beside us or the chatter among the sellers we passed as they set up their stalls for the day. They were all too tired to ask me if I wanted to buy anything, and I was grateful for that. Tariq seemed a master at reading a situation, and he adhered to our tacit vow of silence as we descended an old stone path cut into the rock. High cliffs reached up above us, gleaming in the rising sun. I felt like I could break out into a run, excitement at just being alive overtaking me. I kept walking at the moderate pace Tariq had set. He was pushing eighty years old, but could outpace any teenager I'd met.

After twenty minutes of walking through the meandering gorge, we reached an opening into a small valley. Opposite us stood a massive façade etched into the stone. Tall Corinthian columns held up a second level and the whole scene looked like it had been imported from ancient Rome. The sun had started to peak over the hundred-foot cliffs and poured into the valley, exposing the structure's exquisite detail and bathing it in bright light. Without looking at me, Tariq broke the silence.

"The Treasury."

I said nothing. I simply stood there and took it all in. A single thought raced through my mind. Since the beginning of time people had relied on some version of money to measure work, success, and trade. Too often we mixed up our self-worth with our net worth in a struggle to survive on limited resources. I nearly plunged to my death because of it. It was silly to think that because I had no money that somehow, I as a person had no value. There you have it, the ego unmasked. I breathed in dust and spirit, watching as the ascending sun shrank the shadow over the Treasury, lighting it up. It was a magnificent sight, and I could hear Tariq's slow breath next to me. It dawned on me that this old man was planning to spend a hot summer's day with me walking around rocks in the desert. I turned to him.

"You sure you're up for all this walking?"

"No problem. Not far up the valley is a spot I like to stay in. You can hike all you like, and we'll meet back up later. I'll tell you some of the history before you set out."

We tried to stay on the shady side of the valley, passing several caves where families once made their homes. A huge coliseum lay off to the right and then a long corridor lined with columns. Tariq gave me a history lesson on everything we saw, the types of people who inhabited Petra and its eventual downfall. After the Roman military failed to invade Petra, they wound up competing it into irrelevance. He suggested I stop and sit down in various places and try to picture the civilization at its zenith, with its thriving economy. He made sure I had enough water, and bid me farewell, giving me explicit instructions and directions on where to find the nine-hundred-something step stone stairway up to the Monastery. After a few minutes of walking, I glanced back to find him nestled in with a group of other guides sitting under a makeshift tent made of brown tarp. Everyone seemed to be drinking coffee, smoking cigarettes, laughing, and enjoying themselves. *Not a bad life.*

The trek up the stairs took me a few hours at a slow pace. I had to dodge donkeys trying to catch their footing as they made their way down with tourists who wanted to see the sunrise from the top but didn't want to make the climb on their own. It seemed dangerous enough on foot, given the steep, winding ascent. I felt a twinge of nervousness watching the looks of dread on people's faces as they clutched at their blanketed saddles hoping to control some part of the process. I was glad I was on foot.

When I reached the top and saw the Monastery, which resembled a larger version of the Treasury, I knew what drew people to it. Sure, the ruins were great, but by that point I'd seen enough to know what to expect. It was the view that mattered most. One could see the open desert west of Petra from up there and back down to other parts of the old city to the east. The sun had already started baking everything, but a steady breeze kept the dozen or so of us wandering around relatively cool. A resourceful family had opened a small café in the middle of the flat plateau opposite the monastery, and I bought an ice-cold bottle of water for three Jordanian Dinars (just over four dollars). It was a steep price to pay, but the café was on the winning end of the supply and demand equation. I took the water and scurried around the rocks until I found one where I could look out over the desert.

As much as I wanted to experience that same blissful moment again I had the night before, I couldn't will it to return. One would think the peaceful setting more conducive to quasi-religious experiences, but I guess it didn't work that way. I would come to know how rare mine was and how that glimpse into *heaven on earth* kept me striving on my path hoping to re-experience it all over again. Like a golfer who'd made eighty lousy drives and one clean, beautiful one, it kept me coming back to the fairway. I sat up there considering my life: where I'd been and how much it had changed over the past few years. A few hours later, I made my way back down and we spent a final night in Petra before Tariq drove me out to the Dead Sea.

My experience in the Dead Sea was brief, but noteworthy. Tariq warned me to float, and whatever I did, I was not to let the water touch my mouth. *Not even a drop*, he said. *Just lie on your back and keep your head up.* Of course, just like that time I looked at the sun during a solar eclipse, I disobeyed him and let the point of my tongue touch the tip of my wet pinky finger. My punishment was quick and severe. I spent the next few hours with a horrendous salty taste in my mouth that no amount of fresh water could quench away. Maybe I should have listened, but I also don't regret now knowing just how *salty* the Dead Sea is. As instructed, I spent twenty minutes in there before climbing out and washing off under one of the many outdoor showers set up at the small resort where we'd stopped. Several people were on the beach, spreading some gray mud all over their bodies and lying down in the sand. Not sure what that was all about, but I wasn't interested in getting all dirty. So, I approached Tariq, who was sitting in a lounge chair under an umbrella deep in thought over a newspaper article.

"You look like a new man, Harry."

"Feel like one! My skin feels soft like a baby's bottom. Amazing!"

"You'll be surprised at how long that will last. Maybe weeks." He put down his paper and looked out over the sea. "You said you were headed to Jerusalem, no?"

"Yes, I need to be there by tomorrow afternoon."

"Do you have a plane ticket already?"

"No, forgot to mention that I thought I would cross overland. Can't be more than a few hours."

"The Allenby Bridge?" He dropped his head in a pensive pose.

"I know it's gotta be cheaper and less of a hassle than taking a flight from Amman to Tel Aviv and then having to take a taxi down to Jerusalem."

"Hmm...."

"What's wrong?" I asked.

"It's not an easy border crossing into the West Bank."

"Even for Americans?"

"It doesn't matter who you are, the Israelis control the border. They're suspicious of everyone."

I thought for a moment, considering how much money I spent on seeing Petra and how much more I'd have to spend on a suit and hotel once I got to Jerusalem. I'd grown frugal over the past year, eager to cut a financial corner if necessary. Besides, a trip through the West Bank sounded fascinating. "I'll try my luck at the border. Why not?"

"OK." He gave his head a gentle shake of resignation and pity. "But I would recommend one thing. Take a bus if you can once you get on the other side. Most people already have a ticket booked, so they may ask you some questions."

"What kind of questions?" I felt a pang of nervousness.

"Oh, they will probably ask you questions about where you are going and who you are going to see. Just tell them the truth, but nothing more. Keep your answers short and don't give them any more information than what they ask for."

"Sounds strict?"

"Oh, you will see." He shot me a sardonic smile and threw his hands into his pockets.

CHAPTER 3 | CROSSING ALLENBY BRIDGE

Tariq gave a final wave as he dropped me off at the terminal at the King Hussein Bridge (the Jordanian name for Allenby). A line of cars and buses snaked around a bend, but I didn't see many people in front of the terminal building, hoping I'd chosen an easy day for passing through. There were over a dozen doors, and when I tried to go through one of them, a man in uniform took one look at me and pointed to anther door. When I went through that door I noticed I was in a cordoned-off area that had no one else in it (I noticed the man who'd just helped me). The other side was filled with what I'm guessing were Jordanians and Palestinians.

I paid the tourist tax and turned my passport over to a polite man wearing an immigration badge. All he asked me was how I enjoyed my trip to Jordan. When I told him of Petra and the Dead Sea, he said next time I needed to go down to Aqaba and Wadi Rum. Tariq had told me the same thing. He wished me luck on my journey and informed me that I'd receive my passport once I got on the shuttle bus that would take me to the Israeli terminal. I walked outside and stepped on the large air-conditioned bus with my small suitcase and backpack containing everything I owned in the world. The bus wasn't crowded, and I figured I'd lucked out, eager to hear the swish of the door shutting and to be off to the checkpoint on the other side of the bridge. The door shut, and the driver sat down in his high seat. I was a few rows away, and could make out his right side, watching for movement that suggested we were taking off. After a few minutes, I heard him talking on his cell phone and it didn't seem like we were going anywhere.

A steady flow of people began to climb onboard, and after each group I again expected to rumble to a start, but the bus sat idling. Sometimes he even shut it off and climbed outside to help people stow their large bags under the bus. Once he stood out there smoking a cigarette, which seemed suicidal given the heat had turned up to the point where no sane person would be caught dead in the sun. An hour later, I still wondered what we were doing, realizing that he was indeed waiting until the bus was full before making the trip. Perhaps a busy day would have been better. Eventually, I gave up any anxiety or restlessness, assuming we would be on our way at some point. Two hours after I climbed onboard we made the three-mile journey across the bridge.

I remember feeling hungry, realizing that in my eagerness to get to Jerusalem I'd skipped lunch and not brought any food beyond a few mushy dates. It was silly to assume the trip would take only a few hours from where I started. Even Tariq mentioned something about it and out of foolishness I nixed the idea of stopping before the bridge and heading back to Amman. We filed off the bus and the first thing I noticed were soldiers everywhere with machine guns, even a few working dogs. A throng of porters descended on us and began taking our passports and asking us questions. It was strange having a girl no more than eighteen years old sidle up next to me and begin asking probing questions in an accusatory tone. *Where was I going? Why was I going to Jerusalem? Why didn't I have a hotel? Why didn't I take a flight? Why so little luggage?* With my military background, I knew how to talk to people barking questions just to get a rise out of someone. It reminded me a bit of the first week at the Naval Academy, only a skinny girl asking me questions–and not an unattractive one as well. With her Slavic sounding accent and blond hair tied in a ponytail, she could have swapped the blue uniform in for a little black dress and no one would have guessed where she'd worked if she kept her mouth shut, but she didn't. After a while her questions started growing more intrusive, if not downright odd.

"Who gave you something to put in your luggage?"

"No one."

"But how did you get here?"

"By taxi?"

"Who was in the taxi?"

"Me?"

"*You* drove it?"

"No, there was a driver?"

"Who is he?"

"Tariq."

"He is your friend, no?"

"He was my driver."

"Personal driver?"

"No, he was my guide."

"I thought you said he was your driver. Now he is your guide?"

"He is both."

"But who is picking you up to take you to Jerusalem? Is his brother picking you up?"

"His brother?"

"Yes."

"I don't know about a brother."

"But how are you getting to Jerusalem?"

"I'm not sure yet. I thought there would be a taxi–"

"You don't have transportation arranged?"

"No, I figured I could just get a taxi–"

"From the West Bank? There are no taxis from here, only buses. You need to pre-book it."

"Where can I do that?"

"From your hotel."

"What hotel?'

"Your hotel in Amman."

"But I don't have a hotel in Amman."

"I thought you said you came from Jordan. From Amman."

"No, I was in Petra."

"You did not stay in a hotel?"

"I did. In Petra."

"But how come you didn't arrange a bus from Petra?"

"I didn't think to. I went to the Dead Sea and asked the driver to drop me off here."

"Did he tell you to make this crossing?"

"No, he told me to fly from Amman."

"Why didn't you listen to him?"

"I guess I should have. I thought this would be an adventure."

"Adventure..." She repeated my word and let it hang there in the air, sizing me up with a scrutinizing smirk as though I was playing some game with her. At least Tariq had warned me that someone might ask inane questions to get a rise out of me. That was their job. I was approaching a tipping point, feeling the well of exasperation working its way up my throat. She tapped the passport in the palm of her hand as though it were a paddle, then invited me to proceed to a small desk away from the main line of travelers going towards the terminal. It felt as though I were in trouble, like I'd done something wrong–like all those times I'd been asked if I'd been drinking during a traffic stop, feeling guilty no matter what. I started to feel angry. *I'm an American goddamn it! I look like CIA! Aren't we the good guys giving you all the guns and money?* I glanced at one of the soldiers, who gave me a casual look that said he wouldn't mind shooting me just to past the time.

As I stood there, I watched as others were being pulled from the line, many of them Arab looking, which were most of the people on my bus. There were some grubby backpackers that didn't get much hassle–those would have been the ones I'd target. Of course, it didn't matter because the ones who made it through the gauntlet of crazy questions then proceeded to a line hundreds of people deep, served by a few kiosks on the other side of the sea of people. I marveled at the inefficiency of it all, but I suppose the chaos of people wandering around, some with guns at the ready, kept everyone off kilter and served its purpose of disrupting anyone's plans, good or bad. I resigned myself to amusement since the whole sad spectacle more resembled a circus than anything else.

Fifteen minutes later a short man in his late twenties approached me, holding my passport. He looked at my picture and asked me my name. When I gave it to him he started in on some of the same questions as the girl. *Where was I going? Why? Who was getting married? What were their names? Did I have friends in Israel? In Jordan?* It all seemed like a warped nightmare, and the thought of that struck me. The entire scene and everyone in it, particularly the guards, *did* resemble a bad dream filled with fear. This is what fear looks like in its pure manifestation. *Power without a rudder.* As the young man looked at me with intense, hazel eyes, I felt sorry for him and the whole damn place. Like the child in a dysfunctional family, he tried his best to navigate through a world already set up for him and he'd grown used to. I guess given the option, some people chose to whip rather than be whipped.

I assumed I passed the test because he shrugged and handed back my passport, motioning me to join the line with the others. I caught site of a few young women in *hijabs* being escorted to a door that led to God knows where, both visibly terrified as two female soldiers and another male went in behind them and shut the door. I looked over at a middle-aged Arab man next to me who'd also watched this. He caught my eye and looked down in quiet resignation.

After waiting in the slow-moving line for well over an hour, I wondered if I would have been better off checking my luggage as they wheeled away a cart filled with big 1970s-era suitcases and cardboard boxes wrapped in tape. Because at one point, the same girl who'd interrogated me earlier came up again and asked to inspect my backpack. I unzipped it, so she could peer into it and she also motioned for another officer to take my suitcase. She ordered me to wait and I watched as he rolled it to a small metal desk, where he flipped it on top and unzipped it. Another man brought out a handheld device and they passed it all over the bag as he rummaged through it. I caught sight of a pair of my boxer shorts falling out and laying exposed for everyone to see. Now the entire place knew that I wore shorts with the Grinch's face stamped all over them. *Great.* They were the most comfortable pair I had, so I hoped they wouldn't get confiscated. I noticed the same guy behind me looking at them too and when I caught his eye again I thought he would smile this time, but he didn't. In fact, nobody smiled, ever. I thought of Churchill's quote suggesting that if you find yourself in hell, just keep moving—or something to that effect. So, I did.

After six hours of lines and hunger pangs, I made it through another two checkpoints with metal detectors and more questions, though most of them less disturbing in nature. I saw a bus of people, all Arab looking, being escorted on a shuttle bus back to Jordan. I guess they didn't give the correct responses. I never did see those two women in *hijabs* again.

My passport and bags back in hand, I looked around at the parking lot. Most of the buses were filling back up with people—many entire groups of travelers that seemed to have had their own quick path through security. I deduced that I'd chosen the longest possible route to Jerusalem. I was starving and tired and angry, but in looking back on the experience, I think I gained some insight into a world inhabited by less fortunate people. Though I wasn't sure who was less fortunate, for though the Arabs had to endure harsh tones and rough handling by the Israeli officers, I couldn't help but see parallels between the conduct of a chosen race and what had been done to them for millennia. I tossed my luggage into the trunk of a taxi and slid into the back seat with a mixture of pity and anger. Someone else was in the back seat with me. A diminutive kid that looked fresh out of college, and maybe American. He smiled and said hello to me.

"Didn't know it was a shared taxi," I muttered. "I'm Harry."

"Alex. Nice to meet you." He gave my hand a firm shake, and I could tell by his smile that he had a cheery disposition.

"You American?"

"I grew up there, yes."

"But you live in Jerusalem?"

"No, I live in Ramallah, actually. In the West Bank."

"That's interesting." At that point, the driver, who couldn't have been much older than Alex, bounced into the front seat. He turned to Alex and they started jabbering away in what I assumed was Arabic. I'd heard Hebrew back in the terminal, which sounded more guttural and scratchy. I looked out the window, watching the traffic and everyone else struggling to get on the road out of there.

"Excuse, me. Harry?" Alex turned to me, and I glanced over at him. The driver was looking at me in anticipation. "He's asking for forty dollars to Jerusalem. He'll drop us off at the gate."

"That's fine. The gate?"

"Yes, he's Palestinian. Not allowed to leave the West Bank. So, he can only take us to the Damascus Gate."

"Oh, so you're going to Jerusalem?"

"Yes, just for the weekend."

Alex said something to the driver and I told him I'd lucked out having an Arabic speaker with me, otherwise I would have been lost. The car rolled away, and I breathed a sigh of relief, glancing back once to see the throng of people leaving the terminal and doing their best to get their lives back to together and onto a bus. I reached into my pocket and pulled out what was left of the mushy dates, shoveling them into my mouth and licking my fingers. I played around with the hard pits in my mouth, wondering if I should spit them out the window, but deciding to play it safe and shove them back into my pocket. Alex was texting someone on his cell phone, letting out a sigh of his own. We were passing over a well-paved road, and in the distance I could see little towns, which made me curious.

"What's Ramallah like?" I asked when I guessed Alex wasn't preoccupied. He turned to me with a smile.

"It's amazing."

"Yeah? How long you been there?"

"Going on three years now."

"What's so great about it?"

"Well, the people and the food. Best hummus in the world, and there's something about the Palestinians. No matter what happens to them that light in their eyes doesn't go out."

"Where are you from originally?"

"Connecticut."

"What brought you out here? To the West Bank? Are you part Palestinian?"

"No, my dad's Israeli, actually."

"You're Jewish?"

"Yep," he said with a laugh, "I got interested in Arabic and Islam in college. Came out here for a school trip and fell in love with the culture. Now, half my family won't speak to me because I'm working with the Palestinians."

"That's gotta be tough."

"Yeah, but most of those relatives I wouldn't want to talk to anyway. So, it's alright." He said this with a carefree laugh.

"What are you doing here, exactly? In Ramallah?"

"Microfinance. In fact, I was just at a conference in Amman."

"Really? That's fascinating!" I couldn't help thinking of Zach's philosophy around people of the same frequency finding one another as they walked their path.

"Yeah, I love it. The NGO I work for does a lot of different things—microfinance is just one of them."

"I spent some time in East Asia recently doing a little of that. I was just in Indonesia."

"That's really cool. Indonesia is predominantly Muslim. Did you get involved in Islamic microfinance?"

"Islamic microfinance? I heard some mention of it on Java. So, there is such a thing?"

"Oh yeah. See, in Islam you can't charge interest. It's usury."

"Really? Why not?"

"The Qur'an forbids it."

"Bummer." I didn't know what to say as a flood of confusion washed over me.

"The Old Testament does as well. Jews were forbidden to make loans to other Jews at interest."

"I never heard that."

"Yeah. For a while Christians were not allowed to make loans at interest either. In fact, that's why Jews were pushed into banking hundreds of years ago. I guess the Christians figured we were going to hell anyway, so we may as well be the bankers. Of course, that all changed over time. For Islam it's still restricted."

"That seems so backward."

"Maybe, but when you think about it, it's meant to protect vulnerable people from being exploited by predators."

"I guess so, but how do they get around this prohibition? Somebody's got to take a loan sometime."

"That's the interesting part. Many loan products are asset-based. If someone needs a rickshaw or something the bank buys it and sells it to them at a markup. There are also joint ventures. See, the prophet and his followers were traders and merchants. Basically, loans need to conform to the same ways they did business."

"It all sounds cumbersome and very costly. Doesn't it?"

"A bit, but it spreads the risk around. It also gives people the opportunity to agree on a price that is fair on both sides. Not sure if you noticed this in Jordan, but people in the Middle East like to haggle. It feels better knowing both sides have come to an agreement."

"That's cool. Can't they just game their way around the whole interest thing?"

"Not really. In some parts of the Middle East they'll charge a fee that mimics the interest rates. To be legitimate, the bank or NGO should get a *fatwa*, or a religious opinion from an Islamic scholar. The reputable ones wouldn't approve a simple workaround, especially one that doesn't capture the spirit of the law. If the risk isn't shared in some way, it's no good."

"That's interesting. I didn't know about this *fatwa*–though I've heard that term before."

"Probably in the news."

"Yeah, that must be where I heard it."

"Most people don't know this, but Islam is a scholar's religion with a lot of disagreement. In theory, it should be a fluid, evolving one as scholars discuss rules regarding morality."

"Yeah, but why do people need all those rules? Sounds painful."

"I guess you can look at it that way, but don't most people just want the pill?"

"You're probably right. Better to have someone else do the critical thinking. Anyway, that's meaningful work you do. Super cool!"

We had been driving for about an hour and all the while I was talking to Alex about his work. It all made me want to go to Ramallah. At some point, maybe. The trip was pleasant along the highway, and as we got closer to Jerusalem I noticed more signs of a larger civilization. At one point, we approached a small line of cars and when I asked Alex about it he said it was a checkpoint and that I should get my passport ready. I counted seven cars ahead of us, and each one took about five minutes to pass the checkpoint. Buses were passing by, and it seemed that only cars were being stopped. When it was our turn I realized this was a makeshift checkpoint set up on the side of the road with a few simple concrete barriers, so cars had to zigzag when passing through. It reminded me a bit of the truck weigh stations I'd seen often on the highways back home.

An older man in uniform approached the driver's side with a halting hand, and I could tell our driver was trying to hide a slight nervousness. A young woman with a machine gun approached Alex's window on the other side, peering in, helmeted and ready to shoot us. The driver rolled down his window and spoke to the man in what could have been Hebrew, but I wasn't sure as it sounded like mumbling to me. He twisted his head in my direction, giving me a stern, scrutinizing look. I had my finger on my passport, ready to pull it out when asked. Alex seemed calm as though this were a regular occurrence. I stayed as calm as I could since I had nothing to hide. It had been a long day and I was bushed, which made me nervous since I knew I got punchy when tired and hungry. Eventually, the officer twirled his hand and I followed Alex's lead of passing my passport up to the driver, who handed them over, along with what looked like a driver's license. I noticed that Alex's passport was a blue one with the United States eagle. This made sense because as he'd told me during the drive that he didn't have an Israeli passport, which would have made it very difficult for him to travel in the West Bank. Other than the settlers, Israelis weren't supposed to do that, or so he told me.

The officer looked at Alex and me while thumbing through our passports. His eyes reminded me of the way a small dog looks just before it bites someone—petty fear masquerading as power. After a few moments, he spun around and went to a small kiosk, where he fiddled with our books while looking down at something I couldn't quite make out. Maybe it was a computer or machine. The woman remained beside Alex's window, eying us with curiosity. All of us knew not to say anything, as if we were hiding out, waiting for a drunken stepfather to stumble past us—and just like that, five minutes later he handed back our documents and waved us on through.

CHAPTER 4 | JERUSALEM

Sensing my curiosity, Alex turned to me and said we would soon arrive at the last checkpoint that led to Jerusalem. I was so tired I almost didn't notice the tall wall with barbed wire, graffiti, and old, creaking turnstiles with peeling green paint. As I stepped out of the taxi and looked around, I saw rubble and burned-out buildings on the West Bank side. It reminded me of post-war pictures of Europe. I paid the driver and followed Alex through one of the turnstiles, which seemed designated for non-Arabs because everyone else who looked Middle Eastern was going through a different one. I expected another long dressing down, but surprised when the guard standing in a doorway looked me up and down, flipped through my passport, sent me and my bags through a metal detector, and nodded for me to enter. That was it. I guess by then they'd grown used to my face. Alex was behind me, and received the same treatment. He helped me get into another taxi and told the driver to take me to a budget hotel he knew in East Jerusalem. As it turned out, we both had nothing to do the next morning, so he gave me directions to a restaurant in the old city and we agreed to meet there at ten.

The hotel was cheap and located near the walled city of Jerusalem. A busload of tourists crammed the tiny lobby just as I had checked-in and started making my way up the steps to my room. Most of the people were in their sixties and seventies and overweight with rolls of fat hanging out of their shorts and tank tops. They didn't say much, but it sounded like Russian. I could tell they were relieved to get off the bus. I unlocked the door to my room, glanced around before tossing my bags on the bed, and shut the door again. The room was the size of a jail cell, but that would do fine as I planned to stay no more than three days and needed just a bed and a bathroom. After Java most accommodations, no matter how sparse, seemed luxurious.

It was Friday night and the wedding wasn't until Sunday. Plenty of time to take in a few sites. Sarah's parents were hosting a cocktail reception for friends and family late afternoon on Saturday, and I looked forward to reconnecting with everyone as I had a feeling they'd invited a few of the people I'd encountered when I was with them. If they'd invited me, who knows what other characters might be included in the roundup. So, I set out and grabbed some street food before coming back for an early sleep to maximize my Saturday.

I woke up at first light and went down for the free breakfast buffet in the basement of the hotel. Even though it was 7:00 a.m., the place was full of tourists, and I took a few elbows as I made my way through the chow line. Cucumber, hummus, and a boiled egg were all I could muster before the entire place was cleaned out of food. That was enough to get my energy level up, and I gulped my breakfast down at one of the long tables since the entire group of people seemed to know each other and wasn't interested in knowing me. It felt like being one of the new fish during a prison movie, without a veteran con sitting down to strike up a conversation. No matter; I finished my plate and set out on foot to cross over the stone bridge at the Damascus Gate and into the old city.

With its high stone walls and cobbled streets, the old city resembled a castle. I had a map from the hotel, but wasn't prepared for the sheer size of it and the cloistered streets and winding paths that seemed to lead me in circles. Lots of small shops and Israeli soldiers greeted me at every turn. I made it to the Western Wall, which I was told I should not miss. The first thing I noticed when I entered the open courtyard opposite the towering wall of stone slabs were the various forms of odd dress. Of course, there were the tourists and their usual indiscreet clothes. What struck me were the distinctive clothes of many of the Israelis. I asked Alex about this later when we were eating brunch of falafels and hummus.

"You mean the Orthodox Jews?" he responded.

"I guess so. Men, and even some boys, wearing big round furry caps. It must be eighty degrees out and they're wearing some thick gear. I don't mean to be disrespectful, but it just seems odd to me—almost out of place. Though, so far from what I've seen I'm not sure what is *in place* in Jerusalem."

"You do know you're basically at the center of many religious traditions?" He shot me a playful wink. "I'm not sure the answer to your question. I heard some of the garb harkens back to seventeenth and eighteenth century noble dress from Eastern Europe—Poland and such, but don't quote me on it."

"Interesting. Well, I guess I won't be signing up for *that* sect. Are you Jewish, by the way? Can I ask you that? We are in Jerusalem, so I guess I have license to ask religious questions that would be inappropriate elsewhere."

"No worries. I mean, I was raised Jewish, but after studying world religions I'm pretty sure most of them are way off the mark."

"Which one comes closest to the mark, do you think?"

"Have you heard the joke about the agnostics who die and when they find out there actually *is* a God they start freaking out? St. Peter's leading them down a hall and telling them not to worry, their transition won't be so difficult. As they're passing by a closed door he begins whispering. When the agnostics ask him why he's whispering he says, 'I don't want to disturb the Jehovah's Witnesses. Their transition is going to be much harder, so we take it slower with them.'" I chuckled, and he shrugged his shoulders. "How would I know which religion is closest to the truth? But I'd say I'd have to put my money on the Taoists."

"So, are you a Taoist?"

"Nah. Not for me, but I do like one of their expressions."

"What's that?"

"Shit happens."

"I like that!"

"We all have our own bridges to cross. I'm just trying to keep things as simple as possible. Just doing the best I can to be a good person." He looked out over the crowd for a moment and then turned back to me with a twinkle in his eye. "Harry, you said you'd done microfinance before. You want to see my work in action? I have a few clients to see for this small organization I'm helping. It's in the Arab quarter."

"Sure."

And like that we were off walking through twisting alleys, even passing by a church that Alex told me was supposed to hold Jesus' tomb. "I thought he flew up into the sky and disappeared?" I asked, which made him chortle. He moved faster than anyone else I'd walked with before, even faster than Fr. Jack. A man on a mission and no time to waste. I thought I would lose him a few times as he slid past humans, animals, and all sorts of stuff cramming the streets, which were at times a mere five feet wide. At one point, we were stopped by an Israeli soldier leaning against a corner wall. He'd been chit-chatting with someone as if on break, but suddenly peered up at us and threw his massive arm out to block the way. I looked at him and the alley beyond his arm, which had much less foot traffic than the ones we'd been cruising around. He and Alex spoke a few words of Arabic, and the soldier gave me a scrutinizing once over, then nodded, letting his arm down. As we walked passed him, I looked back to see the soldier watching me, then shrugging and going back to his conversation.

"What was that all about?"

"This is the Arab quarter. Tourists aren't allowed. He thought you were a tourist. Said you couldn't pass, but I told him you were working with me and we had to go see some clients."

"Interesting." I said, considering myself lucky to be going to a place prohibiting tourists. After we were well away from the soldier, I asked Alex about him. "He looked a bit different than the other soldiers I've seen."

"Didn't look Jewish?"

"That's right. He also looked bigger."

"Yeah, he's Druze."

"What's that?"

"They're from the north, near Lebanon. They broke away from the main Muslim sects a long time ago."

"So, they're Muslim?"

"I guess it depends on who you are talking to. They're interesting, actually. They incorporate aspects of many different religions, including Judaism and even Hinduism. They're Neo-Platonist too."

"That's cool. Never met a Neo-Platonist."

"We're here. This is one of my clients."

We were standing in front of a black metal door that was propped open to reveal a small beauty salon with a single chair. In the chair, a woman sat with all kinds of crumpled-up aluminum foil in her hair. The hairdresser stood beside her, and gave Alex a warm smile as he waved and entered with the Arabic greeting *salaam*. She was a young woman, close to thirty years old. The shop was quite small, lined with white tile and a mirror opposite the front door. So, I could see the patron's face, a woman in her forties. To the right of the front door I noticed a stone stairwell and two children, a boy and a girl of about seven or eight years old sitting down on the steps, staring up at us. As Alex spoke to the woman, the children began a quiet inspection of me, unsure what to make of this strange man in their house. The hairdresser seemed reserved, but I could tell by her tone quite comfortable with Alex.

"Harry, this is Fatima."

"*Salaam*," I said to her with a nod, and she repeated my greeting, mimicking my gesture. It was odd that as a hairdresser she herself wore a *hijab*, albeit an elegant pink one. She had strong facial features and a prominent face that said, *Look out world, here I come!* Her shop was simple, but one glance at the satisfied face of her one customer spoke volumes about how much care she took in her work. As she and Alex conversed in Arabic, he was thumbing through a small notebook and talking to her about something. She also stepped up to a wall calendar and it dawned on me that they were comparing dates. Sensing my curiosity, Alex explained that he was setting up a business training session with her.

Later, during the walk back to my hotel, he would explain that his job in Jerusalem was to arrange targeted trainings for women business owners who'd taken a small loan from the organization. The objective was to teach them skills, enabling them to thrive and no longer need to take loans. As he explained, most microfinance borrowers got themselves into a cycle of debt and had merely swapped their payments from loan sharks to a friendlier bank—but they were still stuck in a vicious pattern of perpetual debt. So, his organization attempted to offer value-added services to help them truly climb out of poverty. It reminded me of the work I'd seen in Southeast Asia, reinforcing a growing awareness that loans by themselves did little to help people in the long-run. That without access to trainings or other forms of education, people kept taking loans every year until it just became part of their life—doomed to a lifetime of debt.

Back in her salon, as I watched Fatima and Alex talking, I saw bare feet coming down the stairway and a disheveled man about thirty passing by the children and looking on us. He had the look of a prey animal, waiting to see what the world around him might do to him before making a move. I smiled at him, trying my best not to stir any unnecessary fear in him. He didn't return my smile, just looked at me as he leaned against the railing, and then watched Alex and Fatima flipping through the calendar and writing things down. He looked almost childlike. I also asked Alex about him after we left. He said the man was the woman's husband. He suffered from brain trauma caused by an incident with the butt of a soldier's rifle, and could not work. In a way that explained the blank stare he gave the world, as though he was searching for something missing. Fatima had started the salon to keep the family together. Alex told me when he first met her two years prior, when she had started the business, she was scared and did not know what to do.

The organization arranged for her to attend a cosmetology school and later financed materials for the shop. Over time, she realized her entrepreneurial nature and it was obvious to me that her business was thriving as a result. In fact, she was doing so well that she was starting to teach girls in the neighborhood how to do manicures and pedicures, employing them in her shop. She had asked Alex for a loan to buy a chair for doing pedicures. As he spoke about her and I thought about the look in her eye, it hit me that I'd seen that same spark in the eyes of many an entrepreneur. It was a look easily mistaken for a fearlessness or even assertiveness. Perhaps these *true* entrepreneurs operated that way, but I'd like to think that they saw opportunities and were not afraid to act on them—even appearing risk tolerant to the point of sometimes not recognizing the risk, or even seeing the risk in *not pursuing* an opportunity. In Fatima's case, it wasn't clear whether she was just doing what she needed for her family's survival, but she had that *climbing the ladder* aura emanating from her.

When Alex had finished doing business with her, and another woman came into the shop and began helping the customer with her hair, Fatima invited the two of us upstairs for coffee with her family. We sat on the floor of a large carpet laid out over the concrete floor, without much furniture up there. An older woman came out through a curtain to another room, carrying a gleaming silver pot on a platter, surrounded by small porcelain cups that didn't match. She greeted us with a *salaam* and Alex whispered to me that she was Fatima's mother.

We all sat down on the floor and drank the coffee her mother poured for us. I noticed that Alex dumped more sugar in his cup than most people. It was a beautiful moment, as we sat there next to an open window and I could hear the call to prayer wafting through it and looked out over the smiling faces of Fatima and her mother, appearing pleased to have us there. The husband sat closer to the corner with the children, arms draped around them and watching us but not drinking the cup before him.

That was seven years ago, and I still remember holding back tears that welled up behind my eyes and the lump forming in my throat as we sat there. I'm not sure anyone else in the room realized it, including me, but I was breaking down inside. In fact, it remains a bit of a mystery to me why that moment touched me like no other. Though, I'm sure it was not an isolated event in my mind, especially considering my experiences in Petra and even before that in Southeast Asia and Mongolia. They were all connected somehow, and I even saw semblances of my own father in Fatima's husband. Fortunate for me, we had finished our coffee and bid farewell before I cried. That would happen long after Alex had walked me back to my hotel and I sunk down into my bed before drifting off into a long nap.

CHAPTER 5 | REUNION

Alex said he was meeting friends later for drinks, and I assumed it was the last I would see of him. So, I was startled when after I'd showered and made my way to the open-air deck of the restaurant for Sarah and Mark's party I saw him standing at the bar in a black sport coat, chatting with a few people. At first, I had been looking around to see if I could spot Sarah or Mark, but once I saw Alex I charged up to him.

"Hey, what are you doing here?" he asked.

"Hey, what are *you* doing here?" I responded.

"My friend Sarah is getting married."

"Well, my friend Mark is getting married to another friend of mine, and her name just happens to be Sarah," I retorted with a laugh. The three young men standing next to him all smiled and shot us looks of curious marvel. Alex introduced me to them, though it was obvious that he didn't know them all that well. As this was happening, I felt a hand on my shoulder and turned around to find Mark and Sarah beaming at me.

"Harry!" Sarah half jumped into my arms. She was radiating joy. Even Mark's taciturn manner was on holiday, and he slapped me on the back with a broad smile.

"So glad you could make it, my friend."

"I see you met Alex," she interjected, "I was planning on introducing you two since Alex works in microfinance as well."

"I know, we met yesterday."

"Yesterday?" She gave me a quizzical look.

"Yeah, the Fates threw us together in a taxi at the Allenby Bridge. If it weren't for him and his Arabic, I'd probably be wandering around in some Bedouin village out in the desert."

"Unbelievable! Oh, I'm so glad. So, *so* glad you two are here. Oh, Harry. We really missed you after you left Manila. Such good times. How is

Indonesia? You sounded so happy in your emails."

"Amazing." That's all I could say about the last year or so, and all I could get in before both she and Mark were accosted by someone else who swept them up. She gave me her hand and a deep look of satisfaction before being pulled away, promising that the three of us would hang out sometime over the weekend, for sure.

From the restaurant deck, I could see out over the city of Jerusalem and a large building with a rounded roof of gold not far off. I drifted away from Alex and the others towards the railing. There must have been about fifty people, and I yearned to catch my breath from the small crowd jammed into an even smaller space. It's a good thing we were outside. On my way, I bumped into Stefan and we had a short chat to get caught up, though he was a prolific blogger with a knack for poignant tales of life in Mongolia and I'd read every one of his postings since I met him. He was touched when I mentioned this, looking portly and jolly as ever. I reveled in the idea of spending the next few days steeped among the people who'd introduced me to my new life. I wandered over to the railing, gazing at the gold dot out there among sandstone rooftops vis-à-vis tree dotted hills in the background.

"The Dome of the Rock," I heard a female voice say to someone else who asked her about it. "Seventh century. Ironic, how in a city known for its links to Judaism and Christianity, it's a Muslim shrine that outshines everything else."

I let her comment hang in the air as I continued to look out there, pondering my life since I left the bank. The old one long gone. I had expected tragedy somewhere along the way, especially that first month on Java where all I wished for was death–anything to remove me from the pain of being human–but it never happened. I have a lot of people to thank for that. I spent the next three days in long, deep conversations with old friends and new ones, before traveling around the Middle East and back to San Francisco. "The end of the beginning," as Churchill once remarked.

I have continued down the path of devoting the rest of my life to financial services for those left out of a system designed to keep them out– though not in the way I expected. I wound up going to work for Sarah and Mark in their crowd-funding startup, and so did Alex and a few others from that weekend. Their public website helps people around the world that need access to finance get a low-cost loan from everyday people like you and me. Organizations like the Center in the Philippines can now post a picture of one of their clients on the site, along with a story about them and why they need support. People visiting the website can browse through these pictures and stories and decide whether they want to chip in and finance that person. Mark made the site simple and easy to use, and now anyone with a computer or smartphone can send a few dollars to someone who needs it, knowing that they'll get their money back when the person is finished using it.

After helping to set up their credit policies, Sarah asked me to head up their educational loan program–something dear to my heart after my experiences on Java. I ran that for a few years and still help on a part-time basis, while teaching a course on ethical finance two nights a week at a local business school. The rest of my nights I spend working at a homeless shelter. Never thought I'd be doing all that, but I love it. I suppose it all keeps me from jumping off that cliff.

My one lament is never having gotten to know Mark in a way that I've wanted to–despite our deepening friendship over the years. I guess that's how it is with some people, they influence us in ways we never expected, yet the story in their heart remains forever wrapped in a mystery.

One last thing…

Thanks for reading! If you enjoyed this book, I'd be very grateful if you'd post a short review on Amazon. Your support really does make a difference and I read all the reviews personally so I can get your feedback for future editions of this book.

If you'd like to leave a review then all you need to do is to visit the book's page on Amazon. You can find links to this and my other books here: amazon.com/author/looft

Thanks again for your support!

Michael Looft

Also, please visit me on the web! I would love to hear any questions or suggestions you may have or if you are interested in engaging me as a speaker at your next event. Happy to help!

Email: hola@michaellooft.com
Website: michaellooft.com
Facebook: https://www.facebook.com/AuthorMichaelLooft/

ACKNOWLEDGMENTS

I would like to thank everyone who helped in the making of this book. First, I am very grateful to my initial readers who provided valuable feedback: Margaret Kelly, Cindy Lelake, Nancy Finston, Sharon Taylor, and Mark Barrett.

I would also like to thank the folks at Kiva and Lendahand, for providing me with years of support and showing me ways of helping families that truly make a difference in the lives of people around the world. This book would not have happened without you.

Finally, I would like to thank the inspirational people I met while traveling in the following places and countries over the years that appear in the book: Mongolia, the Philippines, Hong Kong, Indonesia, Jordan, West Bank/Israel, San Francisco, and Baltimore. My life would not be the same without you.

ABOUT THE AUTHOR

Michael Looft has lived a storied life. A globe trotter by nature, he's worked and traveled in upwards of 50 countries around the world. He has spent over a decade working in financial services for the poor (microfinance) and speaking publicly on ethical finance.

Michael holds an undergraduate degree from San Francisco State University, and graduate degrees from both St. John's College and Harvard. He has published two non-fiction books on ethical finance: *Inspired Finance* and *Social Impact Finance* (both published under Palgrave Macmillan, 2014).

When he is not writing or traveling the world eating exotic foods and meeting interesting people, Michael can be found either trail running through the mountains of Northern California or camping with his son.

Contact Information
Email: hola@michaellooft.com
Website: michaellooft.com
Facebook: https://www.facebook.com/AuthorMichaelLooft/